AND
ACTUALLY ...

Denise Deegan

HACHETTE
BOOKS
IRELAND

First published in 2012 by Hachette Books Ireland
Copyright © 2012 Denise Deegan

1

The right of Denise Deegan to be identified as the Author of the Work
has been asserted by her in accordance with the Copyright, Designs and
Patents Act 1988.

A CIP catalogue record for this title is available from the British Library.

ISBN 978 1 444 74297 8

Typeset in Book Antiqua by Bookends Publishing Services.
Printed and bound in Great Britain by CPI Group (UK) Ltd,
Croydon, CR0 4YY

Hachette Books Ireland policy is to use papers that are natural,
renewable and recyclable products and made from wood grown
in sustainable forests. The logging and manufacturing processes
are expected to conform to the environmental regulations of
the country of origin.

Hachette Books Ireland
8 Castlecourt Centre
Castleknock
Dublin 15, Ireland

A division of Hachette UK Ltd
338 Euston Road
London NW1 3BH

www.hachette.ie

To PANTA, with love
Plus a big hello to my friends in Sion Hill

And bon voyage to Matylda
)l(

Praise for the Butterfly Novels

'Think *90210* with a sprinkling of Dublin grit' *Irish Independent*

'This is a gem of a book; intriguing, deep and thoughtful … Teenagers – and adults – will adore this book. It kept me up half the night' *Irish Examiner*

'An engaging and emotional read that leaves you wanting more' *RTÉ Guide*

'[Denise shows] considerable insight into the minefields of adolescent friendships and knows how to keep the pages turning.' *Irish Times*

'It's wonderful … I absolutely loved it. I was so engrossed in it that my family started pulling it out of my hands if they wanted my attention.' Keris Stainton, author of *Della Says: OMG!*

'This is just one of those books that really got under my skin. I just can't stop thinking about it. ★ ★ ★ ★ ✔' I Want to Read That (blog)

'Denise Deegan does a beautiful job of tempering such a serious issue with just the right amount of romance, friendship issues and humour' Anna Reads (blog)

'★ ★ ★ ★ ★ Heartbreaking, bittersweet and simply spectacular' Lauren's Crammed Bookshelf (blog)

'A truly amazing and heartwrenching novel that I couldn't put down' Once Upon a Bookcase (blog)

'I loved every page' I Heart Books and Football (blog)

ONE
Caecilius

Last thing every night, I lie in bed and gaze at a grey face with big, white eyes and tiny pupils, a face with a black line for a mouth which stretches left to right like an equator, a face that has arms and legs. This is my twin. Or at least a substitute for my twin.

I got my Uglydoll when I was seven and my parents moved me into a room of my own. Till then, I'd shared with Jack, my older brother by six-and-a-half minutes. Because Jack's in a class above me at school, people think he's just my brother. My parents have won. They always wanted us to be 'individuals'.

At first, I needed Uggs to see another face before I fell asleep. Now he's like a friend. The night Mark and I got together, I hugged him so tightly I'd have killed him if he'd been real. Actually, he *is* real. To me. The night my friend, Alex, had a baby, I soaked him in tears – it was also the night our friend, Shane, died, leaving Sarah behind, a widow at seventeen. That was two weeks ago. Sometimes it feels like two minutes. Sometimes two years.

Tonight, I stretch Uggs's tiny arms across his non-existent tummy and try to join them together. I make it only because he's a flexible, little guy. I close my eyes and make a wish. That Alex and Sarah will be OK. I make another wish. For myself. Tomorrow, at drama class, I'll hear the outcome of an audition I did for this really popular soap, *Eagle Crescent*. My drama teacher, Charley, who is also my agent, has this thing about discipline. She does not call us with the results of auditions. Even if we get a part. She waits to tell us at drama class. She says, 'we need to have rhino hide in this business'. I don't think it's possible to create rhino hide. You either have it or you don't. I'm not a rhino.

Charley (think Edna Mode from *The Incredibles* but tone it down a bit; she's Irish) calls me back after drama class.

'I've good news and bad news,' she says cheerfully. 'Which do you want first?'

'Bad news.'

She smiles like she knows me. She does. I've been coming here since I was four.

'You didn't get the part in *Eagle Crescent*.'

I close my eyes. There is no good news.

'*But*,' she says. Then stops dramatically. So Charley.

I open my eyes.

'You did get a small part in *D4*.'

'What? How?' *D4* is a medical drama. That I never auditioned for.

'The casting agent interviewed you last year for that play, *Break Even*. She's moved to *D4*. She remembered you.'

'Wow.' My mind is racing. No one I know watches *D4* but it's still TV. And my first ever part. Yaay.

'You're to play a trouble-maker.'

I'm smiling.

'You have to come between a couple.'

'You mean split them up?' I ask enthusiastically.

'I'm not sure yet if you actually split them up.'

)((

I so hope I do. That's what I love about acting. You get to do things you'd never do in real life. 'When do I start?'

'Monday.'

'*Next* Monday?'

She looks a bit guilty. 'Someone else backed out.'

'Their loss.'

She smiles. 'That's the spirit.'

It's a dream come true, a dream I've held since I was four.

'It's a small part, Rachel, but if you play it right, it could lead to bigger things.'

'I'll play it right.'

First thing I do is go straight to Alex's house, where she and Sarah have been spending all their time since, well, since two weeks ago. I'd be spending all my time there too, if it wasn't for school.

I don't tell them straight away. Because when I get there, it hits me how small my news is compared to what's going on in their lives. We go up to Alex's room, which is more like a nursery now. There's all this colour. Bright greens, reds, oranges, yellows. A wall-lamp like the sun. Loads of cuddly toys. A cot that's too big for Maggie. And inside the cot, Maggie's Moses basket.

Sarah is holding Maggie. She kisses Maggie's forehead and passes her to me. (We have this rule that whoever arrives, gets to hold Maggie.) Maggie is Alex's baby but it feels like she belongs to all of us. We each have a job: Alex, mum. Sarah, aunt. Me, godmother. She's only two weeks old, but already Maggie is one of us. I look down at her now and fall in love with her all over again. Happens every time I look at her. She has these hazy, Caribbean blue eyes that gaze up at you like you're the only person in the world. Everything about Maggie is innocent – the tiny creases under her eyes, her little eyebrows that have learned to frown already, her tiny rosebud lips that smile when you least expect or purse for no obvious reason, her little pointy chin, her tiny, expressive hands and, most of all, her gums. I never want her to get teeth.

I sit on the bed, loving the weight of her in my arms. Sarah sits on the floor. She picks up an orange llama, brings it right up to her face and says: 'Hello.'

She's wearing Shane's hat, the one with the flaps that hang down over her ears. She never takes it off. It makes me want to hug her. Constantly.

Alex, smelling the tiny babygros she's putting away, stops for a moment to ask me how drama went. So I tell them about the part. How small it is. How it's nothing to get excited about.

'Oh, my God!' Sarah says so loudly that Maggie jumps in my arms. 'That's amazing.' She drops the llama, hurries over and hugs me. And Maggie. (We're a package.)

'Go you,' Alex says, smiling.

'When do you start?' Sarah asks.

'Monday.'

'Really? That soon?'

I shrug. 'Someone else backed out at the last minute and I got the part.'

'Their loss.'

I smile. 'That's what I said.'

'Have they given you a script?' Sarah asks.

'Yeah but I've just one line.'

'What is it?' they ask together.

'Have you got a light?'

We laugh.

'Right, well, when you get some lines, we're rehearsing,' Sarah says. Since Shane died, it's like she's on this quest. To live till she dies. It was Shane's last wish. And she is fulfilling it, embracing every, little, thing. Always talking, always moving. Always living.

I think she might be expecting too much from my little part. So I remind her it *is* little.

'Yeah but you'll make it big,' Alex says.

And though I smile – because becoming a mum has given her all this authority – I so want to believe that she's right.

When I get home, the smell of baking fills the hall. I drop my bag and go straight to the kitchen. There are buns in the oven and Mum's kneading dough.

'Did you get a job?' I ask hopefully. Mum runs her own catering business. It's been a bit quiet lately. Not that this is, like, a major problem – Dad's a well-known barrister who gets almost too much work – she's just happiest when she's cooking for people.

'No. This is for us.'

I pick up the bowl by the sink that she used to make the buns. I skim the inside with my finger and stick it in my mouth. I lean against the worktop. I've always loved watching her bake.

'How was drama?' she asks.

'Good.' I enjoy the moment before telling her because I know she'll be excited. 'I got a part in *D4*,' I say casually.

'What? Are you *kidding*?' She yanks her hands out of the gooey dough, squeezes me to (almost) death,

)(

then pulls back and punches me gently just below the shoulder. 'We'll have to celebrate.'

This probably means cake.

She puts the dough aside to rise and checks the clock on the oven. 'You're late,' she says questioningly.

'I called to see Alex.'

A look of concern crosses her face. 'How are they doing?' she asks, knowing that Sarah's practically living there now.

'They're great, Mum. It's Maggie. She's so amazing.' It was Maggie who got Sarah out of bed after Shane died. Maggie who got her moving. Maggie who gave her someone else to love.

'Must be hard on Alex, being a mum, without her own mum around.' Alex's mum died, two years ago.

'Her dad's great, though. And Jane, the nanny, is so good.' Three days after Maggie was born, Alex kind of lost it. She didn't think she could do it. She was so scared. And depressed. As soon as she got out of hospital, though, Jane took over, made her sleep. Showed her how to feed Maggie. Showed her that, with a bit of rest and confidence, she could be a good mum.

'So! Tell me all about *D4*,' Mum says. She asks a string of questions that I don't know the answers to. Like who'll meet me when I get there on Monday? How many hours a week will I be working? Will I get a schedule?

'I'll give Charley a call,' she says. She washes her hands and reaches for the phone. 'Would you set the table, pet?'

Though tempted, I don't groan.

Mum gets through, almost immediately. Question. Silence. Question. Silence. Then her voice goes all firm. I stop putting knives and forks on the table.

'Rachel's in Fifth Year, Charley. I don't want her

losing whole days at school for a minor part. They need to understand that.'

I hurry over and start waving my hands to get her to stop. Charley's doing her best. She always does. Mum puts her head down and turns her back on me. They talk some more. Then she hangs up.

'Mum, I can handle this,' I say. 'I'll work so hard. I won't fall behind. I'll . . .'

'I know you will, Rachel. I just don't want you under any unnecessary pressure.'

I look at her. I know what she's thinking about. But that was years ago. 'I can take pressure.'

'I know you can.'

'*OK*,' I say, looking her in the eye, to make sure she does.

After dinner, the doorbell rings.

'That must be Mark,' Mum says to me.

I get up and put my plate in the dishwasher.

'Don't keep him waiting,' she says.

Dad rolls his eyes.

After the first time Mum met Mark, she said to me: 'Go out with him. He's good for you.'

'I am, Mum,' I said.

'*Good*.'

'Why?'

'He makes you laugh.'

She is so in love with him that when he comes in to the house, it takes ages to get back out. I've told him to text when he's outside. He always forgets.

I open the door and burst into a smile. He has that effect.

'Caecilius est in horto,' he says in all his gorgeousness.

'Caecilius is in . . .' *horto? Horticulture?* '. . . the *garden*?' I guess.

He smiles. 'Caecilius is in the garden. Now let him in before he freezes his balls off.'

We have this thing where I have to try to work out something he says in Latin - usually about his hero, Caecilius, a real-life, slave-turned-master who was killed in Pompeii. Mark has worshipped him since First Year. He's loyal like that.

Caecilius hurries inside and gives me a kiss with cold lips. God, I love cold lips. As long as they're his.

'Mark, is that you?' Mum calls from the kitchen.

We look at each other and smile.

She appears at the door to the kitchen. 'You can't go without some of my biscuit cake.'

I widen my eyes at him – as in, *let's go.*

He widens his back – *can't be rude.* When really, he just loves her cooking. His mum's a diplomat and is out a lot. He told me once that the smell of baking makes him happy. He follows Mum into the kitchen like she's the Pied Piper. Dad looks at me from behind a newspaper and shakes his head sadly. I smile.

I sit opposite Mark, drumming my fingers and giving him hurry-up vibes. He looks so cute, though, like a little kid. I feel like tying a napkin around his neck and giving him a glass of milk. Mum calls out the recipe for biscuit cake to him. As if he'll actually go cook something himself. She glances at me like I should be doing this, fussing over him. I worry about her.

When I finally manage to get him out the door, he's biting into a second slice of cake. He catches me looking and holds it out.

)(

'Bite?'

'No, Caecilius.'

He smiles and bleeps his car open. I love Millie, a black VW golf, currently (and mostly always) covered in dust with a bumper sticker that says, 'Meh'. Millie is the one place we can be alone – without anyone walking in.

He holds the cake between his teeth as he starts the engine, then he pulls away. I love watching him drive. It's the only time I get to see him frown, well, apart from when he's reading. I pretend he's moody and mysterious. Possibly French.

He goes through an orange light.

'Fuck the system,' he says.

I laugh and turn to him. 'Why did you do Latin, anyway?'

He shrugs. 'There was a trip to Rome.' *So* Mark.

'Why didn't you give it up after the trip?'

'I liked it,' he says simply.

'Kind of useless, though, isn't it?'

He looks at me, an eyebrow up. 'Tell me one useful thing we do in school.'

'Leave.'

He points at me. 'Exactly.'

Really, though, I love the way he loves Latin. He's a Roman at heart. I look at his profile and picture him in a chariot, reins in hand, shouting whatever Romans shouted at their horses. I imagine women throwing flowers and crowds screaming his name. Marcus Delaneyus.

We drive up into the mountains, listening to his weird taste in music. 'God Save The Queen' by The Sex Pistols. The Sex Pistols were huge – in the last century. I don't

)(

mind most of the punk stuff he listens to. It's actually kind of funny. 'God Save The Queen' is just bad, though. I skip to 'Gordon is a Moron' by Jilted John. Which always makes me smile.

Mark changes it back.

'Hey!' I reach out to change it again.

He play-slaps me away. 'My car, my music.' He starts jerking his entire upper body in time to the song.

I shout-sing 'Gordon is a Moron'. My favourite bit: 'Yeah, yeah, s'not fair. Yeah, yeah, s'not fair.'

He covers my mouth with his hand.

I bite his fingers.

He pulls back, laughing. 'Jesus.'

'That's what happens when you cover someone's mouth. Remember that.'

He's still laughing when we pull into the car park. The city lights twinkle, down below. I look around. There are two other cars here, windows fogged up. Otherwise there's no one around. I think of possible serial killers lurking in bushes. I lock the doors.

'It's OK. I'll protect you,' he says in a macho voice. 'I know karate.' He starts to climb into the back.

'Where you going?'

'Hang on.'

After rooting around, he climbs back in front. He's carrying something. He hands it to me. Oh, my God. It's a present. Gift-wrapped and everything.

'Wow. What is it? Is it like a congratulations present?'

'Open it.' He turns on the light.

I rip off the wrapping. It's a book. *Macbeth*. I look at him. We got together acting in *Macbeth* at school. *Exactly a year ago.* I can't believe he remembered. And I didn't.

I want to find the line he said to me just before he

)(

kissed me for the very first time. I know it's corny but I want to read it out. When I open the book, though, I can't find any line. He's cut a square through the pages, the way people do when smuggling guns into prisons. Inside is a little box. I look at him in amazement, then take out the box and slowly open it. Inside is a charm bracelet. The charms: acting masks, a little turquoise heart and a butterfly.

I look at him. 'I love it.' I try to put it on but he has to help. I hold it up to the light. 'It's beautiful.'

He smiles, like he's glad he got it right.

And he did. He got it so right. I lean over and kiss him. 'I'll get you something tomorrow. I'll go to Dundrum.'

'I'm grand. I don't want anything.'

'Yeah, well, I'll get you something anyway, *sweetie.*' I say sweetie in an American accent, the way Angela from *Bones* says it. It's kind of a thing we do.

He smiles. 'Well done on today.' He pauses, then looks into my eyes. 'You're great, you know that?' he says, hoarsely.

My heart stops. Because this is so not like him. *Oh, my God, could this be it, the moment he tells me he loves me?*

'I'll go in with you,' he says.

'What?'

'On Monday. I'll go in with you to the TV studio.'

'Oh.' I try to hide my disappointment. 'I don't think you can. Only the cast are allowed on set.'

'Oooh. Look at you, sounding all actory all of a sudden,' he smiles.

I smile back and tell myself it's still the most perfect moment. I know he loves me. He doesn't have to say it.

TWO
Miles Finch

'Die, bitchez,' Jack is saying to the flat screen when I walk into the sitting room on Saturday night. His thumbs are pumping away on the Xbox controller. Looking at him, you wouldn't know he was my brother, not to mind my twin. His hair is a weird colour – kind of like that red caramel toffee you sometimes get. His eyes are brown. Put it this way, Jack has never had a problem with the ladies.

'I need to watch *D4*,' I say.

'What, *now*?' he asks without taking his eyes from scenes of destruction.

'Well, yeah. It's on in like two minutes.'

'Shite, Rache.'

'It's the last show before Monday and I have to see the characters and the storylines. I have to at least *know* what show I'm acting in.'

'OK, chill. Let me just get these guys.'

I sit on the arm of the couch and keep looking at him. So he feels the pressure. Jack has loved computers since we were two and we started in a Montessori that ran classes. When we were five, our older brother, Harry, got an Xbox that we weren't allowed use. So Jack would wake me at six every morning and we'd sneak downstairs and play together. We even had 'sneaky breakfasts' of ice-cream or crisps or, if there was nothing else, normal food, like tomatoes. Jack got Harry to teach us the time so we'd have everything put away by seven when everyone else got up. I'm so tempted to forget *D4* and just pick up the other controller and beat his ass. Not that I could. Any more.

'Come on, Jack,' I say. 'It's started.'

'OK, OK.' There's about three minutes of all-out gunfire then, finally, with a sigh, he shuts down. 'How long is it on for?'

'I don't know, half an hour?'

He gets up and leaves. I think he's gone but he comes back two minutes later, his fist lost in a bag of tortilla chips. He collapses into an armchair, draping his legs over one of the arms, like his skeleton has melted.

'Shh,' I say.

'What did I say?'

'I'm trying to concentrate.'

'So concentrate. I'm not stopping you.'

'You're munching.'

Mistake. He munches out loud to annoy me.

I grab the remote and turn the volume up. I block him from my peripheral vision.

D4 is not hard to follow. It has the same formula as most medical shows. It follows the lives of the people working in a clinic and the medical stories of the patients. It's actually not bad. I've always wanted to do medicine, so the stories are really interesting. It'd be good if the doctors were younger, though, like in *Grey's Anatomy*. One of them starts talking about her son, Joe. I sit up. My first scene is with Joe. And there he is, with his girlfriend, Daisy. The couple I 'come between'. They look too perfect. Like Barbie and Ken.

'Hey,' Jack says. He's jumped up and is leaning forward like his skeleton has reformed. 'Isn't that Rebecca French?'

My heart stops at the sound of her name. I can't believe she still has that effect on me. I squint at the TV. And remember she was into drama.

'Pause it,' Jack says. He grabs the remote and pauses it himself. He walks up to the screen. 'It's definitely her. I'd know that ugly cow anywhere.'

'She's not ugly, Jack. In fairness.'

'Trust me. She's ugly. In every way that matters.' He frowns at me. 'Take *no* shit from her, OK?'

'Jack, it was years ago. Stop freaking. We're different people now.' I have a life, friends, confidence. 'Anyway, I probably won't even get to meet her. My part is tiny.' I look at her Barbie features and can't help thinking that I'm glad I'm going to be a problem in her life. Even if it's just onscreen.

'People like that don't change,' he says.

'I'm not afraid of Rebecca French.'

I have one line. Doesn't stop me practising it in front of the mirror all weekend. There are so many ways of saying, 'Have you got a light?' On Sunday, I check my timetable to see what subjects I'll miss on Monday. *Crap, Maths.* I can't fall behind in Maths, my worst subject. I read ahead and try a few exercises. I also read ahead in Biology and French. Then I have to escape. I'm not meant to be at Alex's for another hour – but screw that.

Her dad answers the door. He looks better since he stopped dying his hair and more normal generally since his band stopped touring. For a rock star, he's pretty decent. He smiles hello.

'They're upstairs. Go on up.'

'Oh, Sarah's here already?'

)(

'No. Her brother is.' His voice has turned to ice. And it doesn't take a genius to work out why. Louis got his daughter pregnant.

'I'll just go up then,' I say, embarrassed.

'Yeah, yeah, sure, go on,' he says, like he's waking from a thought.

Upstairs, there's no one in Alex's room except Homer, her golden retriever. I love Homer. And he's been so good since Maggie came. Not one bit jealous. I smile, throw my bag down and go over to him.

'Hey, Homey, how's it going?' I sit on the bed and ruffle his fur. He cuddles up to me. Aw.

'Miles Finch,' comes Alex's voice from the bathroom, over the sound of the fan.

'Easy. *Elf*,' says Louis.

'Yayo,' says Alex.

'*Get Shorty.*'

What are they on about?

'Ron Burgundy.'

'*Anchorman.*'

OOOK. So, now, I get it. Characters in movies.

'There you go, Maggie. All done,' Alex says.

Seconds later, they appear, Alex carrying Maggie. They'd make such a cute family – if Louis was a family kind of guy.

'Oh, hey,' Alex says when she sees me. 'When did you get here?'

'Just now. Hello, baby,' I say to Maggie, getting up and going to her. She is perfection in miniature.

Alex hands her over. I smile down at her. She turns her head towards my boob and opens and closes her mouth like a little fish. Awkward.

'She's hungry,' Alex says.

)|(

'I should go,' Louis says.

'No. You're feeding her, remember?' Alex says.

'It's grand.'

'You don't have to go, Louis. Rachel doesn't mind.' Alex turns to me. 'Do you Rache?'

'God, no! I'm early anyway.'

He doesn't look at me. Ever. It's as if he doesn't like me. Or maybe he thinks I don't like him. I don't know, but there's something.

We go downstairs. Alex zaps a bottle and sits at the kitchen table. Louis feeds Maggie, smiling down at her while she sucks away, her eyes fixed on his. She looks so tiny in his arms.

After a while, Alex's dad walks into the kitchen. When he sees us, he looks like he wants to reverse back out.

'Hey, Dad,' Alex says. 'Look what Louis bought Maggie.' She lifts up a box containing one of those mobiles you hang over cots to lull babies to sleep.

Her dad nods. Then walks over to the fridge and takes out a Coke.

'Come try it out,' Alex says. I'm thinking she should leave it.

Her dad looks like he'd rather eat slugs, but comes over anyway. Alex takes the mobile from the box and hands it to him. He twists a knob. Tiny dolphins start to turn as 'Hush Little Baby' tinkles. Alex's dad nods and hands it back to her. 'Great.'

'Louis is into music,' Alex says. 'He's in a band.'

He looks at Louis, like he's actually curious.

'It's not serious,' Louis says. 'We're just fooling around.'

A beat. Then Alex's dad mumbles, 'Seems to be your speciality.'

'Oh, my God. Dad!'

Louis raises his eyebrows.

Her dad takes off, forgetting his Coke.

Alex's chair grates on the floor as she stands suddenly.

'Leave it,' Louis says.

'No.'

She storms out after her dad. Leaving me sitting at the table with Louis. He starts to make faces at Maggie, widening his eyes and opening and closing his mouth, making a 'bop' sound.

I hear a door slam, then raised voices. I get up and go to the sink so Louis can have some privacy. I pour myself a glass of water and stand looking out the window, my back to him. He starts to sing softly to Maggie, 'Hush little baby, don't say a word. Papa's going to buy you a mockingbird.'

After a while, a door slams again and I hear Alex coming back. I stay where I am.

'I'm *so* sorry,' she says to Louis.

'It's OK,' he says.

'Why did you say you were fooling around?' She sounds frustrated. 'You're so not fooling around.'

'The band's just getting back together, Alex. We haven't even started auditions for the new lead singer yet.'

'That's still not "fooling around".'

'Look. Whether or not I'm in a band isn't going to make a difference to your father.' He stands up, kisses Maggie's forehead, smiles at her one last time, then passes her to Alex. He grabs his coat. 'I gotta go.'

As soon as Louis leaves, Alex, still holding Maggie, closes her eyes.

'He'll never come back now,' she says quietly.

)(

'Course he will.' I hope.

'I can't believe Dad. Louis's been so good, coming to see Maggie every day, feeding her, buying her things. Why can't he see that?'

'He's just upset, Ali. Louis did kind of mess things up.'

'*I* messed things up.'

'In fairness, Louis was nineteen. You were sixteen and you'd just split up with David.' She was so lost. Louis should never have got involved. Alex didn't even fancy him. Just kind of fell into the first pair of arms. He must have known that.

'OK, I was a mess but I wasn't retarded. The main thing is, Louis's here now. Dad shouldn't punish him for that.'

'He's probably just worried he won't *stay*.'

She looks at me.

'He's not exactly into relationships, Ali.'

'He hasn't had one with a baby.'

I smile. 'True.'

'D'you know that today Louis asked me if it'd be OK to tell people he was Maggie's dad. He thought I didn't want anyone to know.' She touches her heart. Then she frowns. 'And now this. Thanks, Dad,' she says sarcastically. Then her whole face brightens. 'I know what I'm going to do.'

'What?'

'Post a photo of Maggie and Louis on Facebook!'

'Is that a good idea?'

She looks at me.

'Everyone in school thinks David's Maggie's dad,' I explain.

'Yeah. So now they'll know the truth. Louis is her dad and I'm not ashamed of that.'

'OK.'

Not only does Alex post a photo, she tags it, 'I love my dad.'

They're going to kill her. But she knows that. She closes the laptop and puts her arms out for Maggie. I pass her over. Alex looks down at her little face then up at me.

'I want everything for Maggie, Rache. I especially want her to have a dad.'

'I know.' I want it for her too. But one day, he mightn't turn up. And we should be prepared.

'You think he's a loser,' she says.

Loser. A word that still causes me to flinch. Especially when someone I love is using it so casually – like it means nothing.

'No. I don't.'

'OK. You think he won't hang around.'

I'm not going to lie. 'He's been great, Ali. But maybe just take one day at a time, or something, for the moment, like.'

She thinks about that then finally nods. 'Yeah, OK.' But she sounds depressed.

'Maggie has so many people in her life, Alex. You, me, Sarah, your dad, Marsha.' Marsha is Alex's dad's partner. She's been quoted as saying, 'I could eat Maggie up.' And I get that.

'I know. And that's great.' But her voice hangs in the air and we both know what's missing, the certainty of a dad for our little angel.

Sarah arrives and I pass Maggie to her. Maggie burps up a bit of milk onto Sarah's top.

'What? You've fed her without me?'

'Sarah you can't exactly hold off on a hungry baby,' Alex says, dabbing Sarah's top with a baby wipe.

'OK but I'm changing her.'

We don't tell her that Maggie's already been changed. Just watch her take the nappy off. I love that she's so obsessed. That she has something to be obsessed about.

'Eh, Alex?' I say.

'What?'

'Your *eyebrows*?'

Her hand goes to them. 'Oh God. I forgot.'

One's plucked. The other isn't.

'I was doing them when Maggie woke.'

'Come on.'

We go upstairs. Before she gets distracted, I put the tweezers in her hand and stand her in front of the mirror. When she's done, we shoo her into the shower. Then, Sarah blow-dries her hair. It's not that Alex doesn't have help with Maggie. She just wants to do everything herself, be the best mum she can.

Later, I take them through some of the stuff they've been missing at school. But neither of them is concentrating. And I'm so tired of studying that we give up and just chill. We go on Facebook and post some pictures of Maggie. On Twitter, Maggie says: 'Yawn.' We go onto the Ikea website and pick out more baby stuff for Alex's room. We watch some clips on YouTube. Monkeys actually share. So cute.

After a while, Alex's eyelids start to get heavy. Luckily, she's lying on the bed. Soon, she's out. She even starts to drool. We cover her up. Tonight, a night nurse is starting so she doesn't have to wake up to feed Maggie anymore. I still can't believe she's back at school tomorrow after only two weeks. But it's what she wants – not to miss

)(

anything. To be normal. Who knows, maybe it'll be good to give the mum stuff a break, be herself again, just a teenager with her whole life ahead of her.

For a guy, Mark has weird taste in movies. He likes all the Will Ferrell stuff, which is normal, and *The Hangover*. But he's not into action stuff. Or violence. Or end-of-the-world movies. He likes real-life stories. Like *The Descendants*.

Sunday night, his parents are out and we watch it on his couch – him sitting, me lying with my head on his lap. He's running his hand over my hair, absent-mindedly. The movie is amazing but so freaking sad because it makes me think of Sarah being left behind. As soon as it's over, I sit up.

'I'm worried about Sarah.'

He looks surprised. 'She's doing *great*.'

'Can a person be too great?'

'No.'

'When her mum died, Alex was in bits. Don't you think it's weird that Sarah's so … up?' I'd die without Mark. Die.

'Rache, you're worried because she's coping.'

I think a bit about that. 'Maybe you're right,' I say finally.

'Caecilius semper iustus est.' He pauses. Then translates, 'Caecilius is always right.'

I smile and lie back down.

He twists a strand of my hair around my ear. I bat him away and sit up again.

'They're going to kill Alex at school, tomorrow.'

'Why?'

'She's posted on Facebook that Louis is Maggie's dad.'

For a minute, he says nothing. Then: 'Rachel. If Sarah and Alex knew how much you worried about them, they'd … worry.'

'We all worry about each other.'

'No. It's like you worry *for* them – so they don't have to.'

'They're my *friends*.' When I moved to Strandbrook and needed friends more than anything, they were there. They treated me like I was normal, not infected. A human being. They actually *liked* me – though it took a while to trust that. I've never told them – or anyone that I'd been bullied – when you get a break, you take it. You leave the shame behind. You don't give people a reason to look at you and say, 'Oh, yeah,' and for it all to start up again. The weird thing now is that they think I'm the strong one, the one with all the answers, the guru. I've no clue how *that* happened.

At two in the morning, I'm lying awake. Part of me is totally buzzed that, after thirteen years of dreaming, I've finally got a chance. The other part is afraid I'll blow it. I tell myself that I've only one line. But that just makes it worse. Everything's banking on that one line. And what about tomorrow? Do I wear make-up or not? If I do, they might have to take it off to put on their own. If I don't wear any, they'll have to put it on. Like I'm a baby. What if I don't fit in? What if I'm the outsider again? And what about Rebecca French? Do I need to worry? God, it would be so much easier not to do this. But that's not a good enough reason to give up on a dream.

THREE
Diva

At school the next day, we don't even make it to the lockers. Robin O'Neill and Orla Tempany come rushing over.

'Welcome back, you guys,' Robin gushes, all highlights and fake tan.

'Oh, my God. Maggie's so beautiful,' Orla says. 'I can't believe she has her own Facebook and Twitter. She looks like a little baby chicken.'

I try not to laugh.

Alex gives her a death look.

'You'll *so* have to bring her to school,' Robin says. These are people who when Alex was pregnant treated her like she had The Plague.

'I can't believe you're with Louis Healy now,' Orla says, getting to the point at last.

'I'm not,' Alex says, totally calm.

'But on Facebook, he's tagged as Maggie's dad.'

'He *is* Maggie's dad.' Alex starts to walk.

We go with her. But so do the others.

'So you're *not* together?'

'No, Orla,' Alex says, like she's tired. 'We're not together.'

'Oh.' Thoughtful pause. 'Shame.'

Alex stops. Slowly she turns. '*Why* is it a shame?'

She hesitates. 'I don't know. I just thought it'd be nice,

you know, to have someone.' Her voice rises at the end, like it's just a suggestion.

'Why?'

'With a baby and that.'

'This may come as a *total shock*. But I don't need a "someone".'

'Oh. Right.' Orla looks confused.

The bell goes.

'Better go,' Robin says, looking relieved.

The two of them walk off, heads together. This information will keep them going for days.

'Like I need a guy,' Alex snaps as we make our way to our lockers.

'I know,' Sarah says. 'You've just had a baby.'

Alex looks at her, like she doesn't get it. 'Sarah, I'm never having another relationship.'

'You can't say that,' Sarah says.

'Just did.'

We get to our lockers, fling our bags and phones in, and grab our books.

'So, what, you're going to be, like, a spinster?' Sarah slams her locker shut.

'I'm going to be a mum.'

'Until Maggie grows up and leaves you all on your own.'

'Don't be a bitch.'

I laugh. 'Guys, we're talking about, like, twenty years' time.'

'Exactly,' Sarah says. 'Alex will have fallen in love a million times by then – even if she tries not to.'

'Excuse me. Love doesn't happen without attraction. And I'm never going to fancy another guy.'

'How do you know?' I ask.

'I just know the way I feel.'

'Yeah, now. You're seventeen,' Sarah says.

'I know. Amazing to be so wise at such a young age.' She smiles like she's won.

And maybe she's right not complicating things right now. Still, I'd so love her to have someone. Eventually. Someone who loves her. And Maggie.

We get to class. Simon, Sarah's ex, comes up to her like he doesn't see anyone else. 'I'm so sorry about Shane.' His voice is full of emotion. Like he's actually apologising. He was really hard on Shane when he was alive, so maybe he is.

Sarah looks at him for a long time. Finally, she says, 'OK,' like it's over. Forgotten.

Then everyone is telling Sarah how sorry they are. She looks like she's been ambushed.

'We better sit down.' Alex says and we walk with Sarah to her seat.

'Is that all you're getting?' Alex says at lunch, looking at my tray. On it is a can of Coke.

I shrug. 'Not hungry.' Mum's coming to take me to the studio in fifteen minutes. And I'm kind of freaking.

'You should have something anyway to keep your energy up,' Alex says.

'You sound like my mum.'

'I *am* a mum,' she says, like it gives her rights. She picks up a banana and points it at me. 'And I'm watching you.' She puts the banana on my tray. 'Eat.'

I smile. 'Thanks Mum.'

'You'll thank me later,' she says bossily.

We laugh.

'Let's go skydiving,' Sarah says, like she wants to drop everything and do it right now.

We laugh.

'I'm serious.'

Alex and I look at each other, then back at Sarah.

'Skydiving?' Alex asks, squinting at her.

'Yeah. Why not? You gotta live till you die. And what do we do every day? Go to school and do homework. That's not living.'

She has a point. But. 'Isn't there something a little less dangerous?'

'It's the danger that makes it exciting,' Sarah says.

'I think I've had enough excitement in my life,' Alex says. 'And now that I've Maggie, I should probably try to stay alive.'

Sarah looks at me. Expectantly. The thought of jumping out of a plane at however many thousand feet makes my stomach plummet. 'Could we do something else exciting?'

'It's OK. Forget it,' she says. 'It was just an idea.'

But she sounds depressed and I'm thinking, I don't know, maybe she needs this. I think of bungee jumping. Then remember the girl whose chord snapped.

'White water rafting?' I try.

'Yeah?' She cheers right up.

Mark comes over and sits beside me. And I cheer up myself. I miss the time when David was going out with Alex and I was with Mark and we'd all sit together. Now he tends to sit with the people he plays rugby with, rather than be the only guy with us.

'Just came to say break a leg,' he says.

'Thanks. I think.'

'Nervous?'

)I(

'A bit.'

'I could come.'

I smile. 'Thanks anyway.'

'All right then, best of luck. Give me a call later, yeah?'

I nod.

His eyes hold mine and I know he wants to kiss me as much as I want to kiss him. We never do. In here.

At a quarter to one, Alex and Sarah come outside with me. We hug and they wish me luck.

'Maybe I won't go.'

'Why wouldn't you go?' Sarah asks surprised.

'It's just not great timing.' I look at them.

'You're going,' they say together. Sarah puts her hands flat on my back and pushes me towards the car. Alex opens the door. Then I'm in. I lower the window. 'You'll be OK, yeah?'

'Shut up,' Alex says.

And I do because I know how annoying it is when someone thinks you can't take care of yourself.

In fifteen minutes, we're at the studio. Mum starts to get out of the car.

'Mum, it's OK! You don't have to come in.' This is a job. You don't turn up with your mother.

She stops and looks at me for a minute. 'You sure?'

'Yeah. Thanks.'

She smiles, then says, 'You'll be great.' She looks a little teary, like she thinks I'm emigrating or something. 'I'll see you when you get out.'

'Mum, I'll be hours. Don't wait.'

'It's fine. I've got my book.' She holds it up.

'You're running a catering business.'

'It's quiet.'

'That could change.'

'I want to be here for you.'

'Mum, it'll probably be rush hour when I get out. I'd actually be quicker in a taxi. There's a whole line of them outside the TV centre.'

She looks at me, unsure.

I check my watch. 'I better go.'

'OK, but if the taxi driver looks in any way dodgy don't get in. Just call me. OK?'

'OK.'

She hugs me tight.

'See you later,' I say and go.

I can't believe the executive producer, the actual boss of the whole show, is showing me around. She's in her, like, forties and looks like the most confident person I've ever met. I nearly drop when she tells me to call her Emily. Then she actually apologises that I've to share a dressing room.

She opens the door to it.

It's a simple room in pale pink with a bench and two dressing tables. They have mirrors with bulbs around them. One side of the room is full of stuff – clothes, magazines, shoes, posters. On the wall are stills from *The Devil Wears Prada*. The dressing table is jammed with make-up, perfume, necklaces and a small bunch of flowers. It's the side of the room that's alive. And it's kind of spilling over into the other side.

'You'll be sharing with Rebecca French, who plays Daisy. We try to put people around the same age together. Unless you and Rebecca are filming at similar times, you'll probably have it mostly to yourself.'

)-(

'It's lovely,' I say. Everything will be fine. It was a long time ago.

She opens a door to a shower room – also full of stuff. 'I'm sure Rebecca will clean that up now that she's sharing.'

Wouldn't bet on it, I think.

'Now, I'll quickly show you around,' she says.

Following her around the studio, I can't believe how small the sets are. The pub is tiny, like a very small room. So's the clinic, the coffee shop, the restaurant.

'Everything looks miniature,' I say without thinking.

'It's to get as many of the cast as possible into one shot. The camera angles make everywhere look bigger.'

'Wow,' I say, fascinated.

It's amazing how many people are involved in the show. Two directors, one for the indoor scenes, one for outdoor. Two cast managers for making sure that all of the cast are where they're meant to be for shooting. And two floor managers to supervise each shoot. Each team needs all its own crew. And then there's the cast. I'm introduced to whoever isn't actually working on something as we pass by. I try to remember names, but it's impossible. Everyone's so friendly when they don't have to be. I'll be gone in three months.

Emily walks me back to the dressing room. 'I was hoping to introduce you to Josh, who plays Joe, but he's not in yet. I'll try and pop down later.'

'Don't worry. It's fine,' I say. 'You've taken up so much of your time already.'

She knocks on the door to the dressing room, then opens it. 'Oh, good. Rebecca's here. I wanted to introduce you two before I go.'

She's sitting at the far dressing table, removing make-up with facial wipes.

)(

'Rebecca, this is Rachel.'

'Oh, *hi*,' she says, bursting into a smile. She gets up and comes over. She stops smiling and starts squinting. 'Do I *know* you?'

'Rachel Dunne. We were in junior school together.' I look her straight in the eye so she knows I've changed. I'm not afraid.

'Oh, my God. *Rachel Dunne*,' she says, as if we were besties.

'I'll leave you girls to it,' Emily says, smiling.

'Rach-*el* Dunne,' Rebecca says again and I know she's remembering. Everything.

I'm remembering. All the names for stupid and what it was like to be called them. Having stuff stolen and worn to my face. How a smile can kill.

'Rebec-*ca* French,' I say back, still eyeballing her.

'So where did you disappear off to, in sixth class?'

'Went and got myself a life.'

'You needed one.' She laughs.

'Do you *always* laugh at your own jokes?'

She looks surprised. 'It wasn't a joke.' Then she laughs like she's joking.

I smile like I don't care, she can say whatever she wants and her words will miss their target.

There's a knock on the door.

'Rachel?'

I turn.

'They're ready for you in Wardrobe.'

'Great.' I don't turn back to Rebecca, I just go.

In Wardrobe, there are racks and racks of costumes, a full-length mirror, a camera and loads of stills of cast members pinned onto a huge board. I'm introduced to someone called Rita who looks me over, then goes to a nearby clothes rail. She selects a costume she has already put together. She collects shoes and hands me a bundle.

'Do you want to try those on in your dressing room and come back to me, and we'll see how you look?'

Five-inch shoes, micro-mini and low-cut top. I know how I'll look. But I just smile.

'Thanks.'

'Oh, nearly forgot.' She goes to her desk, opens a drawer and roots for a minute. The she lifts up ginormous diamondy earrings. She comes over and hands them to me. I've seen the same ones in Penneys. They were nice but not me.

Back in the (thankfully, empty) dressing room, I change into my costume then check it out in the mirror. The skirt is shorter than I thought. *At least I don't have to sit down in it*, I think.

I go back to Wardrobe.

'Hmm,' Rita says. 'The skirt.'

Exactly.

'We need to up it a bit.' She reaches out and turns the waistband over, bringing the skirt so high that it stops just below my bum.

I'm so shocked, I actually thank her.

She takes photos for Continuity, so that she can dress me exactly the same if she needs to - for reshoots or editing. This is so interesting to me.

From Wardrobe, I go to Make-Up. Two actors sit in front of mirrors, having their faces done. One of them is an older actress who made the show on Saturday night. Her face is full of humour and her brown eyes sparkle mischievously. She's chatting to a skinny, male make-up artist. In the mirror, she looks serious. But whatever she's saying cracks the guy up.

'Maisie, you're a riot,' he says.

'You're the riot, Damien,' she says, still serious.

The other actor is Josh Haley who plays Joe. He's even more good-looking in real life – though his lips are a bit weird. Kind of like a baby's.

Damien removes Maisie's cape. She stands and thanks him. On her way out, she smiles at me. Then Damien is on his way over. He's young but balding, his hair shaved tight. He's wearing a grey, ribbed jumper that falls expensively. His belt has a pewter buckle. Strapped low around his hips, like a tool-belt, is a special holder for make-up brushes. His smile is wide.

'Hi, I'm Damien.'

'Rachel.' I smile back.

He shows me to the chair Maisie was in, then puts a cape around my shoulders.

'So just rest your head back against the headrest.' He puts his hands on my shoulders to make sure I do. 'There.'

I look at him in the mirror. It's like being in a hairdresser's. I half expect him to ask him about my summer holidays. Only it's November.

'So, you're new,' he says, like I'm interesting. 'How do *you* fit in to the plot?'

I'm not sure what I can tell him. How that works. We're not supposed to share the plot with anyone. Then again, he works here.

'Oh I've just a small part,' I say, just in case.

'Tell me about it.'

'I think I have to, like, flirt with Joe.'

He widens his eyes at me, then he whispers, 'Lucky you.'

I smile and start to relax.

He lifts pieces of hair and lets them fall. I'm thinking, *Isn't he the* make-up *guy*?

'What do you use to wash your hair?' he asks.

Surprised, I tell him the brand of shampoo.

He tells me another. Just says it. Like I should use it. Like it's an order.

'I'll get it,' I say.

'Do you brush?'

'My hair?'

'No, your teeth,' he says sarcastically. 'Of course your hair.'

'Not really.'

He rolls his eyes. 'Are you telling me you had to get a part in a TV drama for a queen to tell you to brush your hair?'

I smile.

'Ready for make-up?' he says like he's quoting a line from an ad.

'Ready.'

Wearing thin, transparent, plastic gloves he applies foundation with a sponge. I close my eyes. It's so relaxing. Until Rebecca French comes crashing into my mind. Along with all the others. She wasn't even the ringleader. Béibhinn Keane was. Rebecca was the side-kick. I see their faces so clearly and when I start to feel my stomach twist, I remind myself what's different. Back then, I was alone. My parents had just separated me from Jack by moving me down a class. They said I was in his shadow. So they took the shadow away. Leaving me exposed, a turtle without its shell. It was like Rebecca and her gang smelled it, like they knew instinctively that I was easy prey, the

)(

weakling of the herd. When they moved in on me, I was so shocked, I didn't put up a fight. Now, it's different. I've been without Jack for six years. I'm the 'individual' my parents wanted me to be. I don't need anyone now. I can take Rebecca French if I have to.

'Are you OK?'

I open my eyes.

'You feel a little tense.'

'Sorry.'

'Don't be sorry, it's your first time. Just take loads of deep breaths.'

I nod and take one. To keep him happy.

He brushes on powder. I close my eyes again. I can't blame my parents. It was my own fault. I was copying his homework. He was faster. It was easier. If we both finished quickly, we'd have more time outside, playing football. When I started failing, our parents warned us to stop. We didn't. It was our little rebellion. Us against the world. The way it always was back then.

I feel cold running along my eyelids as Damien applies liquid eyeliner.

'OK, now look up.'

He puts more eyeliner on my lower lids. Then under them. I try not to blink.

'It's OK,' he says when I do. 'Nearly finished.'

Then he asks me to close my eyes again and puts more on my upper lids.

When eventually I look in the mirror, I am a different person.

'Wow.'

'Not finished,' he says. There's pride in his voice. And I hope that when I eventually have a job, I'll love it as much as he loves his. He darkens my eyebrows then fluffs up my hair so I look like I'm the kind of person who doesn't care about hair. Or anything. He even gives me black nail varnish. All this for one line.

'Thanks so much.'

'Are you kidding? You're a pleasure to work on.'

'Really?'

'Such cheekbones.'

I smile. And love him. Though I never love anyone that quickly. It took me ages to go out with Mark, to trust that he wasn't just messing me around. Even now, I have to force myself to trust people.

Damien looks at me through the mirror. 'What's your character's name?'

'Naomi.'

'Well, hel-lo, Naomi.'

And while he takes continuity shots, I try to get used to the whole new person sitting in the chair looking back at me.

Back in the, still empty, dressing room, I wait to be called. I sit at the mirror, trying out voices.

'Mess with me, I'll rip your heart out.'

'Daisy, you are *fucking* dead.'

I laugh. But no matter what I say or how many times I say it, nothing sounds right. Finally, I realise why. Naomi would *think* all these things; she'd never say them. She'd use a look. And that would be it.

I wait ages to be called on set. When I finally am, I feel a jolt of nerves, like a shot of adrenaline. This is it. My chance. As I walk down the corridor, towards the exit, in my head I'm singing Eminem. 'If you had one shot, one opportunity …'

)(

For exterior shots, they have a minibus to take us to the lot. It's waiting outside. Onboard is a handful of other actors and crew. I try to climb up the steps without revealing my entire ass.

'Hey,' says a voice.

I look up. It's Josh Haley, sitting just inside the door.

'Oh, hey,' I say back. I sit in the seat behind him.

He turns around. Smiles blankly. 'You're playing Naomi, right?'

I nod. 'Rachel, by the way.'

'Josh ... So this is your first time?' he says, like he's talking about sex.

I can't think of a comeback. And worse, I blush.

'You'll be grand,' he says. 'We don't bite ... Usually.'

Another person gets on and the bus takes off. It's six o'clock now. It's dark and cold and I'm sorry I didn't bring a coat. My teeth are chattering. We arrive at a fake world of one-dimensional buildings. On one side of the 'street' is the coffee shop, the deli, the book shop and the wine bar; on the other, the newsagent's, the pharmacy and the restaurant. Another set, farther down and now in semi-darkness, features the clinic and the homes of the main characters. There are lights, cameras and groups of talking people. A Wardrobe person fiddles with my costume. A Make-Up person dusts Josh's face.

The floor manager comes over to us.

'Right, we'll do one rehearsal, then we'll shoot. OK?'

I nod.

'You know your line?' he says to me.

'Got a light?' I say.

'OK. Good. Now try saying it like you mean, "Come to bed with me."'

I nod in shock.

}{

Someone hands me an unlit cigarette. I hold it between my fingers and try to imagine I've been smoking all my life.

'OK, we're ready.'

With fake confidence, I walk over to the fake pub. I wait in the fake shadow. With my real cigarette.

'Five, four, three, two, one, action.' My heart jumps.

The door of the pub opens. Joe walks out. He turns his collar up against the cold. From his pocket, he takes a pack of cigarettes and a lighter. He taps out a cigarette and lights up. He inhales deeply, then tips his head back and blows smoke into the sky. *Oh God. Here I go.* I walk out from the shadows like a girl who wants *everyone* to come to bed with her. Joe sees me coming. We lock eyes. I move slowly like I've all the time in the world. I go right up to him, gaze into his eyes, let the moment stretch. 'Got a light?'

A smile creeps over his face, like he's imagining all the things he could do with a trouble-maker like me. He flicks open his lighter like he's James Bond – the only good Bond, Daniel Craig. I lean into the flame, still holding his eyes.

'And cut!' the director calls. 'OK, from the top. Places everyone.'

Standing in the shadows, I become Naomi. I don't care about anything or anyone. I do what I want, when I want.

'And action.'

I walk out like I own the world, like this guy with the lighter is nothing. I stand in front of him. I don't ask for a light. Because I'm a taker. I don't use words. I use my body. I put the cigarette slowly, deliberately, between my lips and lean into him. He does *not* have a choice. He looks surprised but totally turned on. And when he lights me up, it is like he's answering a question.

)(

'Cut!'

Crud, crud, crud, crud, crud. What was I thinking? I just ignored the script on my very first day. I'm going to be kicked off the show. Right here, right now. Before I even get a chance to appear on TV. Charley's going to kill me. Oh God. The director's on his way over. His strides are huge for a little guy. He looks so serious. I'm doomed.

'What happened to the line?' he asks me.

I go for honesty. It's all I've got. 'I'm sorry. I just felt that someone like Naomi would use her body instead of words.'

He looks surprised. Then says, 'Right. Do it again. And stick to the script.'

I nod quickly. 'Sorry.'

When he walks away, Josh whispers, 'I thought it was good.'

I'm so embarrassed. It's my first time here and already people think I'm a diva.

We go for a third take. This time I stick to the script. I try so hard to make it as good as the last time. But I know, in my heart, it isn't.

'And cut,' he says.

We turn around.

'OK, that's it,' he says. His face is closed, no expression.

'Thank you,' I say.

He walks off.

'No need to thank him,' Josh says quietly.

I feel like a tool.

'That was good.' He says it like he's surprised. 'Ballsy.'

I look around. People are already setting up for the next shot. 'Are you going back on the bus?' I ask him.

'Nah, I've another scene.'

Course he has. 'OK, see you, I guess.'

ℋ

'Sure. Trouble.'

Trouble? He has no clue how wrong he is. Why didn't I just do what I was told? I *always* do what I'm told. Why break a lifetime's habit the one time I needed to stick to it? I go back to the dressing room, relieved to find it empty. I strip out of the gear. I can't believe I didn't think of bringing casual clothes to change into. I climb back into my uniform. I sit in front of the mirror to remove the make-up. Without it, I look so young. So innocent. So me.

I grab my bag. I'm sorry now I said I'd get a taxi home.

I walk out into drizzle. I pull up my hood. I head for the taxi rank, feeling kind of lonely.

'Yo!' A car pulls up beside me.

I turn. It's Mark. It's so amazing to see him. 'What're you doing here?'

'We'd a match in Donnybrook. Thought I'd drive by and see if I could pick up any stars.'

I smile. 'This is your lucky day.' I jump in and kiss him.

'How did it go?' he asks.

'It was *so* good. Then I acted like a total diva.' I tell him what happened.

'Ah, you'll be grand.'

Sometimes, I wish he wasn't always so casual. 'Mark, it wasn't what they wanted.'

'Yeah, well, maybe what they wanted wasn't what was needed,' he says, so chill.

'You should do debating.'

He laughs. 'Yeah. Imagine.'

We drive to the studio gates. The traffic's jammers.

'Love you, baby,' Mark says to a woman who lets us out. He blows her a kiss.

'Did I miss much at school?'

He shakes his head. 'The usual.'

'That's much.'

'Nah. Anyway. I got you notes.'

'Aw. Sweetie.' He never takes notes.

I call my mum, tell her I'm studying at Mark's.

His mum is out tonight and his dad's due home late. So it's just us and Mark's kid brother Rex having take-away pizza and Coke. Mum would be horrified. Which makes it taste better.

Alex texts to see how I got on in *D4*.

'OK, I think!' I text back. 'Did Louis call 2 C Maggie?'

'Yup. Still here. Better go.'

'Sure. C U tomorrow.' *Yaay.*

Afterwards, we go up to Mark's room, which is a bit like Mark – a surprise. It's got the kind of things you'd expect – basketball hoop, gum ball dispenser – then there are the books, shelves and shelves of them. He even has a wardrobe of books. Like a library. And in a corner of his room, he has a book city, skyscrapers of books like the Manhattan skyline. I never knew he was a reader until I started going out with him. I liked the surprise.

We fly through the homework. Well, I fly. He keeps getting distracted. And trying to distract me. Finally, he gives up and collapses onto the bed with *Lord of the Flies*. He looks so cute, hair all ruffled, eyes following the words. I love it when he reads. He goes all still. Totally in the zone.

'What's the book about?' I ask. The name's familiar.

'Flies,' he says, without looking up.

'Seriously?'

He looks over. 'No. It's about a bunch of boys stuck on an island.'

'What age?'

He shrugs. 'Junior school?'

'Any good?'

'Yeah it's good,' he says, like it's an understatement.

I'd love to have time to be like Mark, to read just for fun, instead of always trying to cram more information into an already full brain. I go back to the notes. And try to be quick.

By ten, I'm done. I run to him, rip the book from his hands and land on top of him.

'About time,' he says, smiling.

We kiss. He smells so good. So Mark.

'I want Caecilius. In a *sexual* way.'

He laughs. Then we're kissing again. We can't get close enough, quick enough. His hands are everywhere at the same time. Magically. I don't want to stop. He struggles with my top. I open his shirt. He rips it off, then pulls me close. I feel a bulge in his jeans. And smile.

'Caecilius est horny,' I say, reaching for his belt.

He puts his hands on mine and stops me. It's not a surprise. Ever since Alex got pregnant, he's been paranoid that it'll happen to us. Even though we never actually do anything that could make it happen.

'Come *on*,' I say. 'We need to release the little guy.'

'Less of the little.'

'Big. Massive.'

'All true, but he's staying where he is.'

'I have condoms.'

'Which aren't a hundred per cent safe.'

'*Ma-rk!* We're going out a year!' Sarah's done it. Alex has. Even if they hadn't, I'd still want to. I just want to be with him.

'I don't want to risk it,' he says.

)(

I can't believe this is Mark. Who never worries. I should be happy, really. He's being so sensible.

'I just don't want that whole situation for you,' he says.

'Or you,' I say miserably.

'OK, or me. We're young, Rache. Let's stay that way. Yeah?'

I think of Alex, all that responsibility. How Maggie always has to come first. Alex last. At seventeen. I know he's right – but that doesn't help.

'Might as well study, then,' I say miserably, shoving my hand into the sleeve of my shirt. I go over to his desk, sit down. But I'm so aware of him, running his hands through his hair, sighing. He drags on his shirt. Goes to the window and opens it. He stands looking out – for ages. And I can't be angry at him.

'Let's go out,' he says.

Five minutes after I'm back in my room, there's a knock. Jack sticks his head around the door.

'Hey,' he says.

'Hey.'

'How did *D4* go?'

It's half-eleven. I'm not going into it. 'Yeah, grand.'

'Did you meet Rebecca French?'

'Jack, you're so predictable.'

'Yeah, OK, but did you?'

'We're sharing a dressing room,' I say, like it's no big deal.

'I don't fucking believe it.'

'Jack, I told you. There's nothing to worry about. I'm not taking any crap.'

'Did she give you any?'

'No. Look, I'm in there for three months. Rebecca French is not important. What is important is that I make an impact so I get other roles. That's it.'

He nods. 'OK. Cool.' He comes in, sits on the bed.

'Jack it's half-eleven.'

'So?'

'There's this thing called school.'

'Since when's school more important than *shootin' the bweeze* with my twin?' he lisps jokingly.

He hasn't called me 'twin' in years. I love that he has. It's like a rebellion. So I let him stay. And 'shoot the bweeze'.

FOUR
Cardboard

The next day, we're sitting in the school canteen.

'I can't breathe,' Alex says.

I stare at her. You can get a blood clot after a baby. 'What is it?' I ask urgently.

'My skirt's too tight.'

I laugh in relief.

'What?' she asks, like I'm heartless.

'Sorry. I thought it was something serious.'

'It is serious. I'm huge.'

'Open a button,' Sarah says.

Alex slips her hand under her jumper and opens her button. 'This is seriously depressing.' She shoves her plate away. Then pulls it back again. 'I'm starving.'

I smile.

Around us the canteen is buzzing. Usual people sitting in the usual places with the usual friends. How can we all make so much noise?

Alex keeps checking the clock.

'You OK?' Sarah asks eventually.

'She's due a feed.'

'Jane's there.'

'I'm her mum. I should be there.'

'You will be,' I say.

'I hated leaving her this morning … Do you think she misses me?' she asks, looking at us like she really needs an answer.

But there is no answer. No, yes – either way you lose. 'You don't have to be here, Ali,' I say gently. 'Leave it for a while. Most people take three months.'

'No. I promised myself my life wouldn't change.' She takes a deep breath, then turns to me. 'Tell us about *D4*,' she says, like it's suddenly the most important thing in the world.

And so, to take her mind off Maggie, I do.

'You diva!' Sarah says to me. But looks impressed.

'I don't know what happened. I just don't do things like that.'

'Wouldn't worry about it,' Alex says.

Which reminds me. There are bigger things.

'So, did you meet anyone famous?' Sarah asks enthusiastically.

I think for a second. 'No one on that show really *is* famous.'

'What's the actor who plays Joe like?' Alex asks.

'Josh? He seems OK.'

'Yeah but d'you like him or not?' Alex asks.

'I've just met him.'

'Yeah but what's your gut feeling?'

I shrug. 'He was nice when I screwed up.'

'How about the actress who plays Daisy?' Sarah asks.

'We're sharing a dressing room.'

'But what's she like?'

'She's OK.'

'So *she's* OK? But you don't know about Josh?' Sarah asks, smiling.

'They're both OK. OK?'

'Only, when you said *she's* OK, you sounded like she's not.'

'What?!'

'You're too nice,' Alex says.

'What d'you *mean*?' I ask.

'You don't diss people. Ever.'

'Oh, my God. That's so not it! I just need time to decide.'

'How much time?' Alex ask.

'I don't know. A year?'

We laugh.

Amy Gilmore comes up to our table and sits down.

'*What*, Amy?' Alex snaps.

People think Amy's pretty. I just see her personality on her face. Cow.

Amy ignores Alex, looking only at Sarah. 'Did you post something on Shane's wall last night?'

Sarah goes white. 'What?' she asks quietly.

'"Cadbury's Flake Allure, yum"?'

'I didn't post that,' Sarah whispers.

'Then how did I read it?'

Sarah says nothing.

'You know, it's kind of messed up that his wall is still up but, like, *writing* on it.'

'OK, Amy, you can fuck off now,' Alex says.

Sarah gets up in silence and walks out.

I stare at Amy. 'What? You just can't help being a total bitch, is that it?'

'I was just trying to help,' she says innocently. 'You know, people are going to rip her apart if she goes on like that.'

'Oh, you mean like you just ripped her apart?' I say, then go after Alex who has just walked out.

In the hall, I catch up with her. Simon is coming towards us.

'Did you see Sarah?' Alex asks him.

)(

'Yeah, she's at her locker, getting her coat.' He looks concerned. 'Is she OK?'

'Yeah, fine thanks.'

When we get to the lockers, Sarah's shutting hers. She turns and sees us. Her face falls even further.

'You think I'm mad, don't you?' she asks quietly.

'No!' we say together.

'I didn't mean to post it.' She sighs, closes her eyes and leans back against her locker.

'So what if you did?' Alex says.

Sarah looks at Alex. 'Sometimes I message him. Just to say hi. Tell him stuff. Silly stuff. Like, OK, "Cadbury's Flake Allure, yum". I know it's dumb but when I press send, I imagine the words going out into the universe and getting to him. Somehow.' Her eyes widen. 'He can't just be gone, you know?'

Her voice cracks and she looks *so* lonely. I want to wave a magic wand and make things better.

'I think it's genius,' Alex says. 'If my mum had Facebook, I'd be on to her all the time, telling her what's happening, telling her about Maggie, how alike they are, every little thing she's missing.'

Now Alex sounds sad.

'You're not just saying that?' Sarah says.

'Why would I?'

'To make me feel better?'

'Sarah, no one knows what happens, no one knows what's possible. You know what I think? I think there's so much energy in a thought that you can send it anywhere. I send thoughts to Mum all the time. And I know she gets them. I feel it. I feel her a lot, especially since Maggie was born. I think that humans have all these powers that we don't use because we're afraid to admit we have them. We have them when we're kids and, over time, we switch them off. There's so much that we never tap into. No one knows what's on the other side, and we won't till we're there. But how pissed off will we be when we find out all the things we could have been doing and didn't?'

Sarah brightens. 'You think?'

'Of course I think. Fuck Amy. She's the emotional intelligence of a fish.'

Sarah smiles. 'Or slug.'

'I'm thinking piece of cardboard,' I say.

We laugh.

'Group hug,' says Alex, half-messing.

But we do hug. It's like powering-up.

When I get home, the kitchen's a mess. Mum is reorganising all her catering equipment. It's everywhere – over every inch of worktop. I get a yoghurt and sit at the table. She stops what she's doing and makes a coffee. Then she sits with me.

She blows on her coffee, then looks up from it. 'Jack told me you're sharing with Rebecca French.' She looks concerned.

I'll kill him. 'When did he tell you that?'

'Over breakfast.'

This is what happens when I leave early.

'Maybe we should ask them to move you.'

'Oh, my God. No! *D4* is an adult production. They don't want to have to treat us like kids.'

'It's just changing rooms.'

'Mum! It's fine. I can take care of myself, OK? If I want to change rooms, I'll ask to change rooms.'

)(

'Are you going to?'

Oh, my God. 'There's no need to. Rebecca's fine.'

'You know what she's like.'

'I know what she *was* like.'

'I'm just worried.'

'Mum, I'm a big girl now. I can handle myself. OK?'

She looks at me for a very long time. 'OK.'

I go up to my room. And for the rest of the afternoon, I listen out for Jack coming in from after-school study. At last, I hear him trudging up the stairs and into his room. I jump up.

I don't knock, just go in and get straight to the point. 'I can't believe you told Mum I'm sharing with Rebecca French.'

He drops his bag and looks up. 'I thought she should know,' he says, like it's no big deal.

'Why?'

'Because it's relevant.'

'No it's not. Stop worrying her. You know what happened last time.' Our parents almost split up. Each of them wanted to handle it differently. Dad wanted to rush in all guns blazing. Mum wanted to go the diplomatic route. She won. Then lost, when it didn't work. Dad wanted to sue the school. She refused. Then he blamed her. And she exploded. Dad almost moved out. Just thinking about it makes me sick.

'You're right. We shouldn't involve them. But we should do something.'

'No, *we* shouldn't. They split us up so I'd be independent. *I'll* handle it.'

'OK but *do*. Don't let it spin out of control like the last time.'

Oh, my God. 'Just trust me, OK?'

)(

'OK,' he says, like he's sorry. 'You'll be fine.'

'I *will* be fine.'

He looks at me as if to say, are you sure?

And because I can read his mind, I say, 'Yes, I'm sure.'

The following morning, my costume is a school uniform – with a *very* short skirt. So short, no school would actually allow it. Then again, Naomi wouldn't care what her school allowed. I stand in front of the mirror. But still look like me. I roll up the sleeves. Loosen the tie. Open the first two buttons of the shirt. Still not there. So I bend down and pull the socks up over my knees.

'Yes!' Rita in Wardrobe says when she sees me. Then she tilts her head to the side. 'Not sure about the skirt, though.'

I open my mouth to say, 'Too short.'

'Too long,' she says. She comes up to me, then turns over the waistband like it's a habit she has, like having a coffee after a meal. She stands back. 'Better.'

For the pervs who'll be watching.

In Make-Up, Damien takes ages.

'My work here is done,' he says finally, proudly.

I hang around the dressing room, studying while I'm waiting to be called. Finally, I am. I pick up my fake school bag. It's way too light so I stick some of my books in.

Climbing onto the minibus at eight in the morning feels like I really am going to school.

'Pretty laid-back principal you have there, allowing that skirt.' It's Josh.

)(

Naomi would have a comeback. I don't. And when I blush, I hope he's not thinking I fancy him. I sit near him to show I'm not intimidated. Despite the blushing.

'So,' he says cheerfully. 'Looks like we're going to get together.'

I look him straight in the eye. Then I have it. 'How d'you know I won't end up with Daisy?' I raise my eyebrows.

He bursts out laughing. 'I'd like to see that.'

And just like that, it feels like we're equal. Not the experienced actor and the newbie.

When we get to the lot, we stand around in front of the clinic. It's freezing. Someone hands me an unlit cigarette. Someone else dusts my face with powder. Another lowers the skirt back down. I'd go over my lines, if I had any. Instead, I try to get inside Naomi's head. I think of something to make me angry. Amy Gilmore giving Sarah a hard time. That works. We rehearse the scene once. Then someone lights my cigarette. I wait for the director to shout 'action', the dreaded word that makes my heart thump in a way that I love.

'And action.'

I take a massive deep breath then walk out onto the set. Smoking. Joe comes out of the clinic, dressed in a school uniform. When he sees me, he stops, looks me over and smiles.

'I see you've got a light,' he says.

I raise an eyebrow and walk past him.

'You know, smoking'll kill you,' he calls after me.

Outside the surgery, I look at him while I drop the cigarette to the ground and stomp it out. Then I turn and march inside. I know from the script that Joe is looking after Naomi 'with great interest'.

'And cut.'

There are two retakes. No one tells us why. Then, just like that, we're done. It's only nine-thirty. We go back on the bus together.

'I enjoyed that,' he says.

Surprised, I say, 'Me too.'

Back in the dressing room, I go into the bathroom. I change out of one uniform, into another. It's like coming down from a high. The skirt that I have no problem with usually makes me feel like a granny. I turn the waistband over. Twice. I take off the make-up and flatten down my hair, but not completely. Then I leave the bathroom.

Rebecca, sitting at her dressing table, turns around when she hears the door open.

'Hey!' she smiles.

Her friendliness feels weird. 'Hey,' I say. Without the smile. I'm not fake.

'So, who was that guy who picked you up the other day?' she asks.

I look at her. She saw Mark? 'My boyfriend.' I'm happy to report.

She looks surprised. Like maybe I'm not still a loser.

'Hot guy.'

'*I* like him.' Oh, yeah.

'Is he an actor?'

'No.'

'Model?'

I smile thinking how he'd laugh at that. 'No.'

'How do you know him?'

'He's in my class.'

She looks disappointed.

'Hey, I must add you on Facebook,' she says.

Wow, I think sarcastically. *A dream come true.*

I've just missed the start of Maths. Mr Harte (ancient, dresses in suits and fires chalk at us) does not look impressed.

'So, Rachel Dunne, you've decided to grace us with your presence.'

'I've permission to be out.' I root for my note, then go up and hand it to him. He scans it then looks up. 'A star in our midst, it seems,' he says sarcastically.

Everyone's suddenly awake, wondering what he's on about.

'All right, sit down.'

I look only at my desk as I walk to it. Next time, I don't care how much I miss, I'm not walking in when class has started.

'Where's your Maths book?' he asks when he sees I don't have it.

'I forgot it.' I left it in the fake school bag in *D4*.

'Do you really think that is an acceptable answer in Fifth Year?'

I look at him with his cheap pen in the top pocket of his short-sleeved shirt, the ordinary glasses on top of his head. I am so close to saying yes. Naomi would. I send him some bad karma instead. It doesn't feel like enough.

Anyway, screw him. The main thing is that I keep up with the class, I concentrate hard and am surprised when the bell finally goes. I've managed it. I'm still OK.

As I collect my stuff, Amy Gilmore turns around in her seat.

)(

'What did he say about a star?'

'No clue,' I say, getting up and legging it over to Alex. 'Let's get out of here,' I say as Sarah joins us.

By first break, I could eat my arm I'm so hungry. I fill my tray. And dive into a packet of crisps before I get to the till. I catch Alex looking at me.

'Missed breakfast,' I explain.

'Thought for a minute, there, you were preggers.'

When she sees the horrified look on my face, she bursts out laughing. 'Joke. You feel like shite when you're pregnant.'

'For the record,' I say quietly, 'we're not doing anything that would make me pregnant.'

'Good! Keep it that way.'

'Yes, Mummy.'

We get to our usual table.

'So how did the "star" get on today?' Alex asks.

'I wish he'd just thrown the chalk.' Wanker.

'How many scenes did you have?' she asks.

'Just one.'

'With Josh?'

'Yup.'

'Does he still "seem OK"?'

Sarah's turning her engagement ring round and round on her finger. I want to ask if she's OK but don't want to drown her in a spotlight. So I distract her instead.

'I'm pretty sure he thinks I fancy him.'

'Oh, my God. Seriously?' Sarah asks, looking up.

'He's an actor,' Alex says, sounding bored. 'He probably thinks everyone fancies him. What were your lines?'

'Didn't have any.'

'Oh,' she sounds disappointed.

'Don't worry,' Sarah says reassuringly. 'You'll get more.'

'It's OK. Naomi's great. I love her.'

'I'm *so* dying to see you,' Sarah says.

I smile and think maybe Sarah really does have the secret to life – just forget everything and live till you die.

The following day, I'm waiting in the dressing room, ready to go on set. I'm struggling with a Maths problem. I just can't get it out. It's killing me. Whoever invented Project Maths should be tasered. In the nipples. Repeatedly.

'I added you on Facebook,' Rebecca says expectantly.

I look up. She's taking off nail varnish like she's all the time in the world. What – doesn't she *get* homework? 'Oh, right. I haven't been on Facebook,' I lie. I did see the request, but the only people I'm friends with on Facebook are real friends, people I trust. Which makes the number small.

'Why don't you do it now? You've an iPhone, right?'

'I'll do it later. I'm trying to figure something out here.'

'Just give me your phone and I'll do it.'

I look at her. 'Do you still hang around with Béibhinn Keane?'

She shakes her head. 'We went to different secondary schools. We're probably still friends on Facebook – but I'm friends with half the world on Facebook.' She thinks for a minute. 'Look,' she says. 'What happened before … can we just forget about that? It was years ago.

Everything's changed. We were different people then. Stupid,' she says like an admission.

'I've no problem with you Rebecca,' I say, but my voice sounds cold.

'So can we be fwends?' she jokes.

I look at her for a long time and think, *fwends might be easier than enemies, as we're sharing a room. Still, fwends is not friends.*

'Sure,' I say.

'So. Facebook?'

'Oh yeah.' I take out my phone but I don't hand it over. Because I am the one in control.

She looks over my shoulder while I accept her friend request. I'm thinking, *I can always unfriend her later*.

'Cool,' she says. Then she's gone, back to her dressing table. She picks up her phone, sits down, puts her legs up on the dressing table and tips her chair back like she's settling in for a while.

First thing she's going to think is how few friends I have. But who cares? I've more important things to worry about. I go over the Maths problem again. I start to underline stuff – like *that's* going to help.

'Are you *friends* with Alex *Newman*?' she asks, eyes still on her phone.

I look up. She's staring at me. Like how could *I* possibly have friends like Alex? 'Sorry, what?'

'Nothing,' she says. I watch her scroll away and know she's checking out every one of my friends.

I go back to the Maths. I give up on the problem and try the next one. I hate having to do that.

'What's your number, by the way?' she asks eventually.

I call it out but change the last digit. It should be 277. I tell her 227. People are always making that mistake.

'Want mine?' she asks.

'Sure.' I pick up my phone and punch her number in. I won't be using it.

I go on set, do my scene. When I come back, Rebecca's still there. I go into the bathroom to change. When I come out, she's sitting at my dressing table, reading what looks like my script for next week.

'Hello?' I say, as in, *What the hell?*

She turns slowly. 'Hey,' she says, all friendly. 'They dropped in our scripts. Good news. They're giving Naomi a terminal illness.'

'What?' I go over. She hands me the script. I look at her, still sitting in my chair.

'Oh, sorry.' She gets up and goes to hers.

I sit and read. It's a scene where Joe's mother tells Naomi she has cancer. Incurable cancer. I don't know why it's such a shock. I knew it was a small part anyway. I put the script in my bag. *Crap*, I think.

'What's wrong?' she asks, surprised.

'Nothing. It's grand.'

'I can't believe you're not excited. I've always wanted a terminal illness.'

Hilarious, I think, glad I've given her the wrong number.

In the taxi on the way to school, I call Charley.

'They've given Naomi terminal cancer.'

'Really? That's great!'

'It is?'

'Rachel, have you *ever* seen a programme where a terminal illness isn't dramatic? If they know what they're doing – and they do – for a while, you'll be the centre of the show.'

'Really?' I feel dumb. And happy.

'I wonder why they never mentioned terminal illness before?' she asks, like she's thinking aloud. 'I'll get on to them. This is great news Rachel. And a huge opportunity to get noticed. Play it right—' she starts.

'Don't worry. I will.'

'I want to see all your scripts from now on.'

'OK.'

'Scan them in and email them.'

'OK.'

'And well done,' she says, like it has something to do with me. 'And I don't need to tell you to keep the storyline to yourself.'

'Of course.' Emily has already warned me about that. 'Thanks so much, Charley.'

And as I hang up, I realise I was wrong about Rebecca. She wasn't being sarcastic. She was actually glad for me.

Still, when I get home, first thing I do is go on Facebook. To check if she and Béibhinn Keane are still hanging out. Rebecca has over a thousand friends. Many of them fans. She even posts photos where fans have tagged her. I can't believe how open she is. But then she's never been bullied. I wade through posts after post, looking for one from Béibhinn Keane. Finally, I stop myself. I have to stop being paranoid. I'm not going back to that.

FIVE
Superbus

Three weeks after shooting my first scene, it's about to be aired. My family has gathered in front of the TV. I tried to talk them out of it – it didn't work for my parents and it only encouraged Jack. Now he'll have something legitimate to slag me about – for the rest of my life.

'Is it the next scene?' Mum keeps asking.

'I don't know,' I keep telling her, until, finally, I say, 'Look, you don't have to sit through the whole thing. I'll record it and then you can play it back whenever you like. It's literally two seconds.'

'No,' she says, appalled. 'We want to watch it. Live.'

'It's not live, Mum.'

'It is to me.'

Daisy and Joe have a scene. I'm waiting for Jack to say something.

He groans. 'They're like Barbie and freaking Ken,' he says, reminding me that we still think the same.

'Is *that* Rebecca French?' Mum asks.

'Yup,' Jack says.

'She's not that great,' she says. That's just for me, because there's nothing wrong with Rebecca's acting.

'Can we just watch it?'

Silence returns for two more scenes.

'Oh, my God,' Mum says suddenly. 'There you are. Shh, everyone.'

'Ooooh, baby,' Jack says.

'Shut up,' I say.

'Shh,' Mum says.

Naomi is going up to Joe. Even though I know it's me, part of me can't believe it is.

Seconds later, Mum is turning around. 'What about your line? Did they *cut* it?' She sounds outraged.

But I'm smiling. They used the take without words – and that makes me *not* a diva.

'It's OK,' I say. 'I cut the line.'

She looks confused. 'You cut your *own line*? *Why*?'

I shrug. 'It felt right.'

'Yeah, but you wouldn't want to be doing that too often.'

'Let's watch it again,' Dad says.

My phone rings. It's Mark. I take the phone upstairs.

'So what did you think?' I ask nervously.

'I'm taking up smoking.'

I laugh. 'Seriously, though.'

'You were really good.'

'Really good?' *That's crap.*

'You were great. Caecilius superbus est.'

'Caecilius is ... I've no clue.'

'Proud.'

'Caecilius isn't just saying that because he's going out with me?'

'Caecilius isn't that kind of man. Anyway, it wasn't just Caecilius. Everyone thought you were great.'

Oh, God. 'Who's everyone?'

'My parents, Rex—'

'Your *parents* watched it?'

)(

'Yeah, we had a big gala watching session,' he says, winding me up.

I groan.

'They thought there was a lot of *chemistry*.'

'I looked like a slut.'

He laughs. 'No, you didn't.'

'The skirt. The boobs.'

'Rex wants to go out with you.'

'Mark, stop, Jesus. Just tell me. Seriously. Was I OK?'

'Rachel. They used the silent take. They closed the whole show on the scene. Would they have done that if it wasn't *OK*?'

He's right. 'Why didn't I think of that?'

'It's obvious,' he pauses. 'I'm the brains of the operation.'

'Shut up,' I say instead of 'I love you'.

At school the following morning, I'm at my locker when Peter Sweetnam comes up to me. Peter hangs around with Orla Tempany and Simon Kelleher, that group. So, not much depth.

'Saw you on *D4*. Hot stuff.'

What did I tell you? 'Shut up, Peter.'

'So are you going to be on it, regularly, now?'

'No. I've just a tiny part.'

'Well, if I was that director, *I'd* want more of you.' He turns. 'Hey Mark! How does it feel to be going out with a star?'

Everyone in the locker room looks over.

'Rachel's on *D4*!' Peter announces.

I close my eyes.

When I open them again, Amy Gilmore is in front of me. '*D4*,' she says. 'Cool.'

'No one watches *D4*,' I say.

'They so do.'

'No one our age.'

'Peter saw it.'

'Exactly.'

'Hel-*lo*,' Peter says to me. '*No* way to treat your fans.'

I actually smile.

Then Amy turns to him for the first time. 'When's it on?'

He blushes then stumbles over the answer. Good God. How could anyone fancy The Queen of Evil? Then again, guys never cop bitches. It's a genetic deficiency.

'Yeah, well I know what I'll be doing tonight,' Amy says.

I close my locker and get the hell out.

'Don't forget me when you're rich and famous,' she calls after me.

In the corridor, I wait for Mark. 'Why didn't you *save* me?'

'He's bigger than me.' I smile. He frowns. 'Maybe you should hire a bodyguard, though. Now that you've your first official fan.'

'You're not volunteering?'

'Busy busy. Though I do have buns of steel.' He pulls up his sleeves. 'Go on, check these babies out.'

'Mark. Buns of steel refers to the general *butt* area.'

He looks like he's about to argue but then the principal comes out of his office. Mark puts away his 'buns'.

'Rachel Dunne, the very woman.' High voice for a big guy. Our principal reminds me of the one in *Ferris Bueller's Day Off*. Except that he's actually OK most of the time. As principals go.

'Excellent performance last night.'

Oh God, he saw it. I think of the skirt, the boobs and can't really believe he's brought it up.

'You'll have to talk to the TY students.'

'It's just a tiny part.'

'For three months,' he says like he's impressed. I wish Mum hadn't had to ask permission for me to miss class.

'Eh, I wouldn't really be comfortable talking about it.' It'd be like I thought I was a star, or something.

'Oh. That's a shame.'

'Sorry.'

'Not to worry.' He looks at Mark. 'Impressive biceps.'

After school, we're walking out of the newsagent's with a range of E-additives, when Sarah's phone starts to ring. She looks at the screen, then kills the line. She puts the phone back in her pocket. It rings again. She takes it out and checks the screen. She looks like she's about to hang up but then catches us watching. She answers.

'Oh, hey,' she says. She listens. Then cheerfully says, 'Oh just living till I die. Listen, thanks a million for calling. I gotta go.' She hangs up.

We look at her.

She just puts the phone away.

'Who was that?' Alex asks.

'Oh. Peter.'

'*Sweetnam?*' Alex asks in surprise.

'No. Shane's friend Peter,' she says like she hardly knows him, like we never hung out. Which we did. For months. Until Shane died.

'How's he doing?' I ask, surprised that Sarah hasn't

)(

kept in touch. Shane wanted them to look out for each other.

She looks embarrassed. 'Yeah, fine.'

I feel like asking how she knows. But I leave it. She clearly doesn't want to talk to him – the one person who really knows what she's going through. But maybe that's OK. Maybe she has to save herself first. Like oxygen masks on planes.

Next day, on the DART to school, I'm standing with Alex and Sarah. The carriage is mobbed with people in uniforms and suits. Two feet away, Katie Burke, a girl in our class, is talking to her boyfriend, Cameron.

'I don't know what the big deal is. She didn't even get to *say* anything.'

'She was good, though.'

'You mean she was hot.'

'OK, yeah. She was hot.'

She slaps him on the arm. 'I can't believe you even bothered looking it up.'

'Got a text from Sweetnam. It's on YouTube. Everyone's watching it.'

They could be talking about anyone, I think. But then Katie catches me looking and turns away immediately. Making it official – they're talking about me.

Walking up to the school, I catch loads of people staring at me, people in other classes I don't even know. Before I even get to my locker, Amy Gilmore comes up to me.

'I thought you said you had a *part*. You didn't even *speak*.'

'Yes, Amy. I know I didn't speak.'

'Then what were you going on about yesterday?'

'I think you're confusing me with Peter Sweetnam.'

'You didn't exactly stop him.'

You see? I think. This is why I didn't tell people.

At lunchtime, I take a taxi to D4. It's so good to be Naomi again. I have my first scene with somebody else – Josh's onscreen mum. I'm sitting opposite her in her surgery in the clinic. She has a kind face that must have been beautiful once.

'I was hoping you'd bring your parents,' she says.

I have no lines. I show no emotion. Don't even blink.

'Isn't there anyone you want with you?'

I barely shake my head.

'I really think you shouldn't receive this news alone.'

I move one shoulder. Hardly a shrug.

And so she breaks the news. Aggressive form of bone cancer. Incurable. No hope. She's sorry.

I'm only acting. I still feel the shock. My whole body moves back an inch like something's collided with it. I don't do this deliberately. It just happens. I keep all emotion from my face. It is closed. Unreadable. Slowly, I get up and leave. Without saying a word.

'Wow,' the director says. 'I felt that.'

'Me too,' I say still kind of dazed. This is how Shane must have felt when he was told he had motor neurone disease. And Alex's mum, cancer.

Rebecca's in the dressing room, dancing to music on her iPhone. It takes a second for her to notice she's not alone. She laughs, embarrassed.

'Oh, hey,' she says. 'I wanted to ask you if I've the right number. I tried to call you.'

'Oh?' What could Rebecca French possibly want?

'Yeah, I just wanted to say well done. Your scene was great the other night.'

'Oh, thanks.'

She scrolls through her numbers. Calls out mine.

'Oh,' I say like I'm surprised. 'You got the last digit wrong.'

'Cool,' she says, changing it.

At home after dinner, I'm only starting into my homework when Mark rings.

'Found a great new video on YouTube.'

'Don't you *ever* study?'

'It's your scene on *D4*.'

'Are you serious?'

'Guess how many hits you have?'

'I don't know, a hundred?' I say only because he sounds so excited.

'One thousand and twelve.'

Like I'd believe him. 'Mark, there aren't even a thousand people in our school.'

'If you don't believe me, check yourself.'

My laptop's open. I go on YouTube. There it is. Oh, my God. He's not kidding.

'That's so weird.'

'Peter Sweetnam posted a link on Facebook. Loads of people shared it. Then people started tweeting it.'

I read the comments. There's a pattern – girls are being sniffy; guys are being guys. It's kind of scary, being up there like that, open, for anyone to say whatever they like.

'I googled you,' Mark says. 'They're talking about you on moan.ie.'

)(

'What's that?'

'A chat room. There are these people who follow *D4*, then go on moan.ie after every episode and, like, dissect it.'

'That's kind of freaky.'

'They want more of you.'

'Really?' This is something I never considered when I got the part. The exposure.

'If the people in *D4* follow moan.ie – which they'd have to – they might give you more work.'

'You think?'

'They'd be crazy not to. This is a seriously big reaction from just one scene. You didn't even speak.'

I try not to hope.

Later, I go downstairs to get a drink. My parents are still sitting at the kitchen table, finishing a bottle of red wine. They look so cosy together, almost romantic. I don't want to disturb. So I hang by the kitchen door in my socks. And see how they are getting on. OK, spy.

'I was thinking,' Dad says, 'why don't you come into town tomorrow? For once, I'm not in court in the afternoon.'

'That'd be lovely,' she says, sounding surprised. 'We could do lunch.'

He takes her hand and runs a finger along the back of it. Then he looks into her eyes. 'How about we book a hotel for the afternoon?'

She giggles. 'Are you serious?'

For most people, the thought of your parents having sex is disgusting. For someone who almost split her parents up, it's still disgusting. It also makes her happy. Married people don't have sex unless they still love each other.

SIX
Muffins

In the dressing room the following morning, I'm trying to finish an essay that's due in this afternoon. Rebecca's flicking through a glossy magazine.

'So, who has Emily introduced you to?' she asks.

I look up and tell her the names I remember.

'So you haven't even met half the cast and crew.'

'I'm only here for three months.' I probably won't have anything to do with most of them.

'Still. It's easier when you know everyone. Come on. Let's see who's around.'

I look at her and wonder if people *can* change.

'Come on,' she says. 'No one did it for me.'

I look down at my essay. Then I get up.

She knows everyone. They all seem to like her. She makes them laugh. Knows about their families. Right down to the names and ages of children.

After twenty minutes, I start to get edgy. 'Rebecca, I have to get back and finish that essay. It's due in today.'

'What's it about?'

'The possessions I couldn't live without.'

She rolls her eyes. 'God. Who thinks them up?'

Funny how normal she seems.

)(

'Let's come up with some ideas over coffee,' she says.

I'm kind of stuck for ideas. Well, original ones anyway. 'OK. Sure.'

In the canteen, she insists on paying. I wonder why she's being so nice. Guilt?

She finds a table.

'So what possessions couldn't you live without?' I ask.

She swirls a coffee stirrer around her glass of Coke, then she sucks it. Finally, she pulls it from between her lips, waves it through the air, then points with it.

'Now *there's* someone you should avoid,' she says, looking at the queue.

I turn. 'Maisie Morrin?' I ask, surprised.

'Yup.'

'Why?'

'She can be a real bitch. Don't look now. Here she comes.'

But I do look.

Maisie winks at me as she passes and ignores Rebecca.

'Total psycho,' Rebecca whispers when she's gone.

I remember how good she was at calling people names.

'So what's Mark like?' she asks.

'Mark?'

'Your *boyfriend?*'

'I never told you his name.'

She waves a hand. 'Checked him out on Facebook. You know, he really could be a model.'

'Aren't we supposed to be discussing possessions?'

'We are.'

'We're discussing Mark.'

'Exactly.'

She's made history. She's made me laugh.

I don't get the essay done. My punishment is the essay plus extra homework. I'm over at Mark's, doing the extra homework first. He's on Facebook, chatting to David who lives in California now. Since he left, Mark hasn't really connected with anyone the way he did with David. They still talk a lot, on Skype or Facebook. Out of loyalty to Alex, I never ask Mark how he is, though I'd like to. I hate the way things worked out between them. They were great together. Mark closes the laptop and comes over.

'Caecilius fessus est.'

This one I know. Bored. 'Go away.'

'I thought you were going to get it done in *D4*.'

'And I would have only for Rebecca. She just wants to sit around and talk about you.'

'Well,' he raises his eyebrows. 'Caecilius bestia est.'

I roll my eyes. Clearly, Caecilius is a beast.

'She thinks you should be a model.'

He bursts out laughing.

'What's she like?'

This is it, the moment I could tell him. But telling him would make me a victim again. And I was a victim for long enough. 'I don't know. She's OK, I guess.'

'What's wrong?'

'Nothing. I just don't want to fall behind at school, you know?'

'It's just an essay.'

'Yeah, I know.'

)(

'We've all missed essays.'

'Not me.'

'Just means you're human, Rache.'

'It's just getting harder and harder to keep up. I'm late to bed every night and up at six when I'm on early in *D4*.'

'Don't worry. Christmas is coming. That'll give you two whole weeks to catch up. This is your dream, Rache. You should be enjoying it.'

I brighten. 'Yeah.'

'Here, get up.'

'Why?'

'Just get up. Come on.'

When I do, he sits on my chair. 'Hey.'

He pulls me down onto his lap and puts his arms around me. Then he jigs me up and down on his lap like a kid. 'That better?'

I try not to smile.

He jigs faster. 'How about now?'

I laugh.

After a few seconds, he starts to slow down.

'Don't stop,' I say.

'My legs are killing me.'

'A *Roman* wouldn't stop.'

He laughs. 'No. A Roman would just ravish you.'

'*Ravish?*' I laugh.

'Here, let me demonstrate.'

The next day, I don't have *D4* so I can get up 'late' i.e. at seven. At breakfast I'm sitting at the table taking my time. Mum is making Jack sandwiches for after-school study. Dad is putting on the kettle. Oh, my God, he's just put his hand on Mum's bum. Ew.

'Get a room,' I say, like they're pathetic. And though it's completely gross, I'm humming to myself when I leave the house.

It's such a relief to be in school for all the classes – and to realise that I'm not as far behind as I thought.

After school, me, Sarah and Alex are walking to the DART when Sarah says, 'Hey! Let's go to the Jitter Mug.'

We haven't been to our favourite coffee shop in ages. Actually, we haven't being going out at all. Since Maggie. And Shane. *It'd be good*, I think.

'I need to get home to Maggie,' Alex says.

I look at her. She's forgotten what she's missing. 'Would half-an-hour make a difference?'

She checks the time on her phone. 'She's due a feed.' She looks stressed.

'OK,' I say. 'No problem.'

'It's just that if I'm not careful, she'll start to think Jane's her mum.'

'No, she won't,' Sarah says.

'Babies know their mums,' I add confidently. The thing about being the guru is they do believe you.

'You guys go,' Alex says.

'We're not going without you,' Sarah says.

There has to be a way of getting her out. All the way down to the DART, I try to find it. Then, just as we're getting on, it hits me.

'You know what we should do sometime? Ask Jane to bring Maggie to school at the end of last class then give her the rest of the day off. We could bring Maggie to the Jitter Mug. You could feed her there.'

)(

Alex's face lights up. 'That'd be so cool. Maggie'd get to see where her dad works.'

'Didn't Louis quit the Jitter Mug?' I ask.

'Yeah but he's started again. He wants to save for Maggie's education. And you wouldn't believe how much Strandbrook costs.'

'Oh, my God!' Sarah says. 'He never tells me anything! You're sending her to Strandbrook? That's so cool.'

'And Louis wants to pay?' I ask, surprised. Alex's dad is minted.

Alex shrugs. 'He says it's his responsibility.'

Wow. I'd so like to believe he's changed. But someone has to be prepared for the worst. Just in case.

SEVEN
Nose

Next morning, I'm at my locker in school. I'm just about to turn off my phone when it starts to ring. It's Rebecca. I pick up, wondering what she wants at eight-thirty.

'Where are you?' she asks impatiently.

'In school. Why?'

'Wardrobe are looking for you. You're on in an hour.'

'What? No. I'm not on till this afternoon.'

'They're looking for you, Rachel. Check your schedule.'

'Shit. OK, hang on.' I put the phone down. Grab my bag and zip open the front pocket where I keep all my *D4* stuff. I fumble the schedule open. My stomach falls like a lift going down. She's right. I must have looked at the wrong date when I checked the schedule last night. I pick up the phone. 'OK. I'm coming. Tell them I'm coming.'

'Get a taxi.'

'Yeah.' I hang up, slam my locker shut. 'I gotta go,' I say to Sarah and I'm running. I don't know if I'd be quicker calling a taxi or trying to flag one down outside the school. I end up calling Mum.

I go to the gates. And even though she's there in five, I've my fingers practically bitten off. I just can't be late. I can't let it happen. Too many people relying on me being there. Time is money and the schedule is law.

Mum breaks the land speed record and two red lights. We're there in ten. I kiss her goodbye and race to the dressing room, sweating.

)(

'OK,' Rebecca says. 'I've got your costume.' She picks it up from the back of my chair.

I throw it on.

'OK now go, go, go,' she says. 'I've told Damien to hurry.'

'*Can* Damien hurry?'

'Good point. Anyway, *go*.'

I look at her, surprised. 'Thanks, Rebecca.'

I make it on set sweaty and hassled. But on time. Thanks to Mum and Rebecca. An unlikely team.

After *D4* I get a taxi back to school. Most of the books I have are for the wrong classes but I manage to get through the afternoon without major hassle. When school's over, Jane is waiting for us at reception. She's about ten years older than our parents, which is weird. But she has all this confidence, which is great.

'Yaay! Maggie!' Sarah says.

We run over. For a second, Jane looks like she wants to protect Maggie from us. But maybe it's my imagination. Or the fact that we're so full of energy, coming straight at her.

While Sarah and I each offer Maggie a finger to hold, Jane gives Alex a pretty formal update on feeds and naps and how her day went. Then we stand aside while she stoops down and gives Maggie a kiss on the forehead. She tells her to be good. I look at Sarah. Like Maggie knows how to be bad?

'Am I imagining it?' Alex asks as we watch Jane walk away.

'What?'

'It's like she's always judging me.'

'I don't get that,' I say.

'She's probably pissed off that I've upset the *routine*.'

'I'd say she's probably delighted to finish early,' Sarah says.

Outside, Jane gets into her car, a clean, unscratched VW Panda. She puts on her belt, checks the mirror, indicates and slowly pulls out. She's the kind of person your baby would be safe with.

'Sometimes I think I'd prefer a Mrs Doubtfire,' Alex says.

'Maggie's too young for a Mrs Doubtfire,' I say in my reassuring guru voice.

'Oh, my God, it's Maggie!'

We turn.

Orla Tempany is hurrying over with Robin.

They stick their heads into the pram.

'Ah, God, look at her little leopard-skin coat,' Robin exclaims.

'She's *adorable*. Her little mouth!' Orla says. 'Oh, my God, she's *yawning*.' She looks up at Alex who I know is dying to get away before a crowd gathers.

'Can I hold her?' Robin asks.

'Eh, we're actually in a huge hurry, sorry,' Alex says and starts pushing the pram.

We're stopped about five times on the way to the DART. Then on the DART, more people in Strandbrook uniforms crowd around Maggie like she's a celebrity. After the walk, though, she's asleep, both arms stretched out behind her, like she's just run a marathon.

As soon as we get to the Jitter Mug, we find a table. Alex takes Maggie out. We go to join the queue while Sarah stays at the table to mind the stuff. When Louis sees Maggie, his whole face lights up, changing from this dark, sultry, Heathcliffy kind of guy into … basically mush. I have to admit there's something kind of adorable about that and I find myself hoping that he never changes how he feels about Maggie, because I want everything for her that Alex does.

'I'm due a break in twenty,' Louis says to Alex. 'If you want me to come over.'

'Cool,' she says.

We order and find a seat. Sarah goes to the loo. Alex takes off Maggie's coat and hat, and turns her to face the counter.

'Look at Daddy. Look at Daddy working,' she says, though Maggie can't see that far yet.

Louis smiles over. Alex waves Maggie's hand at him. He waves back.

I notice this woman about three tables over, sitting on her own with a pot of tea. She keeps glaring at Alex like she so doesn't approve. Luckily, Alex can't see her.

'D'you know what's amazing?' Alex says to me. 'How much I get on with Louis now. Before Maggie, we'd nothing to say to each other – now it's the total opposite.' She shakes her head. 'It's weird.'

'I guess you've something in common now.'

'No. It's more than that. He's changed, Rache.'

'You think?'

'Yeah.' She looks over at him. 'He's happy. Now that he's following his dream.'

'What dream?'

She looks back at me. 'The band. He wants to make it work.'

'Then why did he quit before?'

)(

'Oh, my God,' she says like she's got all this scandal. 'The lead singer was a total dictator. The others couldn't work with him. So in the end they split up. Louis was so depressed. He thought that they really had something and if they couldn't make it work, he'd never be able to make any band work. College came up. And he just went. He put off thinking about the future. Now Maggie's changed everything. She's made him want to do it right.'

I can't help saying, 'What if he doesn't make it?' Most musicians don't. Like most actors.

'That's what he said. So he's going to keep college up till the band takes off.'

'What's he doing in college anyway?' I really don't know Louis at all.

'Economics and social studies.' She wrinkles her nose. 'But the band'll work out. I know it will. Main thing is he's happy.' She looks over at him again and smiles. 'He really has changed.'

I want to remind her that it has only been weeks and Louis has been Louis for twenty years.

Sarah comes back from the loo. She sits down. Looks around, starts drumming her fingers.

'You OK?' I ask.

'Yeah, fine. Why?'

'Nothing.' She looks like she wants to leave already and we've only just got here. She's getting more and more like that, lately. Like she wants to keep moving. Not stop.

Louis joins us. Alex passes Maggie to him.

'Hello, sausage,' he says.

'Sausage?' Alex raises an eyebrow.

'Sausage.' He touches Maggie's nose and smiles down at her like he sees no one else.

For a moment, no one speaks. We all just look at Maggie.

'Have you found your lead singer yet?' Sarah asks. She looks at us. 'You should see the weirdos turning up at the house to audition. Mum's made them use the shed.'

'The right guy is out there. All we have to do is find him,' Louis says.

'Yeah, well he better be a lot hotter than the guys turning up – if you want any chance at the big time,' Sarah says.

'I'll remember that,' he says.

'What are you going to call yourselves?' Alex asks.

'We're working on it,' he says.

'What have you got so far?' Sarah asks.

'You don't want to know.'

'I do,' she says.

'Trust me. You don't.'

Sarah says, 'Here, let me try.' Two seconds later she's calling out, 'The Happy Mondays!'

'Taken,' Louis says.

'What d'you mean, taken?'

'The Happy Mondays are already a band.'

'Really? I was *wondering* how I came up with it so fast. It's a good name.'

'Except there's no such thing as a happy Monday,' Alex says.

'Except *Bank Holiday* Mondays,' Sarah says.

Alex closes her eyes. 'Theeeeee …' she tries. 'No. I can't think.'

'Does it have to start with a "The"?' Sarah asks.

I think of The Script. Then U2. Coldplay. Oasis. 'Maybe better without,' I say.

'The V-shaped Valleys,' Sarah says.

We burst out laughing.

'Where did *that* come from?' I ask.

)(

'Oh, I was clearing out my room last night.' I imagine her, flinging things out of her wardrobe instead of just chilling. 'Found my First Year geography book ... Hey, how about Interlocking Spurs?'

'Wouldn't be bad,' Louis says, 'if we were a country and western band.'

'Spider's Revenge,' Sarah says.

Louis looks at her. 'Are you *high*?'

Everyone laughs, including Sarah. But it *is* like she's high.

'It's hard,' Alex says.

'What about your old name?' Sarah asks. 'The Blue Tomorrows.'

'Don't know *what* we were thinking,' Louis checks the time. 'I better get back.' He kisses Maggie's forehead. 'Bye, Pumpkin.'

'Pumpkin?' Alex asks.

'Pumpkin.' He passes Maggie over. And he's gone.

'Anyone want another drink?' I ask.

'Nah. I think we should go,' Sarah says, looking around, drumming her fingers again. Like she's not living enough.

We collect up all Maggie's stuff. Alex puts on her coat and little hat, and lays her in the pram, all the time telling her how cute she is. The woman who's been glaring over gets up. Oh, my God. She's coming over. *She's not going to say anything, is she? I mean she wouldn't. It's none of her business.* But she *is* coming over.

'Come on, Alex, let's go,' I say.

Sarah follows my eyes. When she sees the woman, she stands up protectively. But the woman just sees Alex – and walks right up to her.

'Is that *your* baby?' she asks, like she's talking about dirt.

'Is that your business?' Alex says, straight out.

'Is that your *nose*?' Sarah asks, staring at it. It *is* pretty big.

We're so shocked, we laugh, reminding me of the first day we met and the uniting force of detention.

The woman looks appalled. She peers at the crest on my uniform. 'What school do you go to?'

'Strandbrook,' Sarah says, like she's daring her.

'Well, I'll be on to your principal,' she warns, then, to herself but aloud, she adds, 'So *rude*.'

'Eh. *Hello?* And *you* weren't rude?' Sarah says, like she's nothing to lose. Which she hasn't. Because she's lost Shane. And he was everything.

'Incredible,' the woman says and starts to leave.

'Hang on, wait,' Sarah says. 'Let me give you my phone so you can call him now.' She goes after her, holding out her phone like she's desperate for her to take it.

We smile as the woman practically sprints from the place.

Sarah turns back to us. 'That woman has a barren and hostile womb. You can tell.'

We snort.

Then I turn to Alex. 'This better not put you off bringing Maggie out again.'

She looks at me. 'No one's *ever* going to make me feel ashamed of my daughter. From now on, I'm showing her to the world.'

I smile.

Later, I'm looking for character traits in the novel we've to study for English, when there's a knock on my bedroom door.

'So how was *D4*?' Jack asks. He doesn't usually do house visits.

'It was good,' I say. 'Rebecca actually saved my ass.' Telling him what happened is like proving a point.

He looks thoughtful.

'What?' I ask impatiently.

'Just trying to work out what was in it for her.'

'Did there *have* to be something in it for her? Maybe she was just being helpful.'

He raises an eyebrow.

Being Jack's eyebrow, I know it means – he'll never trust Rebecca French. No matter how many times she saves my ass.

On Friday afternoon, I'm given my script for the following week. I look up from it and catch my reflection in the mirror. I'm blushing and biting my lip. I look back down. Read the words again. They haven't changed.

'Naomi and Joe kiss passionately.'

OK, I knew this was going to happen. Now that it's next week, though, things I'd never considered are flashing through my mind like the lights of passing cars. Is it going to be with tongues? If not, will it look weird? Will it look weird anyway? And will Josh (who clearly thinks I fancy him) think that I might actually be looking forward to it? I. Am. Going. To. Die.

'What?' Rebecca asks.

The easiest thing is to just hand it to her. She replaces her mascara wand back in its tube, screws it shut then takes the A4 sheets. I don't know why they even *have* kissing scenes. Watching them is just awkward. Even when there's no one in the room.

)(

'Lucky you,' she whispers, handing me back the script.
'*Lucky*?'

'You get to snog Josh. *Obviously.*'

'I'm not exactly looking forward to it, Rebecca.' I think
of Mark. How'll he feel about me kissing someone else –
in front of thousands of people – including ones we have
to face in school every day?

'Don't you think he's hot?' she asks.

'What?'

'Josh. Don't you think he's hot?'

'No.' Especially now that I have to kiss him.

'Come *on*!'

'OK, he's a good-looking guy. Doesn't mean I want to
kiss him in front of half the country.'

'Personally I think it's quite kinky – knowing
everyone's watching.'

I laugh, shocked. 'Pervert.'

'Just enjoy it, Rachel. Thousands of girls would kill for
the chance.'

'Doesn't help.'

'Pretend it's Mark.'

I think about that. 'Maybe I could squirt a little Ralph
Lauren on him when he's not looking.'

'I could distract him,' she says, like we're
masterminding a heist.

I smile.

She takes up her mascara again. 'So. Doing anything
interesting for the weekend?'

'Not really, no.'

'Want to do something?'

'Oh, thanks,' I say when I recover, 'but even though
I'm not doing much, I'm doing it with people, if you
know what I mean?'

'Sure.'

'What about you?'

'Oh, I'll probably go out with friends and that.' She sounds weirdly lonely.

And I feel weirdly bad. 'I'm sure it'll be a lot more fun than just hanging around.'

'Yeah,' she says.

That evening, Mark arrives over with popcorn and a two-litre bottle of Coke.

'I brought refreshments,' he says. He's wearing a hoodie and tracksuit bottoms as if he's settling in for the night. I should never have told him I'm on *D4* tonight.

'We're not watching it,' I say.

'Yes, we are.'

'Mark, I'm on for, like, two seconds.'

'That's OK.'

'I don't even have a line.'

'I know.'

'And everyone's going to be sitting in the room.'

'I can live with that.'

'Maybe *I* can't,' I joke.

'Come on, don't be a wimp.'

Turns out, it's just Mum. Dad's working late. And Jack has gone to a friend's.

Mark shares out the popcorn and Coke, like a dad dealing out sweeties at a party.

We're sitting comfortably when the show starts. It's good, after all, to see all the scenes, filmed randomly, coming together to make a story. After a while, Mark nudges me and looks over at Mum. She's sitting forward, eyes glued to the screen. *Aw*, I think. Sometimes, you forget that they love you.

The show's almost over and I haven't appeared. I'm thinking maybe I got the night wrong.

'Ooh. I *like* the uniform,' Mark says appreciatively.

Mum looks back at me and smiles.

The show ends on the scene.

Mark turns. 'OK, I'm *definitely* taking up smoking.'

I smile and reach for the remote.

'Don't turn it off,' Mum says to me. 'I want to see your name.'

'Aw,' Mark says and rubs my head like a proud parent.

'Get off!' I laugh, shoving him over.

'Rachel!' Mum says like she's appalled by my 'unladylike' (a word she actually uses) behaviour.

Finally, she turns off the telly. 'Right, let's celebrate,' she says.

I want to escape in Millie. But Mark's following her into the kitchen.

'Back in a sec,' I say. I run upstairs and go on moan.ie to see what they're saying about *D4*. They're talking, but not about my scene, which is good. I go on Facebook. No comments at all. I go on Twitter and put in the *D4* hashtag. Nothing about Naomi. I go back on moan. ie. Oh, God, here we go.

'That Naomi's got attitude.'

'And great legs.'

'Makes a change from Daisy. What a moan.'

'Total nag.'

Poor Rebecca. I hope she's not reading this. I wonder if I should text that they're a bunch of losers but decide that that would make it worse – her knowing that I'd read it.

)(

I hear someone pounding up the stairs. Mark sticks his head in. 'What're you up to?' he asks, walking in.

'Nothing. Just checking moan.ie.'

He comes over. 'You're up here half an hour. There's only so much cake a person can eat.'

'Yeah, sorry.'

He stands behind me, looking over my shoulder at the computer screen, just as one of the regulars, BatmanReturns, comes online.

'Daisy might be a moan but that Rebecca French is one great actress.'

Phew, I think. *Everyone listens to BatmanReturns.*

Then he adds, 'With even better legs.'

'Why are you reading that crap?' Mark asks.

I turn. 'I need to know what people are saying about me.'

'It's called moan.ie. They will *eventually* moan about you.'

'Especially when I move in on someone else's guy,' I say.

'They already know you two are going to get together and they still like you.'

I think about the kiss. I have to tell him.

'No,' he continues.'It'll be about something else.'

'You're right,' I say, depressed. I close the laptop. But immediately want to open it again. Instead, I grab my coat from the bed. 'Let's go.'

We run downstairs.

'Drive carefully,' Mum calls from the kitchen.

All the way up into the mountain, I'm thinking, *Just tell him.* But I keep finding an excuse to put it off. Don't want to interrupt the soundtrack. Don't want to interrupt the snogging. Don't want to interrupt the soundtrack,

)K(

again. Until we're coming back into the city. If I don't tell him today, it'll just be weird.

We stop at the lights. I take a deep breath. I look at him. And can't do it.

'What?' he asks.

'Nothing.'

'What?'

'You know Naomi *will* have to kiss Joe eventually, right?' Notice, I use the characters' names.

'Inevitable,' he says calmly. It encourages me.

'OK, well, we're shooting that scene on Monday.'

'Monday?'

'It seems quick because of the gap between shooting and screening.'

He says nothing.

'I'm dreading it.'

He looks at me and smiles for the first time. 'Just pretend it's me.' He runs his tongue over his top lip and moans sexually.

I laugh. 'Stop. Jesus.'

He goes quiet again. And for ages neither of us says anything.

'What are you thinking?' I ask finally.

'If we cut up that road and onto the dual carriageway, it'd probably be quicker.'

Not worried, then, I think. And collapse into the seat in relief.

On Saturday, Alex wants to bring Maggie to the zoo. It's Maggie's first real outing and I feel like thanking the woman in the Jitter Mug for her general obnoxiousness.

We wrap up warm. Possibly overwrap Maggie.

)(

We walk through the African Plains, Sarah pushing the pram.

'Look at all the *sky*,' Alex says, gazing up at it like someone who's just been released from captivity.

A lion roars, sounding like a giant clearing its throat.

'I was hoping Louis'd come,' Alex says.

We both stare at her.

'Yeah. I thought it'd be like a little family outing.'

'Weren't you just going to take it one day at a time?' I ask.

'I am,' she says, looking a bit guilty.

'Are you *sure*?'

'Jesus, Rachel. I'm sure.'

I put my hands up 'OK. Just checking.'

'I can't believe you asked Louis,' Sarah says. 'Hanging out with my brother is *not* my idea of fun.'

'Oh, God, sorry. I didn't think,' Alex says, grimacing.

I think about how Jack and I used to hang out together all the time and how natural that was. It wouldn't be now. I guess that's normal.

Alex gets a text. She takes out her phone, smiles and looks up.

'He's found a lead singer!' she says.

'Better be the guy who looks like Kurt Cobain,' Sarah says. 'Here, text him.'

'Does he look like Kurt Cobain?' Alex reads as she texts.

Seconds later, her phone goes again. She smiles. And reads. '"Well, he *is* skinny."'

So, Alex and Louis are texting each other now?

Alex catches me looking. 'So. Have you told Mark about the kiss, yet?' she asks.

)(

'Yeah. He was fine about it. I don't know what I was worried about.'

'He wasn't jealous?' Sarah asks, like that's weird.

'No.'

'Wow. Because Josh is *so* caliente.'

'He's not *that* caliente,' I say.

'He's caliente enough to be jealous of.'

Then I start to think, *should* Mark be jealous?

'When are we doing the white water rafting?' Sarah asks out of nowhere.

I try to look keen. 'I don't mind.'

'I googled it. They do it Palmerstown.'

'Where's Palmerstown?'

'I don't know. Somewhere in Dublin. On the Liffey.'

'Cool.'

'Maybe we could do it next Saturday,' she says.

'OK. Sure.' *Crap.*

'D'you mind if I don't go?' Alex asks. 'I have motherly responsibilities.'

Good move, I think, joking her way out of it.

When I get back from the zoo, Jack's studying at the kitchen table. He moves around the house. If he stops concentrating in his bedroom, he moves to the kitchen. I remember what Sarah said about brothers. I look at him, bent over a book, his hair spiking up, and think, *He's more than a brother. I don't care what Mum says about individuals.*

I sit opposite him with a glass of water.

'I can't believe you're doing your Leaving Cert.'

He looks up. 'Believe it,' he says glumly.

'Do you know what's really freaky? If I hadn't stayed back, I'd be doing it too. I *so* wouldn't be ready.'

'Course you would.'

I look down at the book open in front of him. 'Is it going OK?'

He shrugs. 'I'm working. That's a start, right?'

'You were always the smart one.'

'OK. That's complete crap,' he says like he's genuinely annoyed.

'Then why did I have to stay back?' I ask simply.

'Rache, I'm quicker, not smarter. And that's just because of computer games.'

'What are you talking about?'

'If you don't react quickly, you die. Makes you think fast. You're just as smart as me. Just nowhere near as good-looking.'

I laugh.

But he looks suddenly serious. 'You still believe them, don't you?'

'Who?'

'Those losers who called you stupid.'

'What? *No!*'

'Then why do you work so hard?'

'I don't know. I just don't want to fall behind, I guess.'

'Rachel, there is no danger of you falling behind. You're a straight-A student. Who still thinks she's stupid.'

'I don't think I'm stupid.' *Just not good enough.*

He looks into my eyes and says, 'You *are* good enough.'

Sometimes I wish he was just a brother.

EIGHT
Mouthwash

On Monday morning, I head for Make-Up with a knot in my stomach. I so don't want to do this scene. I've washed my teeth and gargled a half a bottle of mouthwash. Now I'm chewing gum. I bet he doesn't give a damn. Oh, God, here he is, sauntering along the corridor on his way back from Make-Up like he's out for a morning stroll. He bursts into a smile when he sees me.

'All set for later?' he asks, like something's hilarious.

'All set,' I say casually, as if I do these scenes every day, like breathing.

'Maybe we should rehearse?' His face is serious now and I can't work out if he's being professional or a dick.

I think quickly. 'Nah. It should look spontaneous.'

'You're right. Let's make it *spontaneous*,' he says, sounding like he means something else.

'What, the kiss?' Rebecca asks loudly, walking up to us. She turns to me. 'You'll be grand,' she says. Then, she looks at Josh while saying, 'He's actually a pretty good kisser.'

Josh looks at her and deadpans, 'I'm holding judgement on you.'

She tips her head back and laughs. Then she stops as quickly as she started. 'Oh, by the way. Newsflash, Josh. Rachel doesn't think you're hot.'

He fakes horror. '*No!*'

)(

I stay cool. 'It's OK, Josh, loads of people fancy you,'
I say, looking at Rebecca so it's clear she's one of them. I
may even be doing her a favour. 'Anyway, I gotta get to
Make-Up.'

'See you *later*,' he says to me, his words full of meaning.

I close my eyes and shake my head, like he's seriously
sad.

He laughs.

They so better do this in one take.

I sit in Make-Up, eyes closed, going over what just
happened in my head. I can't believe she said that. What
was she thinking? Did she *want* to embarrass us? At least,
now, he knows I don't fancy him. Damien, who has been
going on about the world's best party towns, stops mid-
sentence.

'You're very quiet,' he says, like he's just noticed.

'Oh. Sorry.' I open my eyes.

'Something up?'

I make a face. 'I have a kissing scene.'

'With Josh?' he asks eagerly.

I nod.

'Ooh, lucky you.'

'Why is everyone so keen to snog Josh?' I ask quietly.

'There's this thing called sex appeal, Rachel?'

Lost on me, I think. But just smile.

I'm a professional. I can do this.

'And action.'

I am Naomi. And I'm in charge. This is *my* kiss. I stride
up to Joe, take his face, roughly, in my hands and kiss

him. With tongues. After a while, he pulls me to him. But I'm done with him. And push him away. He looks totally shocked and I don't know if he's acting or it's for real. I smile, then turn and walk.

'And cut.'

It's like waking up. Frank, the director, is coming over. This time, he really is going to kill me. Or worse, make us do it again.

'Excellent. Excellent,' he says. 'Well done, you two.'

'I doooon't knoooow,' Josh says. 'Maybe we should go again. You know, just in case.' He's grinning.

'Thanks, Josh, for your commitment. But we have it.' It's the first time I've seen Frank actually smile. He slaps me on the shoulder like I'm a good soldier, then walks off.

'So *that* was spontaneous,' Josh says, smiling. 'Loved the little shove.'

'Well, I *was* finished with you.'

He laughs. 'For now.'

Back in the dressing room, Rebecca's removing her make-up. When she sees me, she beams. Her teeth are so perfect, almost like one big unitooth.

'Hey!' she says, all friendly.

'I can't believe you said that to Josh.'

She looks at me innocently. 'What?'

'You know what.'

'That you don't think he's hot?' She says it like it's no big deal.

'Yeah. It was so awkward. Why did you *do* that?'

She shrugs. 'So you guys could relax about the kiss.'

'What?'

'So, it was just business.'

)(

'Seriously?'

'Did it work?' she asks.

'Actually, yeah,' I say, surprised. I got her totally wrong.

'So. Good kiss, then?'

I smile. 'You're unbelievable.'

'Wonder what they'll think of it on moan.ie.'

'You go on that too?'

She grimaces. 'I hate it. But I can't help looking. It's addictive.'

'I *know*. Mark tries to talk me out of going on it.'

'Yeah, but he's not acting, is he?'

'Exactly!'

'So, you still don't think Josh is caliente?'

Oh, my God. She's using 'caliente'. Only Sarah, Alex and I use 'caliente'. Where did she get it? Then I remember – Facebook.

'What's wrong?' she asks.

What can I say, *Don't use 'caliente'*? 'Nothing.'

'So. Caliente or not caliente?'

'Not hot.'

'Good,' she says, 'because he's mine.' Then she laughs at her own joke.

'What's Mark's mum's name?' Mum asks when I get in. She's bought herself lilies and there's a candle lighting. Which usually means good news.

'Grace,' I say. 'Why?'

'And she's a diplomat?'

'Yeah.'

'Wow.'

'What?'

'She's just asked me to cater for her.'

'Oh, my God, seriously? Mark never said.'

'Maybe he doesn't know. It could just be a coincidence.'

'What's the job?'

'Dinner for sixteen, Saturday night.'

Easy for Mum but because she hasn't had work in ages I ask, 'D'you want a hand?'

'I should be OK, thanks. I have Jessica.' A woman she calls when she has an event. 'I'm so excited. If this goes well, there'll be more work. Diplomats are always entertaining.'

It's so good to see Mum excited. I go up to my room and call Mark.

'Did you know your mum has asked mine to cater for her on Saturday?'

'No.'

'Well she did. What a coincidence.'

'Maybe not *that* much of a coincidence. I brought her home some of your mum's cookies. And happened to mention she was in catering.'

'That's so sweet.'

'Rachel, we get the leftovers.'

I laugh. 'Thanks, Marcus.' I use his Latin name when I think he's being particularly amazing.

'I like your mum.'

'Yeah, well, she likes you.'

'I know.' He laughs.

'You're unbelievable,' I say.

'I know,' he says, like it was a compliment.

Much later, after my homework's done, I get into bed and go on Facebook. I usually love this time, last thing, when I can just chill with Alex and Sarah, maybe post something

)(

on Maggie's page. Since I've started getting to bed so late, though, they're often not online. And since my first scene was aired, there are all these friend requests from people I don't know. Tonight, there's one from Béibhinn Keane. I can't believe she thinks I'd accept. Does she think I've no memory? Doesn't she *get* that I want her to rot in hell and as soon as possible? I close my laptop and reach for Uggs, the face of calm.

Even if I wasn't watching *D4*, I'd know what episode was going out by the questions people were asking at school.

'Is there *definitely* no cure?' Peter Sweetnam asks at the lockers the next morning.

I smile. 'No.'

'That's terrible,' he says. I don't know if he's concerned for Naomi or the fact that my part will come to an end. I don't ask.

'But will she get together with Joe before she dies?' asks Amy, who's not supposed to be watching the programme.

'That's classified,' I say to annoy her.

'She definitely will,' Peter says. 'I'd put money on it.'

Orla Tempany comes over, then – even though she and Amy hate each other. 'Speaking of money, how much d'you get?'

I turn to put my bag in the locker and get out my books for our first class. 'Not much,' I mumble.

'*How* much, though?'

'Less than you think,' I say, closing my locker and starting to walk.

I widen my eyes at Mark. He closes his locker and walks with me. Ever since *D4* has gone out on air, it's like he's become invisible to people. They see us together, they talk to me. It's like he's stopped being interesting. I hate it.

Out in the corridor, he makes his hands into little fists and shakes them like he's excited. 'Oh, my God. I'm going out with a celebrity.'

'Shut up.'

'Can I've your autograph?'

'Not funny.'

We walk down the corridor together. 'How about a photo?'

I hit him. 'Feck off.'

'By the way. How much *do* you get paid?'

'Three hundred a day.'

'Three hundred euro?'

'Yeah.'

'Not bad. What are you going to do with it?'

'I don't know. Depends how long they keep me on. Maybe a cheap second-hand car. With loads of personality.'

'What about Millie?'

'Millie's your car.'

'Millie's *our* car.'

I smile, relieved he thinks like that too.

Once you appear on TV, people think they can come up to you and ask you anything. The canteen is the worst. Total strangers just sit beside us and start shooting questions at me, killing whatever conversation we were having and ignoring Sarah and Alex. Most want to know what's going to happen and don't believe me when I tell them I don't know. Some like to give their expert opinion on what

)(

has happened, like they could write the telescript in the morning and make it better. Today, we watch a First Year go back to her friends like she's got the inside scoop. All I told her was that I share a dressing room with Rebecca.

Sarah turns to me, 'What are you doing about all your friend requests on Facebook?'

I grimace. There are hundreds now. 'I don't know. I don't want to seem stuck up. But I don't know these people.'

'You should do a fan page,' Alex says.

'I don't know. People could post *anything*.'

'They're fans,' Sarah says. 'What are they going to say? We love you?'

'Even if someone posted something iffy, you just delete it,' Alex adds.

'Hey,' Sarah says. 'We could all set it up together. It'd be fun.'

'Yeah, maybe.'

We walk back to our lockers. Two people I'd normally say hi to, blank me as they pass. I get this a lot – people who don't want to look as if they're being friendly because I'm on TV. I also get the opposite. People who never normally say hi, starting to. Even I've changed, not wanting to act like I think I'm some sort of celebrity acknowledging everyone. The easiest thing is to just not look at people.

When I leave school, it's already dark. People, including Mark, are running out onto the pitches, their breaths frosting up. I wish I'd time to still play hockey. Maybe when *D4*'s over, I'll take it up again.

As we walk down to the DART, Alex gets a text.

'Yes!' she says.

'What?'

'Undertow are having their first gig this Friday.'

'Undertow?' I ask.

'Louis's band. They were trying to get included in a competition for new bands. They've just been accepted. It's on next weekend.'

'Are they going to be ready?' I ask.

'They only have to play three songs. So they're going to perform two of their old ones and one that the lead singer, James, has written.'

'So *that's* why they're rehearsing all the time. He never tells me anything,' Sarah says.

'We should go,' Alex says. 'The judges look at the reaction from the crowd. It's so dumb. The group with the most friends has the best chance.'

'Then we have to go,' Sarah says.

'Don't look now,' Alex says to me. 'But there's a woman over there who keeps staring at you.'

Automatically, we look.

'I said, "Don't look now,"' Alex says, sitting back and looking out the window.

The woman is small and old. I've never seen her before, but she seems to know me. I smile to be polite. She gets up and comes over. Maybe I do know her, just don't remember. I try to think. Is she a friend of my gran's? She sits beside me. Her lipstick has gone over the edges. And she has plum-coloured nail varnish. Her handbag is triangular and wooden. She reaches out and clasps my hand in hers, the way people do at funerals. I look at Alex and Sarah. They're as baffled as I am.

'I just wanted to tell you that you're a *very brave* girl.'

OK so she *has* got the wrong person. Awkward.

'Most people fall to pieces when they are diagnosed with cancer.'

Oh, God. She thinks I'm Naomi. I start coughing so I don't laugh.

'Thank you so much,' I say, because it is cute that she cares even if Naomi isn't real.

She squeezes my hand in sympathy, then leans towards me and whispers, 'I'll be praying for you.'

'Thank you.'

She gets up to return to her seat.

Alex and Sarah snort.

I frown at them. Then I look over at her and smile.

After a while, she gets up like she's reached her stop. As she's passing, she starts to look confused. 'You've changed your uniform.'

I look down at it. 'Oh,' I say.

Then, luckily, she has to go.

When she gets off the Dart, Sarah and Alex collapse laughing.

'Why didn't you tell her it's not real?' Alex asks.

I shrug. 'It is to her.'

In *D4*, I put fairy lights around my mirror. And little Santas and angels on my dressing table. I turn on the lights. They wink and glow Jelly Tot colours. *Ho, ho, ho,* I think.

'Cool,' Rebecca says when she sees them. 'I must get some.'

My scene, which is to go out in the Christmas Special, is an interior shot in the clinic with Naomi's doctor:

'Naomi, I'm recommending surgery,' she says.

'Why?' I ask and allow the tiniest bit of hope to reach my eyes.

)K(

'*To slow the progress of the disease.*'

'*Forget it.*'

'*Naomi, I need to speak with your parents. You should not be dealing with this alone.*'

I shake my head.

'*Naomi, you're seventeen. I need their consent for surgery anyway.*'

'*I'm not having surgery. If I'm going to die, let me die in peace,*' *I get up and walk out.*

I go back to the dressing room thinking about Shane and Alex's mum and what it must be like to have a deadline on your life. I should be removing make-up. I should be putting on my uniform, grabbing a taxi. Instead, I just sit here.

Rebecca walks in with all this energy, singing along to her iPhone.

'Back in a sec,' I say and leave before she can even think.

In the canteen, I stare into a bowl of Cornflakes, watching the sugar melt and the flakes slowly go soft. After a while, I feel someone beside me. I turn. It's Maisie Morrin, standing there with her tray.

'We haven't been introduced,' she says.

'Oh. Sorry. Hi. I'm Rachel.'

'I know.'

'Oh. Right.'

'Mind if I sit?'

'Eh. Sure.'

'Thank you.' She lowers her tray onto the table.

'Am I the *only* person you haven't been introduced to?'

She pretty much is. And I blush.

She waves a hand. 'It's OK. I'm joking.' She pours milk on her muesli then looks up. 'You'll get used to me ... So, the Queen Bee has taken you under her wing.'

Queen Bee. Sometimes it does feel like that.

'Make sure it doesn't get too hot under there.'

I give her a 'what-do-you-mean?' look.

She ignores it.

'I just came over to congratulate you on that scene you've just shot. Powerful.'

'*Really*?'

'I'm a huge fan of your work,' she says.

I laugh.

'I was actually being serious, that time,' she says.

'Oh. Sorry.'

'So how're you getting on? What do you think of *D4*?'

'I love it. It's amazing,' I say genuinely.

'Can be difficult, at times, though.'

I look at her.

'You felt the emotion in that scene. Didn't you?'

I nod. Thinking about the scene I start to tear up. 'Sorry,' I say, embarrassed.

She smiles for the first time. 'You remind me of me. A long time ago. Actually, still me. Nothing wrong with feeling empathy with your character, Rachel. In fact, I'd recommend it.'

I nod.

'Oh, oh. Queen Bee alert,' she says.

Rebecca's on her way over with a tray.

Just as she reaches the table, Maisie stands. 'Well, I'll leave you two young whippersnappers to it.'

I follow her eyes and almost laugh.

Rebecca sits down, with a frown. 'I thought I said not to bother her.'

'She sat with me.'

'That's weird. What did she want?'

I can't help it: 'To know why you hadn't introduced us.'

'Seriously?' She actually looks worried.

I laugh. 'She was joking.'

'Jesus.'

'She's nice, Rebecca.'

'Yeah, well, don't go getting all cosy. She bit my head off once. For, like, *nothing*.'

Knowing Rebecca, it probably had something to do with personal space.

'Then again,' she says, 'maybe it's just me she doesn't like.' And even though she says it like it's a fact and she's not worried, I feel bad for her.

We go back to the dressing room together.

'What time are you on?' I ask.

'Five.'

'Then what are you doing *here*?'

'Ah, sometimes I just like to keep my face in front of theirs. You know, so they don't forget to write me into the script.' She laughs.

'But the scriptwriters work from home.'

'Emily doesn't.'

'Is it worth missing school over, though?'

'You are *way* too obsessed with school. Hey! What are you doing for Christmas?'

'Nothing much. Sleeping. Eating.'

She looks shocked. 'Be careful. You don't want to put on any more weight.'

'What?' I laugh, shocked. *Any more*?

'I'm just saying. The camera adds ten pounds.'

'Thanks, Rebecca, for the concern.'

'No probs,' she says, missing the sarcasm.

Maybe she was just being helpful, I think. *In her usual speak-first-think-last way.*

In the shower room, I change back into my uniform.

)(

Standing in my knickers, I look in the mirror. Properly. I'm not fat, am I? I turn to my side. Try to pinch my skin. I've never worried about my weight before. Should I start?

As soon as I get home on Friday, I have to get ready to go out. We have to be in town at half-seven.

'Rachel can I ask you a huge favour?' Mum says.

I look at her. 'Sure.'

'Jessica's come down with a bug. She can't help me out tomorrow.'

'What about Maeve?' She's Mum's fallback.

'She has a christening. She can help me serve but not prepare. Could you help me? I'll pay you.'

'Sure.' Then I remember the white water rafting. I don't want to let Sarah down. But Mum's stuck. This is a huge gig for her.

'Yeah, I'm sure it's fine. I just have to ring Sarah. I said I'd go white water rafting with her – but I'm sure we could do it another time.'

'I really need you, Rachel.'

'I know. It's fine. Sarah won't mind.'

'Thank God,' she says and her whole body relaxes in relief.

I go upstairs, call Sarah and explain the problem.

'Could we do Sunday instead?' I ask.

'I don't know. I've booked for the morning.'

'Could you ring?'

'There'll be no one there now. And we're meant to be there at eleven. Pity you didn't tell me before now.'

)(

'Sorry, Mum only just asked me.'
'It's OK. Don't worry about it. I'll ring first thing.'
'I'm so sorry. I'm sure they'll be able to change it.'
'I'll tell them that if we like it, we'll go back.'
'Good idea. Sorry, Sarah.'
'It's OK. I'll see you later.'

NINE
Mad

We get there on time but the queue is really long.

'I wonder how many people are here for Undertow,' Alex says.

'How many bands are there?' I ask.

'Eight,' Sarah says.

'OK, so they've a one-in-eight chance,' Alex says.

'Very good, Alex,' Mark says.

She hits him. 'I know they're not here to win, just to practise gigging live – but imagine if they did.'

After about ten minutes, the queue starts to move. Soon, we're in. There's another queue to hand in coats. Alex takes hers off. She's wearing a short, tight, white dress that I've never seen before. She looks amazing.

'Oh, my God,' Sarah says. 'You're so skinny.'

'I had to do something,' she says. 'Yuri, Dad's trainer, started me on a fitness programme. His favourite words are "pooosh it".' She rolls her eyes.

'The dress is amazing,' Sarah says.

'It's not too much?' Alex asks, looking around. The girl in front of us is wearing a T-shirt that says, 'Dirty Girl'. She's pretty much pierced everywhere. Her friend's hair is blue and her arms are completely covered in tattoos.

I look at Alex again. 'Right. That's it. I'm going on a diet.'

'Are you high?' Sarah asks, looking me up and down.

'The camera adds ten pounds.'

'Which would make you just about right. If you lost weight, you'd be a stick insect,' Alex says.

'Yes, Mummy,' I joke, but a little would help. I'll be careful over Christmas.

We go inside where it's dark and mobbed. Alex gets a text.

'Louis has reserved us some seats up near the front,' she says excitedly.

'Quick,' Sarah says, 'before someone nabs them.'

They're good seats.

'What's everyone drinking?' Mark asks.

'Diet Coke,' I say.

'*Diet*?' he checks.

'Good idea!' Alex says. 'I'll have one too.'

'I'll just have Coke,' Sarah says.

'Eh, Mark, could I have vodka in mine?' Alex asks at the last minute.

'Sure.' He disappears into the crowd.

Alex starts drumming her fingers on the table. 'Will we go back stage, say hi? Actually, no. Dad hates anyone coming near him before a gig. I wonder if anyone's filming this. Imagine if they put it up on YouTube. God, they *so* need a manager.'

I think it's cute that she's so nervous for him.

'Here he is.' Sarah announces. Louis is coming our way. He's wearing a tight, white T-shirt. His hair's gelled which makes it even darker. He has a pair of drum sticks in the back pocket of his faded denims.

'Everyone OK?' he asks, like we're his guests.

'Yeah, great,' Alex says.

'You look nice,' he says to her.

)(

She looks down at the dress and laughs. Oh, God. Don't tell me she fancies him.

'I was just thinking,' she says. 'You guys need a manager.'

'Yeah. We're looking for one.'

'I could talk to Dad.'

'We're grand.'

'He knows the industry.'

'Alex, I don't need your dad.' His voice is firm.

'But he's so many contacts. And that's what the music business is all about.'

'I don't need a leg-up. Especially not from him.'

'You hate him, don't you?' she asks miserably.

'No. I get him. I'd kill anyone who got my daughter pregnant.'

She looks surprised. 'Me too,' she admits.

'Let's make a pact,' he says. 'Maggie's never going out with anyone.'

'Never?' She's smiling now.

'Never.'

'No boyfriends at all?'

'None.'

They laugh. 'I better go,' he says, looking behind him.

'Good luck up there,' Sarah says.

'Thanks. And seriously loud clapping from over here – even if we're crap.' He winks, then he's gone.

The first band are wearing a lot of black. And a lot of eyeliner. They look a bit like The Cure and I'm expecting them to be kind of dreamy-sounding. The minute they start, though, it's noise. Very loud noise. Like screaming. They're all jumping around, jerkily. I can't work out the lyrics. Except maybe, 'over'. I'm hoping they soon will be. We sit, kind of stunned. *Finally*, they leave the stage, all sweaty and quiet. The silence is a shock. There's buzzing in my ears. We look at each other.

'Christ,' Mark says.

We laugh.

Some backstage guys come out and change around the equipment.

The next band are totally different. Skinny and pale with really cool haircuts and too-big clothes. When they introduce themselves, they sound timid but funny. Their music reminds me of the *Juno* soundtrack. I imagine their fans clap quietly. I'm wrong.

Next up is a solo artist, making me wonder how entries are selected. This guy is doing ballady stuff. A bit like Ed Sheeran.

'Hard to take the guy seriously with those shades,' Mark says.

'He's good, though,' Alex says, like it's a bad thing.

The next band are all girls. I think, *yeah*. They're loud and seriously talented. I'm beginning to think that Louis was right in not expecting to win.

The next two bands are a bit like the first and have me hoping again.

Last up are Undertow. And when I see Louis walk on stage, I suddenly feel nervous, like I'm about to walk on set. They take their places and pick up their equipment. Louis takes out his drumsticks. The lead singer stands at the mike. *Be brilliant,* I think.

'Testing one, two. One, two,' James jokes.

People laugh.

Sarah is squinting up at him. 'He *does* look like Kurt Cobain, doesn't he?'

Louis taps his sticks together, one, two, three. Alex is on the edge of the seat, looking worried and beautiful. Then they're playing. I've never heard the song before, but I like it. Somewhere between Coldplay and The Script. When it's over, they don't go straight into their next song like other bands.

'Hello, *Dublin*,' James deadpans. 'We are *Undertow*.'

We go wild, whooping and stomping our feet.

He looks over at us. 'Who let them in?'

Then he's straight into the next song. I love that you can hear his Irish accent. Louis looks so different up there. At first, I don't know what it is. Then I get it. He looks happy, like this is what he was born to do. Alex was right. I glance at her. She's looking up at him, smiling.

After their last song, the whole place goes wild. They don't rush off the stage like some of the others, they walk off slowly, looking at the audience. James holds up an arm. Louis smiles.

One of the organisers comes on stage. He thanks the entrants and says that judging will take about fifteen minutes, and to sit back and enjoy ourselves until the winner is announced.

Then, Rebecca French is standing in front of us. She's wearing this really tight, short, red dress and seriously high, very cool shoes. Mark and possibly every guy in the place is staring.

'Hey!' she says. 'They were *amazing*, weren't they?'

'Yeah, amazing,' I say. 'What are you doing here?'

'Oh, I saw you guys plugging the gig on Facebook and thought I'd bring some friends along to support.'

'Cool. Where are they?'

She waves casually. 'Oh. Over there somewhere. You must be Alex,' she says.

'Eh, yeah.' Alex looks at me.

'This is Rebecca from *D4*,' I say.

'Can I join you guys?' she asks.

'Won't your friends mind?' I ask.

'What? No. Sure I'll go back in a minute.' And just when I think she's going to love bomb Alex, she surprises me and squeezes in beside Sarah.

'Sarah, right?'

Sarah smiles. They start to talk.

Louis arrives, smiling, a towel draped around his neck. 'What are you all having?'

He raises his arm, instantly catching the attention of a girl with a tray. She takes our order. Louis wipes his face with the towel. The tips of his hair are wet.

'So, what did you think? Have we a hope?' For a second he looks almost vulnerable.

'Oh, my God, you were so amazing,' Rebecca says.

He looks at her as if to say, who are you?

I introduce them.

Louis says hi, then turns to Alex and says something I can't hear.

'That last number was *incredible*,' Rebecca calls to him.

'Thanks,' Louis says, looking at her properly for the first time.

But she turns back to Sarah and they chat and laugh together for ages. Which means I get to snuggle up to Mark. After a while, Louis has to get back.

'Hey, thanks for the support, guys,' he says. 'No matter what happens.'

'See you, Louis,' Rebecca says, like she's known him all her life.

Alex looks at me. I shrug. Then Rebecca buys everyone drinks.

)(

Up on stage, the judges are asking all the bands back and, one by one, they walk out. The main judge, some guy from a music magazine I don't read, talks about 'the talent' and how hard it was to make a decision.

'Just get to the point,' Alex says.

Finally he does: 'And the winner is …' He pauses and looks up. 'Overbite.'

Oh.

The girl band go mental. Jumping up and down. Hugging each other. Screaming. I kind of go off them.

'Aw, shame,' Rebecca says.

'It's OK,' Alex says, almost to herself. 'They did great.'

James goes over to shake the lead singer of Overbite's hand.

'That guy is going places,' Mark says.

'The whole band is,' Alex says.

Louis comes over again.

'Hard luck,' Alex says. 'You guys so deserved to win.'

'Nah. Tonight was just thrown together. We were lucky not to screw up. What about James, though, right?' he asks, laughing and shaking his head.

'A real showman,' Mark says.

'We're still in shock. Anyway, I better get back. We're going out for a few pints with Overbite.'

Oh, God. Alex's face.

When the drinks run out, we start to get ready to go. Rebecca finally remembers her friends. She stands.

'So, I'll see you tomorrow,' she says to Sarah.

'Great. Are you sure it suits you to pick me up?' Sarah asks.

'Yeah, sure, no probs.' Rebecca looks at the rest of us and gives a little wave. 'See you guys.'

'Yeah, see you,' I say. As soon as she's gone, I turn to Sarah. 'You're seeing her tomorrow?'

'Oh yeah,' Sarah says brightly. 'You don't have to worry about the white water rafting. Rebecca's coming with me so I don't have to change the dates.' She looks at me. 'I know you didn't really want to go anyway.'

I can hardly speak. 'You're going with Rebecca?'

'Yeah, I was telling her the story and she said she's always wanted to try white water rafting.' She shrugs. 'It seemed like a no-brainer.'

I nod. I should be glad I don't have to go. Instead of feeling shoved aside.

'I can't believe you never told us what good craic she is,' Sarah says. 'She's mad.'

I don't care how mad she is, Rebecca French is going white water rafting with one of my best friends. There are no words.

'I think you're right about a manager,' Sarah says to Alex on the way home in Millie. 'They so need one.'

Alex says nothing. She hasn't actually spoken since Louis mentioned going for a drink with Overbite.

'Are you OK?' Sarah asks.

'Yeah, why?'

'You've gone really quiet.'

'I just want to get home to Maggie.' She sounds upset and lonely, like maybe she shouldn't even have come out.

Mark speeds up a bit and changes into fifth gear. He taps on the wheel. I keep thinking about the white water rafting.

'So, Alex has the hots for Louis,' Mark says when we let the others off.

'Is it that obvious?' I ask.

'A bit.'

'I thought maybe I was imagining it,' I say, and I must sound disappointed because Mark feels the need to say:

'He's not a bad guy, Rache.'

'I know. But one fling with an Overbite and Maggie might never see him again.'

'He could just be winding down with a few pints.'

I try to be positive. 'Maybe it's good this has happened. Before she gets too into him.'

'He's just going for a drink, Rache.'

'I know. And I hate to sound like Orla Tempany here, but I'd love someone to love her, you know? Someone she can rely on to stick around.'

'She'll find someone.'

No one like David, though, I think.

'Rebecca seems nice,' Mark says.

'Mark, you were drooling.'

He laughs. 'Actually, I like brunettes.'

'Then why were you drooling?'

'If I *was* looking at her, it's because I was thinking how like her character she is. Her part isn't as challenging as yours.'

Interesting.

'So what do you think of her going white water rafting with Sarah?' I ask.

'I think it gets you off the hook.'

I spend Saturday cooking. And imagining Sarah bumping over rapids with Rebecca.

'Are you OK?' Mum asks.

'Yeah, fine,' I say cheerfully.

'You seem quiet.'

'Tired. After last night.'

'Was it good?'

I tell her about it, but not about Rebecca turning up.

'This is nice. We never have time for a chat any more.'

I smile.

'So, how are you getting on in *D4*?' It's a Rebecca-loaded question.

'Great.' I talk all about Naomi for a bit.

'And how's Rebecca?'

I talk her up, so Mum doesn't worry. Surprisingly, it's not that hard. All I have to do is tell her about how she's introduced me to everyone and how she helped me out when I was late.

She looks so relieved. 'Oh, I'm glad.'

Finally, Maeve turns up and I'm free. I spend the afternoon catching up on homework and then go to a movie with Mark.

Later, in bed, I go on Facebook. I freeze. Rebecca has added Sarah and Alex as friends – and has posted loads of white water rafting shots. Sarah has already commented on most of them. I look at the photos and comments, and my stomach cramps. It's like she's moving in on my

)|(

friends. I tell myself to stop. She's friends with over a thousand people. And posts photos of everyone. Still ...

At my place on Sunday, Sarah nags so much about setting up a fan page that I give in. If Rebecca can be friends with all her fans, I can at least go that far. We're all supposed to be working on the page, but soon Sarah takes over. She's so creative when it's stuff she doesn't have to be creative for. She uploads stills from *D4* that she finds on Google Images. She puts up links to You Tube of clips from the show. She finds the *D4* logo. She asks me to repeat the lines I've had. I know them by heart and call them out. By the time she's finished, it looks amazing. Really professional.

'You're so talented at this,' I say. 'You should do it as a job or something.'

'Meh.' She hates talking about stuff like that.

'How did the white water rafting go?' I ask. Part of me doesn't want to know; part of me can't stop thinking about it.

She smiles. 'Really good. Rebecca's completely mad, isn't she?'

'Yeah. Mad.'

'We might go again, sometime.'

'Cool.'

'I wonder if she would do the skydiving.'

I feel like shooting my hand up and saying, '*I'll* do the skydiving.' But. They get on. And how can I deny Sarah this friendship because of something Rebecca did to me years ago? Sarah needs something extra now and maybe Rebecca is it.

TEN
Hoarse

The next time I see Rebecca, she's covering her mirror in tinsel. Loads and loads of silver tinsel. She hangs blue baubles from the lights. It's not great.

'Oh, hey,' she says when she sees me. 'Wasn't Friday night amazing?'

'The gig? Yeah it was good.'

'They're so talented.'

'Yeah.' I drop my bag at my dressing table and turn on my fairy lights.

'Was Sarah telling you about the white water rafting?' She talks so familiarly, like we're sharing our lives now.

'Yeah, she told me.'

'It was insane. Such a rush. I thought we were going to fall out. I seriously thought the boat was going to turn over. On Sunday, I was hoarse from all the screaming. Luckily, I've my voice back for today.'

'Luckily.'

'You should have come.'

'Couldn't.' Didn't Sarah tell her?

'OK, well, next time.'

The thought of hanging out with Rebecca French doesn't exactly thrill me, but I smile.

The dressing room phone rings. Rebecca lunges for it, like she always does. She ends up handing it to me. It's Emily's PA, calling me up to the office. He doesn't say why. It's like being called to the principal's office. An explanation would help.

'Where're you going?' Rebecca asks.

'Emily wants to see me.'

'Oooh,' she says, like I'm in trouble.

Hilarious, I think. Then tell myself to stop. If I resent her friendship with Sarah what does that make me?

Emily's PA is like a young, even hotter Antonio Banderas. It's so cool that he can wear denims at work. He smiles and tells me to go on in.

I take a deep breath, knock and open the door.

Emily stands up from behind her desk and smiles. 'Rachel.'

Her office is neat and tidy. Trophies and photos of her with celebrities line the walls. It smells of success. Ambition.

'Sit down,' she says.

We both do.

'I wanted to have a chat with you about where we're going with Naomi's part.'

Oh, my God, are they going to renew my contract?

'As you know Naomi got together with Joe. And that's gone well. We'd like to take it a step further. We're considering a sex scene.'

I swallow. I think of all the people who'd be watching. Thousands of complete strangers. But worse – my family, friends, people at school, teachers. Mark.

'I just wanted to make sure you're OK with it.'

Do I have a choice? I mean, really? I want to keep my part. Do a good job. I want the story to stay the story. And not be a diva – and if that means a sex scene, I'll do a sex scene. This is an adult world. Backing out is not an option. Her asking is a formality.

'It's fine.' My voice sounds high.

'Are you *sure*?' She looks at me from under her eyebrows.

I nod. 'Sure.'

'Have you any questions?'

Just millions. But they all boil down to one. 'Will I have to take my clothes off?'

'No, no, not at all. It'll be handled very tastefully.'

Which means what, exactly?

'Rachel, if you're not comfortable with it, you must tell me now. Before we go ahead.'

'It's fine. Honestly.'

'Would you like me to run it past your parents?'

'No. No. I'll tell them.' *Maybe. How, though? And how much time do I have?* 'When will it be shot?'

'Oh, not till after Christmas.'

I nod. *OK. I managed the kiss. I can do this.*

The week before Christmas, the episode with the kiss goes out.

'So, Mark, some kiss last night, eh?' Peter Sweetnam smirks.

I freeze.

'Great kiss,' Mark says.

'So you weren't jealous?' Peter asks.

'Why would I be jealous?' Mark puts an arm around me.

It's like I've cleared my first hurdle.

On our last day in *D4* before breaking for Christmas, notices go up. They're auditioning for new parts. Teenage parts. Rebecca's not happy.

)(

'There are enough of us on the show,' she says, collecting up all her stuff to bring home for the holiday.

'Don't you think that if they want more teenagers, we must be doing something right? Charley thinks the viewership figures have gone up for our age.'

'Maybe, but, *at some point*, they'll realise they've too many teenagers in the cast and some of us will have to go.'

'Well, one of them will be me. With my three-month contract.'

She waves her hand. 'Oh they'll extend that. They did with me.'

'Really?'

'Of course. You're great.'

I stare at her in shock. She just zips up her bag as far as it will go and drops it onto the floor beside her dressing table. Then she flops onto her chair. For a while she just sits there, watching me while I check my drawers for stuff I might need over the holiday.

'Isn't it so sad about Shane?' she says.

'*Shane*? As in Sarah's Shane?'

'Yeah. We went shopping last night. She told me all about him. I was trying not to cry. You know what she said?'

I wait, not believing that maybe Rebecca knows more than I do about my friend. Sarah never talks about Shane. And she never said anything about shopping.

'She said, "He was in a wheelchair but he held me up."'

Wow.

)(

'Her whole attitude is amazing. The way she wants to live till she dies. She's an inspiration.'

When I get home, I call Sarah.

'Hey, how's it going?' I ask.

'Yeah fine. How was *D4*?'

'Good. Last day.' I pause. 'Rebecca was telling me you guys went shopping.'

'Oh yeah.'

'Good time?'

'Yeah, it was good.'

I wait, but she says nothing else.

'Buy anything nice?' I ask, for something to say.

'Nah, not really. It was just good to get out.'

I feel bad that I haven't had more time for her. 'Sarah you know if you ever want to talk about stuff …'

'Yeah, I know. Thanks.'

I can't help feeling that she's already got someone to talk to.

Later, there's a knock on my door.

'I can't believe you set up a fan page,' Jack says as he walks in.

'What, you're spying on me now?'

'Yeah, I'm spying on you.' He rolls his eyes. 'Someone in school was slagging me about it.'

'Who?'

'No one. Just an idiot. Look, you're leaving yourself open. People can post whatever they want.'

'And I can delete whatever they post. Jack, you worry too much.'

He looks at me for a long time and quietly says, 'Last time, I didn't worry enough.'

It hits me in the chest. And for a moment I can't speak. 'Worry doesn't change anything. Just makes it worse. The page is up now.'

'Do you want the bullying to come back?' he asks desperately.

'Yeah, Jack. Life's just so freaking boring.'

'I'm just saying you should be careful. People get jealous.'

The only person getting jealous is me. Jealous of Rebecca's friendship with Sarah. And I hate myself for it. 'Jack. I can handle myself, OK?'

'OK.' He puts his hands up. 'OK.'

'Don't make it sound like I'm wrong.'

'There was a time you listened to me, Rache.'

'And look where that got me.'

He shakes his head, turns and leaves.

And I can't believe that hurting him is still like hurting myself.

ELEVEN
Serviettes

I love Christmas. The traditions. Going to buy the tree with my dad, just the two of us. Taking ages to select the right one. Coming home to a blazing fire and hot chocolate, and decorating the tree to Christmas carols. Buying and wrapping presents. I even love the crowds. The buzz of looking forward.

The first day of the holidays, I always go shopping with Sarah and Alex. It's tradition.

'Would it be OK if Rebecca came along?' Sarah asks the night before.

No, I think. But can't exactly say it. And shouldn't anyway.

'I don't mind,' I say, looking at Alex.

'Yeah, sure,' she says. 'If you want.' I know she's as guilty as I am about not having more time for Sarah.

Louis, who didn't go off with an Overbite after all, offers to mind Maggie. Before the total crowds swamp Dundrum, we meet Rebecca at nine-thirty. She looks amazing in a leather jacket with a hoodie underneath and skinny jeans. She hugs us all like she's one of us.

'Where to?' she asks.

'Can we start in B Cool?' Sarah asks. It's this gadget shop that's great for presents.

She and Rebecca walk ahead. Every so often someone recognises Rebecca and stares. If she notices, she doesn't show it, chatting away to Sarah.

)(

'You're not going to believe what I did,' Alex says to me as we walk along. 'I asked Louis not to smoke while he was minding Maggie.'

'So?'

'He was totally offended. He said he'd never do anything to harm her.' She holds her forehead.

'You were thinking of Maggie.'

'I was thinking of *cot death*. But it was *Louis* I was talking to. He'd never do anything to hurt her. I know that.'

'He's a relaxed guy. He'll have forgotten it tomorrow. Actually he's probably forgotten it already.' I imagine him singing to Maggie and calling her pumpkin or making faces at her. Whatever he's doing he's enjoying himself.

'Should I buy him something for Christmas? You know, to make up for it.' She looks unsure.

'I don't know. What do you think?'

'I kind of want to. After today. But what if he thinks it means something?'

'Then don't.'

Sarah turns around. 'What are you two talking about?'

Alex shrugs. 'I was just wondering if I should buy Louis a Christmas present.'

'Of course you should,' Rebecca butts in.

'I don't know,' Alex says.

'You could make it from Maggie,' Sarah says.

'That's a great idea,' Alex says, cheering up.

And I get what Sarah likes about Rebecca. She's just like her. Impulsive. Optimistic. She just goes for things. Doesn't worry.

'What are you getting Mark?' Sarah asks.

'I don't know. I was thinking a Kindle. But he likes books. You know, physical books. He likes to hold them.

)(

Smell them. Feel them. Re-read them. Build cities with them.'

Sarah and Alex laugh.

'Build cities?' Rebecca asks, as if that's weird.

'Yeah, cities,' I say, like I mean, do you've a problem with that?

'Cool,' she says.

Sarah and Alex look at me like they can't believe I'm being so touchy.

It's tradition to go back to my place after Christmas shopping. Mum makes us homemade cookies in the shape of Christmas trees and stars. We have them with hot chocolate, then wrap our presents together. It wouldn't feel right with someone else along. All day, I'm waiting for Rebecca to say she has to go. She doesn't. At around three, we're all ready to collapse when Alex says, 'Will we head?'

'Yeah, OK,' I say.

Sarah turns to Rebecca. 'Hey, we're going back to Rachel's if you want to come.'

Excuse me? Hello? I think. But then, this is just Sarah being Sarah. It'd never occur to her that I wouldn't want Rebecca to come.

'Yeah, that'd be great,' Rebecca says excitedly, like she's been formally invited into the group.

Alex looks at me as if to say when did we become a foursome? And I feel a bit better.

We get a taxi because it's so hard to get to my house from Dundrum. On the way home, disappointment changes to nerves. I don't want Rebecca in my house. I don't want to expose my mum to her. I don't want to expose everything

I love to her. I know she's changed. They're still my family. And how are they going to react to her? I know Mum won't say anything. But *Jack*. Jesus. He better not be home.

When I open the front door, Mum has Christmas carols on. The house is warm and a fire is blazing in the front room. I have this awful feeling that Rebecca's going to laugh at everything.

'This is so cosy,' she says, like it's great.

We drop our bags in the hall and go into the kitchen. Mum's halfway through hugging Alex when she realises who the extra person is. She's staring. I think, *Oh shit*. But then she recovers, finishes Alex's hug and moves on to Sarah. But she just smiles at Rebecca.

'Mum this is Rebecca,' I say. Because I don't want her to have to say she recognises her from TV.

'Hi, Rebecca. Welcome.' Then she turns to us. 'So how was Dundrum?'

'Packed,' Alex says.

'But good,' Rebecca adds.

'Why don't you all sit down and I'll make some hot chocolate?' Mum says.

'That'd be so cool,' Rebecca says.

Mum looks at her, then at me, then goes to make the hot chocolate. Everyone sits down. I go and get the cookies. Mum's bought schmaltzy Christmas serviettes, the kind you'd never put in front of a bully. I'm so close to leaving them behind. Then, I think, *Mum got these*. I carry them to the table with the cookies.

The minute the plate hits the table, three hands automatically reach out. Which makes me want to laugh.

'Oh, my God, you're such a great cook,' Rebecca says to Mum after her first bite.

Mum's smile is polite. 'Thank you.'

)(

We chat about the decorations in Dundrum, about what we're going to do for Christmas – sleep basically, we talk about our favourite presents. Then Jack comes into the kitchen.

He says hi to Alex and Sarah. Then he cops Rebecca. He looks at me as if to say, are you mad? Then he just stands and glares at her.

'Jack, this is Rebecca from *D4*,' Sarah says.

'I know who she is.' Ice.

'Eh, Jack,' Mum says. 'Can I've a hand, here?'

He walks right up to us, still glaring at Rebecca. He takes three biscuits, then finally goes over to Mum. She speaks so quietly, we can't hear. Luckily.

It's the first time I've ever seen Rebecca blush.

And I know when he leaves that he's holding himself back.

When we've finished, we collect all our bags from the hall and carry them up to my room.

As soon as we get inside, Rebecca turns to me, 'Rachel, your brother is seriously hot.'

I stare at her. Didn't she *see*? Or is she just pretending she didn't? Will I ever fully trust her? I say nothing, just take the wrapping paper out of its cellophane cover. I've three pairs of scissors and three Sellotapes ready for action. We all sit on the floor.

'What about the presents we got each other?' Rebecca asks. 'We can't exactly wrap them now, can we? Why don't we just give them to each other now? I hate waiting.'

I look at Sarah and Alex. They look at me. That awkward moment when someone buys you a gift and you don't have one for them.

'Yeah, no,' Sarah says. 'Wrap them at home. We'll swap closer to Christmas.'

OK, she's saved our asses. But now we have to a) buy Rebecca a gift and b) see her again before Christmas.

'Cool,' Rebecca says.

At around six, the others leave. I close the door and turn to see Jack on the stairs.

'You're hanging out with Rebecca French? Are you fucking kidding me?'

It's like hearing my inner voice. 'She's OK.'

'Yeah, like Hannibal Lecter is OK.'

'She's changed.'

Mum comes out from the kitchen.

'It's good that they're friends,' she says to him. 'What do they say, keep your enemies close?'

'She's not my enemy.'

'I know,' Mum says, 'but if you're friends, she can't exactly give you a hard time.'

Jack rolls his eyes. And I know what he's thinking: *How can she have survived in this world for so long?*

'For the record,' I say, 'we're not friends. Sarah asked her along today. I don't know why she's good for Sarah, but she is. And I'm not going to get in the way.'

'Don't tell me I didn't warn you,' Jack says and heads up to his room.

'Thanks, Jack,' I say sarcastically.

On Sunday morning, I'm having breakfast. I've caught up on everything now – sleep, study, life. The forecast says it might snow, so I'm feeling pretty good.

Dad grabs a coffee and sits at the table. It's nice that it's just the two of us, he reads the paper and I enjoy having nothing to do. I help myself to the glossy magazine section. I put it on the table next to my bowl and flick leisurely through it with my left hand. God, it's good to read rubbish.

Dad starts to read aloud from the paper. 'Spotted on the town, two new besties, teen stars of *D4*, the gorgeous Rebecca French and newcomer Rachel Dunne, out Christmas shopping together in Dundrum. Isn't it wonderful when rivals can be friends?'

I drop my spoon and put my hands out for the paper.

He passes it over. 'Bottom right-hand corner,' he says.

It's a tiny piece in a social column. And it's exactly as Dad read it. How did it get in there? How did they know we were in Dundrum? And *besties*? What will Rachel and Sarah think? I hand it back to him.

'Don't show Jack.'

'Why not?' he asks. And I realise Mum hasn't told him.

'He thinks I should avoid her.'

'He might be right,' he says, his opinion the opposite of Mum's as it always is when it comes to me. Suddenly, I've lost my appetite. I get up and throw the rest of my cereal into the bin. I go upstairs, hoping no one reads the paper.

I'm heading for the shower when my phone rings.

'Did you see the paper?' Rebecca asks excitedly.

'How did they know we were in Dundrum?'

'I told them.'

'What?'

'Yeah. I met that columnist once, at an opening or something. He said to give him a shout anytime I'd news.'

'Is this news?'

'For some people, yeah.'

'People who've no lives.'

She laughs. 'Doesn't matter. It's good to keep your name in the paper. *D4* are less likely to cancel your contract. And they love the publicity for the show.' It's as if life is a game she knows how to play. She's forgotten something though.

'I'm kinda surprised you didn't tell me you were doing this.'

'I wanted it to be a surprise. I thought you'd be blown away.' There's a pause. 'You're not, though, are you?'

'I'm just glad you didn't mention Alex's name. She hates publicity.'

'I kind of got that vibe, which is why I didn't.'

'OK.'

'You don't mind, do you, that I did it?'

'It's OK. But if you're ever going to mention me in the paper again, it'd be great if you'd check with me first. Just in case.'

'Oh. OK. Sure.' She sounds surprised. 'Sorry,' she says.

'Don't worry about it.'

And now, before it gets any later, I have to go around Dundrum wondering what to buy the girl who made my life hell for Christmas.

It's almost Christmas. Sarah wants us to meet Rebecca to exchange gifts. We get the DART into town. Alex brings Maggie, to show her the Christmas lights. Not that she'll actually see them she's so small. But it's the thought. We arrange to get the same DART as Rebecca, who lives closer to town. She misses it. So we have to wait for her in town. We find a coffee shop, so Maggie's not cold.

Half an hour later, she shows up. 'I'm *so* sorry. Oh, my

)(

God, is that Maggie?' She raves about how beautiful she is, how like Alex.

'Really?' Alex asks enthusiastically. 'The only other person who thinks she looks like me is Louis. Good to know that there's a bit of me in her too.' Alex smiles but she sounds almost hurt. And I can't believe I never thought of that.

'Oh there definitely is,' Rebecca says enthusiastically. 'I think she's *really* like you.'

It's seriously cold outside, so we stay in the coffee shop to exchange presents. Prize for the best one goes to Rebecca. A trip to a day spa for Sarah.

'It's too much,' Sarah says.

'No. I got a special deal because I booked for two people. You and me.'

Sarah touches her heart. 'That's so sweet.'

And I have to admit it is. And thoughtful. Not only is it exactly what Sarah would love, she hasn't embarrassed her with the price of it.

On the way back, we're all standing on the platform, waiting for the DART. It pulls up in front of us.

Suddenly I'm back in time. I'm with Rebecca. And Béibhinn Keane. And two others. The doors of the DART slide open. I walk forward. They walk with me. I step onto the DART. Suddenly, I'm alone. I turn around. Out on the platform, they're standing looking at me, laughing and then turning to high five each other, as the doors close. And as the DART pulls away, I want to die.

'Don't mind them,' a woman says.

I turn in surprise. She's seen it all. I look around. Everyone in the carriage has. I'm a loser even to strangers.

Now, I take my seat, remembering what it's like, trying not to cry on public transport.

TWELVE
The Princess and the Pea

My older brother Harry's coming home for Christmas dinner. This is good. He's bringing his new girlfriend, Jessica – which is not so good. I was looking forward to us just being a family again, not having to be polite to some stranger. I have told Mum we are *not* watching the Christmas special with non-family members. She's taping it.

They arrive late. She looks like Snow White. Her hair is black and shiny, like an ad for shampoo. She doesn't have individual hairs but one shiny curtain. I imagine her swishing it around. Oh, my God, he's pulling out a chair for her. Nobody does that. Especially not Harry.

I help Mum serve the dinner, like I always do at Christmas. It's the one time I don't mind. Today, though, I feel like a waitress, serving a princess.

Mum and Dad make polite conversation with Jessica. Where she's from. (Terenure.) How many in her family. (Four.) How they met. (College.) It's exhausting.

Jack and I stay quiet. I hope they're not hanging around for the whole afternoon.

'So, Rache,' Harry says, finally. 'Got enough Brussels sprouts there?'

I stop shaking the salt and look down at the plate. Everyone does. There's not an awful lot on it, besides the Brussels sprouts. And I hate Brussels sprouts.

)(

'Are you on a diet?' Jessica asks.

I feel Mum, especially, look at me. 'No.'

'You don't even like Brussels sprouts,' Harry says.

What's he doing, trying to act the big man? Impress his new girlfriend? He's never like this.

'What's it to you?' Jack asks.

I hate the way he thinks I can't stand up for myself.

'How's the *study* going, Jack?' Harry teases.

'Harry, why are you being such an asshole?' I ask calmly.

'Rachel!' Dad says. 'Language.'

Jessica smiles. And it hits me – when Jack falls in love, I'm going to be like one of those mothers who no girl will be good enough for. I look at Jessica.

'What d'you think of that fairytale, *The Princess and the Pea*?' I ask her.

'I'm sorry?' She looks confused.

'You know the one where the princess can't sleep because there's a pea in her bed.' She's that precious.

'Is that a trick question?' she asks. Which means she's not completely stupid.

'No,' I say innocently.

'Let's pull some crackers,' Mum says cheerfully. She knows I hate *The Princess and the Pea*. She knows what I'm doing.

Mum points a cracker at me.

I can't help it. I smile. Because she gets me.

The holidays go way too fast. As usual. The day before we go back, I still haven't told Mark about the sex scene. We get back to his house after being out all day. In the hall, we hang up our coats, then he takes off, racing up the stairs.

'Where are you going?' I call after him.

But he's actually gone.

When I open the door to his bedroom, he's draped across the bed, fake seductively.

'I've been expecting you,' he says, raising and lowering his eyebrows.

I laugh.

He gets up, comes over and kisses me. After a while, he pulls back.

'You know, I was thinking, what if Naomi has the surgery?'

'You're as bad as Peter Sweetnam.'

'Can't help it. I've developed *feelings* for her.'

He always makes me laugh. Like a lifetime guarantee.

'Seriously, though,' he says. 'If they're talking about surgery they might want to keep you on.'

'It's surgery to relieve her symptoms.'

'I know but what if they operate and somehow get the tumour? Maybe that's where they're going with this. Think about it. The amount of hits you get on YouTube now. The ratings must have gone way up since you joined. Don't be surprised if they want to keep you on.'

'Don't be surprised if they don't.' The only thing I'm sure that's going to happen is the sex scene.

'What?' he asks.

'Nothing.'

'There's something.'

'It's nothing. I'll tell you later.'

I go sit on the bed and pick up the book that's lying open on it: *The Rules. A Man''s Guide to Life – Revised and updated (Because being a man has gotten much harder).* I flick through it and start to smile.

'It says here that calling your penis Señor whatever won't make you appear more worldly.'

'True,' he says seriously.

I flick forward a few pages. 'It also says that when trying to impress the ladies with your musical skills you should never opt for an accordion, your knee, cymbals, or a lute.' I smile. 'True,' I say.

'Damn. I've just bought a lute.'

I smile then flick on a few pages. 'Apparently, you shouldn't trust a woman who refers to her boobs as separate entities, like "the girls".'

'You don't do that do you?' he asks.

'No, Mark.' *If only he was an actor. Then I wouldn't have to explain about sex scenes. He'd just get that it's part of the job.* Out of that thought comes the most amazing idea. 'Guess what? They're auditioning for teenage parts in *D4*.'

He picks up his sponge ball. 'Yeah?' he says, like he's trying to sound interested.

'Why don't you go up for one?'

He laughs. 'No, thanks,' he says, slam dunking the ball into the hoop on the back of his door.

'Why not? It'd be great. Think of all the time we'd have together.'

He holds the ball to his chest. 'Acting's your thing, Rache. Not mine.'

'That's so not true. You were an amazing Macbeth.'

'I took the part to be with you. You know that. I didn't actually enjoy prancing around in tights.'

'There's no tights in *D4*. Come on. It'd be so much fun. We could rehearse together.'

'We already do.'

'Yeah, but you'd get paid for it.'

He shoots again. 'I'm a behind-the-scenes man, Rache.'

'Come *on*,' I almost beg.

))(

He stops shooting and comes over. 'I'd hate it. The attention. People coming up to me all the time.'

'*I* hate it. Especially when they act like you're invisible. But the attention's only a small part of the whole thing.'

'I like being invisible.'

'It'd just be so much easier with you there.'

His face gets serious. 'Why? What's up?'

I turn away and walk to the window. 'I have to do a sex scene,' I say without looking back.

He laughs.

I turn back. 'It's not funny, Mark.'

'Sorry.'

'I don't want to have this other life from you. I mean, the only time I share it with you is when I embarrass you.'

'You don't embarrass me,' he says simply.

'Even if I have to get my kit off?'

He looks worried. 'Will you?'

'I don't know. I don't think so. Emily said it will be "tastefully done" – whatever that means.'

'You'll be fine. You always are.'

'Mark, I've never had sex.'

'You've never had cancer either.'

'I wish I'd said no.' Though, I didn't really have the choice.

'You'll probably end up proud of that scene.'

'Eh. *No!*'

'You *might*.'

'So you're not going to audition?'

'No. Sorry.'

'You did it for me before – took a part so we could be together.'

)(

'That was a school play. This is national television.'

'So?'

'I don't want my life to change. I'll rehearse with you. I'll be there for you. I'm your biggest fan. You know that. But, like I said, I'm a behind-the-scenes man.'

I sigh. And can't help feeling that he's got me now, why should he bother?

THIRTEEN
Batman Returns

On my first day back at *D4*, I meet Maisie in the corridor.
She is practically grinning.

'I was just coming to look for you,' she says.

'Really?'

'Want to go for coffee?'

'Eh, sure,' I say, surprised, but glad. As we walk to the
canteen, we joke about our Christmases.

She gets tea and a scone. I get a Diet Coke.

'No brekkie?' she asks.

'Had it at home.' It's my second lie today. I told Mum
I'd have breakfast here. I've only two pounds to go. And
I'm the most determined person I know.

'Did you watch the Christmas special?' she asks, way
too enthusiastically for her.

'No, I missed it. We had family over.'

'Your scene was breathtaking.'

'*Really*?' It means so much coming from her.

'I'm sure it's what got you the IFTA nomination,' she
says.

'Sorry?'

'You've been nominated for an Irish Film and
Television Award.'

'Really? Are you *serious*?'

She smiles. 'Don't sound so surprised.'

'But how do you know? Was it announced?'

'No.'

'Then how … '

She smiles like she's enjoying this. Finally she says, 'I was just up with Emily. I'm getting an award for my "contribution to the industry".'

'Oh, my God. That's amazing. Congratulations. You *so* deserve it.' I want to hug her but a) she's across the table and b) I don't know her well enough.

'I'd prefer yours. Mine's for geriatrics.'

'No, it's not.'

'So. Are you excited?'

'I still can't believe it,' I say. 'I mean, I've only just started.'

'Now, when Emily calls you up, act surprised.'

'I am surprised.'

'Then it won't be hard.'

I want to call my parents. Mark. Charley. Alex and Sarah. I want to scream and jump up and down.

'It's usually a good night,' she says.

I look at her blankly.

'The Awards night.'

'Of course. Sorry. I'm not thinking.'

She smiles like she gets that. 'Would you like to sit with me?'

'That would be amazing.'

'Good. Then I'll make sure of it.'

'Thank you.'

I don't know what Rebecca was talking about – Maisie is lovely. She didn't *have* to tell me. I go outside to call everyone. Then I remember: Mark, Alex and Sarah are in class so I call Mum.

I have to hold the phone away from my ear, she's so excited.

)(

'It's not official yet,' I say. 'So don't go telling anyone.'

'Not even Dad?'

'No, you can tell Dad, just warn him not to say anything to anyone, though.'

'Rachel, I'm so proud of you.'

'I haven't won it, Mum.'

'I know, I know. But being nominated is such a vote of confidence.'

I can't stop smiling.

Next, I call Charley.

'This could open so many doors for you, Rachel,' she says. 'In fact, I'm going to make sure it does. I'll come with you to the Awards ceremony. There'll be so many people there I can introduce you to.'

'Aw. Thanks, Charley.'

'I'm your agent. It's my job.'

'Thanks anyway.'

'This is just the beginning,' she says.

Walking back to the dressing room, I feel like I'm walking an inch off the ground. I keep wanting to say, 'Yay.'

I'm in the dressing room five minutes when the phone rings. It's Emily's assistant, asking if I'm free to come upstairs. My heart leaps. But I check the time.

'I've about ten minutes till Make-Up,' I tell him.

'Perfect,' he says. 'Won't take long.'

'Who was that?' Rebecca asks as soon as I hang up.

Emily's PA.

'What's up?'

'I don't know,' I say because I'm not supposed to.

I practically run to Emily's office. At the top of the stairs, I take a deep breath. Check myself in the glass of a painting and flatten my hair a bit.

I'm told to go straight in.

So I knock, and do.

Emily's already halfway to the door, smiling widely.

'Rachel. Great. Come on in.' She places her hands on my shoulders and guides me to my seat and actually sits me down.

I feel so giddy, I'm afraid I might laugh.

'I have some great news. You've been nominated for an IFTA.'

'Seriously? Oh, my God. Wow.'

She takes her seat behind the desk. 'It's fantastic news. We're so proud of you.'

'Thank you.' I'm smiling again.

'You're nominated for Actress in a Supporting Role in Television.'

I nod slowly like this is news to me. Then I think of Rebecca. 'Is anyone else from *D4* up for an award?'

'Yes, actually. Maisie Morrin is going to receive the award for Outstanding Contribution to the Industry.'

'She so deserves it.'

'We think so. The nominations will be officially announced at noon. So say nothing till then. You can tell your family obviously. But I'd leave it at that.'

I nod. 'So there's no one else up for an award?'

'We're delighted with two.' She looks at me for a long moment. 'I put your name forward, Rachel. I have a feeling about you.'

Wow. 'Thanks so much.'

'Our ratings have been rising steadily since you joined the show.'

So Mark was right. I want to hug him and tell him and kiss him and laugh. I start to hope that maybe they *will* keep me on longer. She stands and puts out her hand.

)I(

'Well done, Rachel. You're surpassing all our expectations.'

'Thanks so much,' I say, shaking her hand. I could hug her. That's how high I am.

'Well?' Rebecca asks the minute I get back.

I can't tell her. She's been in the show a lot longer than me. It's her life. 'Eh, nothing really,' I say lightly.

'You were called up to her office for nothing?' She looks doubtful.

'Well, no. Emily was just saying that they're happy with me and stuff.'

Luckily, I'm called on set.

Then we're filming.

I don't get back to the dressing room till twelve-thirty. Rebecca's there.

'I can't believe you didn't tell me,' she says. 'That's why you were called up to the office this morning, wasn't it?'

I make a 'sorry' face. 'They asked me not to say anything.'

'Yeah, but we're friends. We share a dressing room. I'd have told you.'

'OK. I didn't know how to tell you. Your part is so much bigger. And you're so good.'

'I *know*,' she says. 'I mean, you're great and everything. It's just that I've been on the show longer and stuff.'

'I know.' I give her that.

'Have you told your parents?'

'I rang my mum, yeah.'

'And Charley?'

'Yeah.'

'Alex? Sarah? Mark?'

It's freaky the way she says everyone's names, like they're part of her world too.

'They're in class,' I say, 'so no, not yet.'

She forces a smile. And when she says, 'Congratulations,' I know she doesn't mean it. And I kind of understand that.

'OK. We're going to have to get you a dress,' Sarah says after she's squeezed me to death. 'A totally fuck-off dress.'

I laugh.

'Marsha!' Alex says. Alex's dad's partner is a fashion designer. She's amazing.

'Oh, my God. Yes!' Sarah says.

'Anything else just wouldn't be lucky,' Alex adds.

'What if she's busy?' I ask.

'Are you kidding? This will be great for her profile. Red carpet publicity.'

I get a bit freaked at the thought of red carpet.

'Will I need a tux?' Mark asks when I tell him (and he's stopped bouncing me up and down).

Oh God, I think. *Can I bring someone? And if Charley's coming, is that my someone used up?*

'Let me check.'

'It's black tie, right?'

'I think so.'

'Then it's a tux.'

'Mark? I have to check about bringing someone. Like, if we can. I'm sure it'll be fine.'

He doesn't say anything for a few seconds then he smiles. 'Sure, no worries.'

'Charley wants to come to introduce me to people.'

)(

'Charley's going? Well then, there probably won't be room for me.'

'I'd love you to come, though. Let me ask, OK? Maybe I can bring two people.' What about my mum, though? I owe her so much. And she was so excited on the phone.

'It's OK. Don't worry.'

If he came, he'd be invisible again. 'Would you prefer not to come?'

'No, I'd like to. But it's work for you. You should make contacts and stuff.'

'Let me see, OK?'

'It's OK. Honestly. Work the room – that's more important. I'll watch it on TV.'

'I'm still going to check.'

As soon as I get home, I google the IFTAs. I'm up against three other actors, three seriously good actors who've been around a lot longer than me.

'I haven't a hope,' I say to Mum.

'Rachel, it's great just to be nominated.'

'Yeah.' I have to remind myself of that. I still can't believe it.

'When is the ceremony?'

'February.'

'Can you bring someone?'

'I don't know. They didn't say and it's not on the IFTA site. Charley said she wanted to come, though.'

She looks kind of disappointed. I want to bring her. And Mark. I don't want to let anyone down. 'I'll ask Maisie.'

'Who's Maisie?'

'Maisie Morrin.'

)(

'You're friends with Maisie Morrin?'

'Not friends. But she told me about the award. She's nice.'

I go on Google to check out Maisie's career. I knew she'd acted in Hollywood, but I'd no idea about all the films she'd been in, all the leading roles she'd played. She was so beautiful. I go on YouTube to watch some clips. She so deserves this award. After, I go on moan.ie to see if they're talking about the nominations.

It's like a punch in the stomach. I sit, stunned, staring at the screen. Then, reach for my phone.

'Have you seen moan.ie?' I ask Mark.

'I thought you weren't going on that.'

'But did you see it?'

'No. Why?'

'There's this comment that's so not fair. It's like personal.'

'What is it?' He sounds concerned.

'There's this guy who posts and he's popular? He's never said anything bad about me before. Now he's saying I don't deserve the nomination. He says I'm a crap actress. And I've a fat ass.'

He laughs.

'Jesus, Mark. People are reading that.'

'People on moan.ie.'

'They're still people.'

'Bored, angry, vengeful people —'

'Who are being angry and vengeful to me.'

'Rachel, why go on that site if it's just going to upset you? It's not like you can do anything about it.'

'It's just that everyone likes this guy. He's cool and

)(

funny and so *right* – usually. You *want* to agree with him, you know?'

'Is that the guy you mentioned before?'

'BatmanReturns, yeah.'

'Rache, you've just achieved something amazing and you're worrying about some anonymous computer geek called *BatmanReturns* who's moaning on some stupid site for moaners. If that guy was any good, he'd be out acting himself.'

'I guess.' I like that he's angry for me.

'Haters gonna hate, Rache.' And though he says it in a jokey voice, I know he means it.

'You're right,' I say, relieved.

But then the minute I hang up, I look at my ass in the mirror. I am *not* eating till dinner tomorrow. Then I'll have an apple.

FOURTEEN
Eyebrows

On Saturday, Sarah and Rebecca spend the day in a spa. I'm over at Alex's, where Louis has just finished feeding Maggie. He takes a small cellophane bag from his pocket. From it he pulls out a piece of raw carrot. He starts to gnaw at it.

'What are you doing?' Alex asks.

'Oh sorry. Want one?' He offers the bag around.

No takers.

'What's with the carrots?' Alex asks.

He shrugs. 'Just having a carrot instead of a smoke.'

'Oh, my God, you're quitting?' she says.

'No. Substituting.'

'But ultimately quitting, right?'

'Only if I *end up* quitting.'

She looks confused and I don't blame her.

He shrugs. 'I'm just taking it one smoke at a time. I like them way too much to quit.'

Alex's face softens. 'You're doing this for Maggie, aren't you?'

'Alex, you know I'd never smoke around Maggie,' he says, suddenly serious, borderline offended.

'I know you wouldn't.'

'But. I do want to be around for her. Someone has to fight off all those potential boyfriends,' he says, getting up and grabbing his jacket. He bends over the Moses basket and smiles. 'Bye, bye, sweetie pie.'

Alex looks like she's going to melt.

As soon as I hear the front door close, I turn to her.

'You fancy him, don't you?'

'No, I don't. OK I do.'

I laugh. 'Didn't take long to get that confession out of you.'

She groans. 'I'm kind of mad about him.'

'I noticed.' I smile.

'Is it that obvious?'

'It's kind of obvious.'

'Even to him?' she asks, eyes suddenly wide.

'No. You're fine.'

'Good because Louis doesn't do relationships. And I don't want to fool around with anyone. Not any more. Not after Maggie.'

'Pretend you're related to him or something.'

'Uggh, gross.'

I laugh. 'OK maybe not.'

She looks at Maggie. 'Maggie, your dad is way too caliente.'

Maggie gurgles. Proving, once again, she's one of us.

Saturday night, I go out with Mark. Afterwards, we go back to my place because my parents are out.

'What's this?' he asks, holding up an eye pencil he's just accidentally sat on.

'Eye pencil.'

'For what?'

'Oh, just darkening around the eyes or the eyebrows.'

'The eyebrows? Aren't yours dark enough?'

Ж

'You can never get dark enough.'

'Can I try?'

'What?'

'Darkening your eyebrows.'

I shrug. 'If you want.'

'I want. OK, go lie on the bed, so I can get at you.'

I smile. And do as instructed.

He starts running the pencil over my eyebrows. I close my eyes. It's relaxing.

'Now I'm just going to extend your eyebrows.'

'What?' I laugh.

'Humour me.'

I'm too tired to do anything else.

I feel all these little strokes, firstly on my eyebrows, then coming out into my temples, then right down the sides of my face as far as my jaw. I open my eyes. He's frowning in concentration, like he's Michelangelo or something. I smile.

'Can you sit up for a sec?' he asks.

'No. Too tired.'

'Come on. I've done all this work.'

I groan and sit up.

He holds my chin and turns my face from side to side, examining his work. Then he takes a step back and cracks up. 'You're beautiful.'

I get up, look in the mirror and burst out laughing. I look like I've half a handlebar moustache over each eye.

'You should go into school like that on Monday,' he says. 'Just go in and say nothing.'

'Yeah, right.'

'No. It'd be hilarious. Just to see how long before someone actually says something.'

'About a second, Mark.'

'You're right. We shouldn't make it so obvious. Just take them right out to the side.'

'We're not doing it, Mark.'

'Come on. It'd be a laugh.'

'You do it.'

'OK!'

'I'm messing.'

'I'm not. Here, do it on me.'

'No.'

'Come on.'

I smile and pick up the eye pencil. 'Go, lie down.'

He does – with such enthusiasm you'd swear he was getting a massage.

'It tickles,' he says.

'Don't move. I'm trying to keep a straight line, here.'

When I've finished, he gets up. We go look in the mirror. And laugh. He picks me up, carries me back to the bed and drops me onto it. Then he climbs over me, so that he's kneeling a leg on either side of me. He licks his fingers and starts to rub my fake eyebrows out. I look up into his eyes. It hits me how lost I'd be without him.

On Sunday, when Sarah shows up at Alex's, Rebecca's with her. She stayed the night at Sarah's. Now she's here. And I don't know if she senses I'm pissed off about that because she looks at the others and says, 'So did you hear about the IFTA?'

'Yeah, it's amazing,' Sarah says, smiling at me.

'I *know*,' Rebecca says. 'I'm so proud of her. She is *so* good for a beginner.'

I look at Sarah and Alex. But they don't hear what I hear. They hear, 'so good'. I hear 'for a beginner'. And that is the difference between someone who's been bullied and someone who hasn't. I know I'm too sensitive. Still, I hate this. I hate that she's in my life again. And I hate myself for being jealous of her with my friends. I'm not this kind of person.

Later, Rebecca leaves with Sarah.

I know I should be rushing back to study. But I can't. 'What do you think of Rebecca?' I ask Alex.

'She *seems* very nice,' she jokes.

I smile. 'Seriously though.'

She thinks about it for a while. 'She's kind of like Sarah, isn't she? Makes sense they get on.'

I nod. 'Sarah told her about Shane.'

'Seriously?' She looks at me. 'It's good she's talking. I was worried about her.'

'So was I,' I say, surprised.

'It was like she was blocking it or something, you know?' Alex says. 'It's great she has Rebecca.'

'Yeah.' She's right of course.

'Your new pal sent me a friend request,' Jack says, appearing in my room on Sunday night.

I don't believe it. 'Did you accept it?'

'You *really* think I'm that dumb?'

'She's got the hots for you Jack,' I say, trying to make a joke of it.

'You know what I should do?' he says, 'Go out with her, then dump her. Show her what it's like to be treated like shit.'

Jack might be tempted but he'd never do it. Even to Rebecca.

'Are you still hanging out with her?'

)(

I grimace. 'It's kind of spiralling out of control.'

'If I was you, I'd unspiral it.'

I nod but I can't do that to Sarah. My tummy rumbles. Loudly.

'Jesus,' he says.

I laugh. 'Impressive, right?'

'Scary. Anyway, better go study. Roll on summer.'

He goes back to his room.

I run downstairs for a glass of water to kill the hunger pangs. I'm knocking it down when Mum comes into the kitchen.

'Have you lost weight?' she asks.

'No.'

'You're not on a diet, are you?'

'No,' I say, filling the glass again.

'Because you don't need to be.'

'I know.' I start to leave.

'Is everything OK?'

'Yeah, fine.'

'You're still enjoying *D4*?'

'Yup.'

'And everyone's treating you well?' She means Rebecca.

'Yup.'

'Nervous about the IFTA?'

'A bit,' I say so she thinks that's why I'm not eating.

'We must get you a dress.'

'It's OK. Marsha's making me one.'

'Marsha, Alex's dad's stylist?'

'Girlfriend now.'

'She made Sarah's wedding dress?'

I nod.

'That was amazing. How much does she charge?'

'Nothing.'

We have this long discussion about why we need to pay for the dress.

'It's red carpet publicity for Marsha,' I say.

'You better give me her number. They're the IFTAs, not the Oscars.'

Why, all of a sudden, is everyone driving me mad?

'Have you seen moan.ie?' Rebecca asks, next day in the dressing room.

'I don't look at it any more,' I say. 'Why?'

'No reason,' she rushes. 'You're better off.'

They've said something about me, I know.

She goes into the bathroom.

Immediately, I open my laptop.

'You could start a fire with her, she's that wooden.' It's BatmanReturns' latest comment on my acting.

'Every house should have a Rachel Dunne. It'd be like having a fire-lighter,' from someone called LittleDevil. Funny guy.

'She's more plastic than wooden.'

'Thanks, Sionara, whoever you are,' I say, aloud.

I don't hear Rebecca come back out of the bathroom until she's right beside me. 'They're completely wrong, by the way. You're a great actress.' She looks over my shoulder. 'It's just a pity it's BatmanReturns. Everyone listens to him.'

I know, I think. But say nothing.

'And everyone tries to impress him with their comments,' she says. 'It's sick.'

It's the one thing we're together on. Our hate for moan.ie.

)(

She leans forward and closes my laptop. 'Screw them,' she says. 'What's your scene today?'

'Naomi starting to get sick.'

'Could I watch?'

'Sure. If you want to.'

'Cool! I just have to go to Make-Up. Wait for me, yeah?'

I'm not due on for about half an hour. 'OK.'

Forty minutes later, I'm called on set. I text Rebecca. She doesn't answer. I hold on for another few minutes. But then the cast manager calls and tells me to 'move my ass'.

I run.

Even so, I'm holding up the scene.

'Sorry,' I say to him.

'Don't go all Lindsay Lohan on me now that you're up for an IFTA.'

Christ. He's serious.

'Sorry.'

I'm so stressed, it's hard to get into Naomi's head. But then I just use my own worry and frustration. When we're finished, I go up to the cast manager.

'Sorry, for earlier.'

He winks. 'You made up for it.'

I'm annoyed with myself for waiting for her.

When I get back to the dressing room, she's typing away on the new Apple laptop she got for Christmas.

'Where were you?' I ask.

She jumps. 'Jesus. You scared the shit out of me.' She closes the laptop.

'I held up the scene waiting for you.'

'That was dumb.'

I just look at her.

She shrugs. 'Yeah I was talking to Damien and didn't realise the time. Soz.'

Soz? That's it? I go into the bathroom to change, my mind racing. There was a time when she'd have done it on purpose, made me late. They used to trick me all the time. Tell me I'd been called to the principal's office when I hadn't. Give me the wrong homework when I'd missed class. Invite me to parties that weren't happening. Tricking me was their running joke until I began to suspect everything they did and said. But I can't think like that. I can't go back to that – reading stuff into everything a person says or does. I'll go crazy. I have to believe her. She just got carried away with Damien. It could happen. Easily.

When I've changed, I take a deep breath and go back out. My script for next week is lying on my dressing table. Rebecca is reading hers. I pick up mine and start to read. I sink into my chair. I can't believe it.

'So what's happening with Naomi?' Rebecca asks cheerfully.

'She starts to bully her sister.'

'Let's see.'

I pass it over.

'That's rough,' she says. And I don't know whether she means for the sister. Or for me.

I spend the night awake. Naomi is not a bully. She's angry and sad and wild. But not mean. They're ruining her character *and* the story. How will I act it?

First thing the next morning, I bump into Emily in the corridor. The words are out before I know it. 'Why does Naomi start bullying her sister?'

She frowns. 'Why do you ask?'

Oh God, I'm questioning the story. No one questions the

story. I try to explain. 'She's not a mean person. She's messed up. She's angry. But she's not mean.'

Still frowning, she nods. 'It's complicated. Which makes it good.' She smiles. And I almost collapse in relief. 'Firstly, Naomi's jealous of her sister, Mel. *She* gets to live. *She* gets to have a healthy relationship with their parents. Two things Naomi doesn't have. *But*. Naomi also *loves* Mel and doesn't want her to drop out like she's done herself. It's tough love, a kick in the ass, if you will. She wants to push Mel so hard that she fights back, becomes stronger, more determined, so she'll survive when Naomi's no longer there.'

Oh, my God. 'That's so good.'

'Of course, none of this will be clear at first.'

'So people will think she's just a bully?'

'It increases the drama. Don't you think?'

I nod. 'I do. I really do.'

She smiles.

'Thanks so much, Emily.'

'No,' Emily says. 'Thank *you*, for being concerned enough about the story to ask. I was in your shoes once. I know the courage that took.'

I smile. She's just so amazing.

Rebecca walks by, looking like she's dying to know what's up.

Emily taps my shoulder. 'Keep up the good work.' Then she's gone.

I'm so happy. It makes total sense now. I can do it.

'What was that about?' Rebecca asks, when we get back to the dressing room.

'I just asked Emily why Naomi has to be a bully.'

'You did *not*.'

'I did.'

)(

'Are you mad?'

'Probably.' I laugh. If I'd thought about it for one second, I'd never have done it.

'What did she say?'

I tell her.

'Wow. She's not as scary as I thought.'

FIFTEEN
Flab

It's eight-thirty on Saturday morning and Mike, Alex's dad's driver, is taking us to a drop zone. Sarah and Rebecca are skydiving. Alex and myself – and Maggie – are doing the cheerleader thing. Alex's idea.

'Did I really mean it when I said I wanted to skydive?' Sarah asks as we drive along.

'You'll be grand,' Rebecca says. 'We'll have jumping buddies.'

'Jumping buddies?' Alex ask.

'Experienced skydivers who jump attached to you.'

'Yeah. That made me feel safe when I was booking it. Now I'm not so sure,' Sarah says.

'You don't have to go,' I say.

'Yes you do,' Rebecca says.

They laugh.

'You sure you guys don't want to try it?' Rebecca asks myself and Alex.

'Yup, sure,' we say together.

When we get to the hangar, they change into orange jumpsuits covered in straps and harnesses. They frown in concentration when getting instructions from the pretty hot instructor guy. Then they all put on leather helmets and goggles. Next thing I know, they're waving us goodbye and walking towards a plane.

'Is that it?' I ask Alex. 'Don't they need, like, more

instruction or something? They're jumping out of a plane.'

'They'll be grand. The buddies will do all the work. All they have to do is scream and not wet themselves.'

Outside, there's the noise of an engine starting up. We go to the door and watch the plane take off. We stand in silence, staring as it gets higher and higher. I look at Alex.

'Should they be going above the clouds?'

'That's what I was thinking,' she says.

Then the plane is gone.

I try not to think about things like parachutes not opening.

'He doesn't fancy me,' Alex says out of nowhere. 'He doesn't even *see* me.'

I look at her. 'I thought you weren't going there, Ali.'

'I can't help it.'

'Do you want to go out with him?'

'No. Yes. I don't know. Maybe I just want him to like me back, you know?'

'That's OK,' I say.

'No, it's not. It's dumb. Because he doesn't look at me like he used to. He doesn't talk to me like he used to. He doesn't think of me like he used to. It's because I'm a mum, a boring frumpy mum.'

'Oh, my God, you're so not frumpy. You are so *good-looking*, Alex. Seriously.'

'For a mum.'

'You're better looking than you *ever* were.'

'Yeah, right.'

'Maybe you don't see it, but you have this softness about you that you never had before.'

'You mean flab.'

I laugh. 'After Yuri, there is no flab. I mean, softness –

it's in your eyes. Especially when you look at Maggie. It's like you've become this really loving person.'

'Boring person.'

'Loving.'

'Boring.'

'You talk yourself down one more time and I *will* kill you. It will be painful. And there will be blood.'

She smiles.

'Are you ready to actually go out with someone?' I ask.

She looks at me for a long time. Then shakes her head.

I put an arm around her. 'Well then.'

'I think I hear a plane.'

We look up. Nothing but cloud.

After a few minutes, a parachute comes through. 'There!' I point. It looks like a jellyfish.

'There's the other one.'

They look so peaceful and silent as they glide, swaying from side to side. Still, I bite my knuckles till the first two land on their bums. The buddy gets up, says something, then unhooks and starts to roll up the chute. Sarah or Rebecca, whoever it is, stays sitting on the grass like they're in shock. The second couple lands.

'Phew,' Alex says.

I want to run out, but we were told to stay here.

The second person gets up, takes off the helmet and shakes her hair. It's Rebecca. She walks over to Sarah and sits on the grass beside her. They laugh. They stay there for ages, talking excitedly. Finally, they get up and start walking towards us. The closer they get, the more alive they look. When Sarah sees us, she runs to us and hugs us. Tightly.

)(

'Oh, my God that was amazing. You guys have to do it.'

'Yeah,' I say.

She laughs. 'I'm serious. It's amazing.'

'I'll take your word for it.'

She turns to Rebecca. 'My legs are still shaking.'

'Me too.'

They get out of their gear, thank the buddies. The buddies give them their business cards. Walking back in the car, they're buzzing.

'I was freaking till the chute opened,' Rebecca says.

'Wasn't it amazing then though, so peaceful, when all the wind stopped.'

'Did your buddy chat to you?' Rebecca asks.

'Yeah.'

'Mine asked me out.'

'Seriously?' Sarah asks.

And just when I'm thinking, *Rebecca always has to get one better*, she says, 'He probably asks everyone out. I'd say he's a total player.'

'Hot, though,' Sarah says.

'Definitely hot.'

They've filled the parts they were auditioning for. Emily makes the introductions the following Monday. Holly. Tom. Patrick. Holly and Tom look around fifteen. Patrick is more our age. The good thing about them is they look real, the kind of people you'd meet at school. When Emily calls to the dressing room to introduce them to myself and Rebecca they remind me how I was on my first day. Nervous. In awe. Green.

'Wow. It's so great to meet you,' Holly says when Emily introduces us.

'Congratulations, by the way,' I say.

Emily turns to me. 'Rachel, Holly is going to be your kid sister.'

Oh right! When the notices went up, I never imagined what parts they were going to be for. Now Naomi has a sister. And I have to bully her.

'Sorry in advance for what I'm going to do to you,' I say.

She laughs politely.

Emily takes them off to show them around.

'No beauts,' Rebecca says as soon as they're gone.

I'm so shocked, I laugh.

One thing. It's good not being the new kid any more.

On set, I have to tell Mel, my onscreen sister, that she's dumb, thick, stupid and retarded. My voice is weak, the words unconvincing. When I say them, I feel like the victim, not the bully. There are five retakes.

'I was so *bad*,' Holly says to me afterwards.

'What makes you think it was you?'

'I'm new,' she says, like it's obvious.

'Everyone starts new. You won't believe what I did on my first day.' I tell her.

'I saw that scene. It made me want this part. I love Naomi.'

'Even now?'

She shrugs. 'I think she loves Mel underneath it all.'

'You get that?' I ask, surprised.

She shrugs again. 'It's what I feel,' she says simply.

'You're good,' I say.

)(

She bursts into a smile. 'I can't believe how nice everyone's being. Rebecca has invited me for lunch tomorrow. I can't believe it.'

And I can't help thinking Rebecca wants to control everything.

That night, on Facebook, Rebecca has posted photos – of Sarah and Alex in the Jitter Mug. They were in the Jitter Mug, today, without me? What's going on? I start to freak. What's she doing, trying to take them from me? In panic, I pick up the phone.

'Were you in the Jitter Mug today with Sarah and Rebecca?' I ask Alex.

'Yeah.'

'Without me?'

'You were working.'

'You didn't even tell me you were going.'

'I didn't know I was going. It was just supposed to be Sarah and Rebecca but when Rebecca turned up at school, they bullied me into going.'

Bullied.

'If I'd known you'd be so upset, I wouldn't have gone,' Alex says.

'I'm not upset.'

'You sound upset.'

'Yeah, well, I'm not.'

'OK.'

I talk myself down. Rebecca is Sarah's friend, Alex tagged along. They weren't excluding me. And I *was* working. But I can't help thinking that they better not go without me again, which makes me the kind of person I hate.

)(

It takes ages for me to get to sleep. When I do, I'm ten again. I've just been disinvited to a party. Rebecca and Béibhinn are turning people against me.

'You didn't invite *that* loser?' Rebecca whines.

'Oh, my God, you're not hanging out with *her*, are you?' Béibhinn says in disgust.

When I wake, the insides of my cheeks are sore. I run my tongue over them. They're all cut up. I've been biting them in my sleep. Just like I used to do. It's like I'm back, like it's started all over again. The tightness in my stomach. The uncertainty. The analysis of every little thing. The fear that my world is about to fall apart. What can I do to forget the past? What can I do to stop becoming this person I hate?

SIXTEEN
Decency

The *D4* episode where Naomi starts bullying is about to be aired. Mum and Dad head for the TV room. I make for the stairs.

'Aren't you coming?' Mum asks, surprised.

'Homework.'

'Can't it wait?'

'No.'

She smiles. 'I'll tape it for you.'

'Thanks,' I say, but I know I won't be watching it. It was hard enough acting it.

In my room, instead of my school bag, I reach for my favourite medical encyclopaedia. I've named it Carson after the butler in *Downton Abbey* because like Carson, it is solid and reliable. The logic of the body, how things go wrong and how to put them right, always calms me down. I'm reading about Ménière's Disease when there's a knock.

I look up.

Mum comes in. 'Hey,' she says. She sits on the bed. She tucks my hair behind my ear like she used to do when I was a kid.

'Rache, if this is too hard for you, I want you to say.'

'I'm fine,' I say cheerfully. I should have made myself watch it so she wouldn't worry.

'You sure? Because the storyline …'

)|(

'Is fine,' I say firmly now.

She nods slowly. 'OK.' She stands. 'I'm bringing up some tea and toast. You'd hardly any dinner.'

'Are you sure? Thanks.' Last thing I need is more calories.

'You're fading away.'

'I'm grand,' I say, hating that I'll have to eat it all.

As soon as she goes, I reach for my laptop. They're giving out about bullying on moan.ie. Maybe they don't realise that they are bullies themselves. On Twitter, *D4* and bullying are trending. Major hate for bullies. You can feel the hurt in the comments, people who've been bullied, people whose kids have (or are still being), all venting. I can't believe the power of one programme – to get all these people talking. And still, nothing's going to change, because no one is prepared to tackle individual bullies. No matter how many people tweet. Or moan. It's the victim who has to move school – never the bully.

First thing next day, I'm in the canteen in *D4*, sitting alone when Emily comes over.

'The very woman,' she says. 'Can I join you?'

'Sure,' I say, surprised.

She sits, takes her latte and croissant from the tray, then smiles at me. 'How're you doing?'

I smile back. 'Good, thanks.'

'I just wanted you to know, there's been a very strong response from the media to last night's show. This happens sometimes when we touch on a topical issue, like bullying. We've had journalists and researchers contacting us, wanting to feature bullying.'

I'm suddenly angry. This is just the latest sexy topic. They don't care. Not really. 'They're wasting their time,' I say. 'It's not going to change anything.'

She looks surprised. And I'm immediately sorry I spoke.

'You're probably right,' she says. 'But they thought that speaking to a cast member who had personal experience might make a difference.'

I say nothing.

'So I'm asking around. You don't have personal experience, do you, Rachel? Not that there would be any compulsion on you to talk.'

'No, sorry. I haven't,' I rush.

She smiles. 'That's fine. Even if you did, we wouldn't expect you to go public. Just thought I'd ask. Since they did.'

'Sorry.'

'Nothing to be sorry about. If we can't help them, we can't help them. End of story.'

Even if I thought it would make a difference, I couldn't do it, and there's something depressing about that.

I get to school in time for lunch. I sit with Alex and Sarah. It is so different when it's just us. I'm actually normal. We've hardly landed our trays down when Peter Sweetnam pulls up a seat beside me.

'Rachel, they're screwing up your character,' he says.

'Hello, Peter,' Alex says. She gives a little wave.

'Oh, hey, Alex,' he says distractedly then looks back at me. 'You used to be hard ass; now you're just mean.' He says it like his dreams have been shattered.

I shrug. 'I'm not the screenwriter, Peter.'

'I think I'll write in to complain,' he says.

'You'd *write in* to the show?' I know people do. Just not people our age.

'Yeah. They're wrecking Naomi. I mean, OK, I got the whole anger thing and the whole need for, like, intimacy and that.' I look at him with new eyes. 'I just don't get the bullying,' he continues. 'Naomi's not a mean person.'

'I know. You're right. I thought that too. But it'll all be explained.' I can't believe we're having this conversatin. Sarah and Alex are gaping. I actually want to tell him. Because it's nice when you find someone who gets your character, like he does. And who questions things like you do.

'Don't worry, Rachel. We've got your back,' he says. Then he gets up and goes.

The others look like they're trying not to laugh.

'Shut up,' I say. 'Leave him alone.'

'We've got your back,' Alex says, an eyebrow raised.

I try not to laugh. 'Stop. Seriously. It's nice that he cares.'

'Let me get this right,' Alex says. 'The way to your heart is through Naomi?'

'Yup. We're a package.'

'Like Jekyll and Hyde,' Sarah says.

'Exactly like Jekyll and Hyde.'

Going home on the DART, they're slagging me about Peter Sweetnam again, calling him my stalker. I'm telling them to shut up – obviously – when Alex whispers, 'Oh God. It's her, that woman. And when I say don't look now, I really mean don't look now.'

'The old woman who came over to me before?' I ask.

'Yup and she's coming again,' Alex says, suddenly looking at her fingernails.

I turn. It *is* the same woman. This time, though, she's

not smiling. I look out the window, hoping she'll change her mind, somehow realise that I'm just an actress, playing a role. She's standing beside me, now.

'*That* was uncalled for,' she snaps.

And I have to look at her. God.

'I don't care how awful your life is, that poor girl did not deserve that.'

I feel myself blush as the whole carriage turns to see what the fuss is.

'I'm an *actress*,' I say quietly, so only she will hear.

'No. You're a bully. And you should be shot.'

Alex covers her mouth, gets up and goes to the door. Sarah bites a bent index finger.

'There's a thing in life called decency,' she snaps. Then she's gone, leaving everyone staring, wondering what atrocity I've committed.

The thing is, I agree with her. There's a thing in life called decency. I'm just not Naomi.

Alex comes back.

'Oh, my God,' she says.

'We have to stop getting the DART,' I say.

On Friday, my Biology teacher hands back a test paper she sprang on us, Monday.

'I'm surprised,' she says to me quietly, disappointedly.

I look at the mark. My heart stops. I knew I'd done badly, but not *that* badly. I haven't failed a test – any test – since junior school. And it's Biology, my best subject. While she hands back the rest of the papers, I scan my answers. So many red crosses. A question mark at my stupidity. A comment: 'You should have put *something* in', where an experiment should have been. I fold it in two and shove it into the back of my book. But I have to take it out again because the teacher wants to go through the answers.

'Did we even *cover* that?' I ask Mark afterwards.

'She told us to read it at home.'

'You never told me.'

'I'm sure I did.'

'If you'd told me, I'd have done it.'

'It's not an important test, Rache.'

'It is to me.'

'OK, sorry,' he says, as in *jeez*.

'Sometimes you're just so dozy.'

He gives me this look like he can't believe I've said that. And I remember all the notes he's taken for me, when he never usually takes notes.

'Sorry,' I say. 'I just don't fail.'

'OK.' But then he says, 'I'll see you later,' and goes off.

At break, Sarah says she's meeting Rebecca for coffee in the Jitter Mug after school and asks us to come. It's the last thing I want to do. But I don't want Sarah to think we don't have time for her any more, so I go.

Mistake.

I feel like killing Rebecca. Every time I open my mouth to speak, she cuts across me.

'Oh, my God, I think Louis fancies you, Alex,' she says. 'He keeps looking over.'

'Does he?' Alex is suddenly on full alert. She glances at Louis. He's busy and doesn't see.

'He's actually looking at Maggie,' I say. Because he *is*. And I don't want Alex getting her hopes up.

)(

Alex looks at me like I've insulted her. Then she turns to Rebecca. 'D'you think?' It's like she values her opinion over mine.

'Yeah, *definitely*,' Rebecca gushes. The love guru. Oh, God, I need to stop.

Alex looks up at the counter again. This time she catches Louis's eye. He smiles. Innocently. She smiles back, like it means something. Does Rebecca even *know* what she's done?

After a while, Sarah starts taking photos of Maggie. Then she scrolls through them.

'Let's see,' Rebecca says, holding her hand out for the phone.

Sarah gives it to her.

'Ah, God. She's such a sweetie.' Rebecca scrolls back over photos. Then she looks up. 'Rachel, you're *so* photogenic.' And when she smiles, it's like she means 'you don't look that well in real life'.

'Thanks,' I say sarcastically.

Alex and Sarah stare at me, like they don't know what's wrong with me. I feel I'm losing them. I stand up because it's too much. 'I gotta go.'

'What, *now*?' Sarah asks.

'Yeah. I've work and that.' I grab my bag and leave before anyone sees how close to crying I am.

Outside, I stop and take a deep breath. I tell myself I'm overreacting. All she said was that I'm photogenic. But she smiled. She *smiled*. I hurry to the DART, walking so fast I must look crazy. So I make myself slow down. When I get to the station, I take out my phone and scroll through my own photos of Maggie. Her little face. I look at her and think, why can't we all stay like that? When do we change, start hating each other, hurting each other, hiding stuff from each other, being afraid of each other? We start off so perfect. Smile without expecting one back. Look into a person's eyes like they're the only person in the world. Trust that no one will harm us. Eat when we're hungry. Sleep when we're tired. Burp and fart without caring. And we do it all with such *enthusiasm*. Why does it have to change? Why does it have to get complicated?

I get the DART to Mark's.

'Hey! I was just going to see if you wanted to go for pizza,' he says, and I know he's forgotten about earlier.

I hug him. Maybe it's more of a cling.

'What's up?' he asks.

I bury my face in his chest. 'Nothing.'

He kisses the top of my head. 'You sure?'

'Yup. Let's go.'

Driving in Millie is like driving back to normality. As we come into Dalkey, the rain is really coming down. People are hurrying along, heads down. Water gushes along drains and disappears into gutters. There's a huge puddle on the road. And a woman walking on the path.

'Will I get her?' Mark asks.

'Oh, yeah,' I say. Whatever else happens, I have Mark.

He slows down and goes around the puddle.

'Wimp,' I say.

'Couldn't do it.'

He was never going to.

He pulls up outside the tiny pizzeria in Dalkey. He tells me to run in while he goes to park. He's sweet like that.

'I shall return,' he announces.

)l(

I kiss him then hurry inside. In those two seconds, I get seriously wet.

The waiters fuss over me. They fuss over all women. So it's not totally embarrassing.

When Mark finally arrives, he's soaked through. He takes off his jumper and laughs. 'Jesus.'

'Want my hoodie?' Not that it would actually fit him. With his 'buns of steel'.

'Nah I'm grand. What are you having?'

We order. It's so good to be out, just the two of us, away from everyone else, from hassle, stress. When our pizzas arrive, I eat a whole meal, for once. But the worry doesn't go away, not really. It's lying under my skin – and I can't help scratching.

'If someone told you that you were photogenic what would you think?' I ask innocently.

'They fancied me.'

I laugh. 'Seriously?'

'Why else would they say it?'

'To imply you weren't as good-looking in real life?'

'No, Rachel.' Then after three seconds, he asks, 'Why?'

'Oh, no reason.' I'm not bringing it here to infect our evening.

'Is some guy in there telling you you're photogenic?' he asks in a mafia voice.

'No, Tony, no, I swea'.'

'Cause I'd fill him fulla holes. I'm telling ya.'

I smile. Maybe it *was* that simple. A compliment. And the smile was just a smile. Maybe I'm the problem here.

On Saturday morning, I call over to Alex.

'Do you think I was a bit, like, snappy yesterday?'

)(

She smiles. 'A bit.'

'Sorry.'

'What's up?'

'Nothing. Sometimes I want it to be just the three of us, like it used to be.'

'Me too.'

'Seriously?' I'm so relieved. 'Sorry, by the way, that I said Louis was looking at Maggie. I just didn't want you getting your hopes up.'

'Yeah and I wish I'd listened to you.'

'Why, did something happen?'

She lets her head fall back till her neck is fully extended, then she says to the sky: 'Disaster.'

'What?' I ask anxiously.

'Last night, there was this moment – or what I thought was this moment. We were going to kiss. At least, I thought we were. Oh, God. I closed my eyes and moved closer. Nothing. So I opened them again and he was on the other side of the room, grabbing his stuff. I was so embarrassed. What if he doesn't come back to see Maggie now?'

'He will.'

'It was just so *awkward*, though.'

'He'll be back. He loves Maggie.'

'He must really think I'm yuck. Not able to even kiss me.'

'He doesn't think you're yuck.'

'I feel so stupid.'

'That makes two of us.'

'Why *you*?'

'Yesterday, in the Jitter Mug, I totally overreacted. When she said I was photogenic, I thought she meant that I wasn't good-looking in real life.'

She hugs me. 'You dope.'

I feel my shoulders sag in relief. 'So maybe when Sarah calls over, we'll say about just the three of us?'

'Sure.'

Half an hour later, Sarah arrives. I'm relieved she's alone. She's playing with Maggie when Alex says, 'Hey, Sarah. We were thinking, next time we go out, let's just make it the three of us.'

'*Why*?' She looks from Alex to me like there's some sort of conspiracy. 'What's wrong with Rebecca?'

'Nothing's wrong with Rebecca,' I say.

She turns on me. 'Are you *jealous* of her?'

'*What*? *No!*'

'You act like you are.'

Oh, my God. 'Thanks, Sarah. So, basically, you're saying I'm immature?'

'No. I'm saying you're jealous. You know, Rebecca *said* she got a jealous vibe from you. I told her you weren't like that – but maybe you are.'

'OK, then, you believe Rebecca. You know, why don't the three of you just go out together. Then no one will be jealous.'

'Now you're definitely sounding jealous,' Sarah says.

'Oh, fuck off, Sarah.'

Alex's eyes widen.

Sarah's just lost Shane and I've told her to fuck off. What am I doing? She's one of my closest friends, one of the most important people in my world. 'Sorry,' I whisper before I literally run. What's wrong with me? I'm losing my friends all by myself.

SEVENTEEN
Trespassing

Neither of them calls me for the entire weekend. So it's official. I'm a jealous cow. Or maybe just Sarah thinks I'm jealous and Alex is pissed off with me for attacking Sarah. Or maybe they both think I'm jealous and are pissed off with me for attacking Sarah. *Fine, let them. And let them go off with her,* I think, but don't really mean it. I'm stressed and moody and feel like screaming. 'Jealous vibe' my ass.

On Monday, I'm in *D4* first thing. Cramming Biology. It's not the only thing I need to cram. I'm missing a whole day, today.

Rebecca swans in, carrying breakfast. 'Rachel, you work too hard.'

I ignore her.

At her dressing table, she opens the tinfoil on her breakfast. The most amazing smell fills the room. I look over. It's just a bagel. But I'm so freaking hungry.

'You're putting yourself under way too much pressure,' she says, then sinks her teeth into the bagel. 'Sarah was saying how narky you've got.'

I stare at her. 'Shut up, Rebecca.'

'Oh, I see what she means.'

I could kill her. I could actually break her neck. There's no way I can study now, with murder on my mind and nothing in my belly. I get up, grab my bag and go to the canteen, where I have a full Irish breakfast. Screw her. And the diet.

When I get back, she's gone. I still can't study. I take out Carson to calm myself down. I open it randomly, the way I always do. It lands on the thyroid gland. I run my fingers under the words to help me focus. The thyroid gland controls metabolism. An overactive gland results in hyperactivity, sweating and weight loss. *Weight loss*, I think. I read on, interested now. If I could speed up my metabolism I'd burn more calories without having to starve myself. Carson says nothing about this. I need Google. I've only a few minutes before Make-Up, not enough time to turn on my own laptop. Rebecca's is on, just closed over. She owes me.

I go over and open it. I click on Safari. It opens into moan.ie which she mustn't have closed. Good to know she's still as obsessed as I am. This is weird. She's in the middle of posting something – under the name BatmanReturns. Oh. My. God.

I sit staring at the screen, as the truth sinks in. She *is* BatmanReturns. She's the one who's been dissing me all this time. In public. Ever since the IFTA nomination. I think of all the things she's said. About my ass. About me being wooden. About *her* being a great actress. With great legs. I have to stop myself firing the computer at the mirror. I want to rip her skin from her bones. Pull her hair out from its roots. But I'm called to Make-Up. Then Wardrobe. Then on set – where I've no problem working up some serious anger for Naomi. I've no problem being an onscreen bully. And I've no problem getting back to the dressing room fast. To let her have it.

She's removing her make-up when I walk in. 'Hey,' she says, all friendly, like I'm an idiot. 'How did it go?'

)(

'Well, my *ass* looked fat. And I was so *wooden* you could set fire to me.' I glare every word home.

Her whole expression changes, twice. First, she freezes. Then, recovers. 'What are you talking about?'

'Don't act dumb. I was on your computer.'

'Oh, my God. That's trespassing,' she says, trying to turn it.

'No, it's borrowing. And what you've been doing is libel,' I say, glad we had that Law Day in Transition Year.

'Jesus. Relax,' she says, like I'm a mental patient. 'It was just a *joke*.'

'You think *Emily* would see it as a joke?'

I see her tense. She tries to hide it. Slowly, she puts down the lip gloss. 'Don't,' she says. 'I was just messing.'

'Like all those times you wre "messing" in junior school?'

'Look, I'm sorry. I don't know why I did it. I thought that maybe your part would get bigger and mine would end. You do all this study. I've dropped out of school. I don't have a fallback.'

'And I should feel sorry for you, is that it? For all I know, you're making it up.'

'I'm sorry. I really am sorry.' She looks like she's going to cry.

'Yeah, well, you will be.'

'Where you going?'

'Where do you think? It's not just me you've been dissing. It's Maisie. Even poor Holly. Emily needs to know.'

'Please, Rachel.'

Please, my ass. She's a two-faced cow. I don't believe anything she says. I can't. So I go. Run upstairs. But the office is locked. I check my phone. Damn. It's ten-past-one.

)(

They've gone to lunch. Fine. I'll wait. I sit on the ground outside the office. I can't believe it. I still can't believe she would do that. To all of us.

A throat clears. I turn.

It's Rebecca. And she's smiling as she walks the empty corridor towards me. 'Oh, isn't she there?' she asks, as if it's a shame.

Something's changed.

I stand so we're at eye level. 'I've no problem waiting.'

'Wait all you like. You're wasting your time. I've deleted the account.' She smiles. 'So you've no evidence to back up your *story*.'

Why did I say anything? I should have just come here and told Emily.

'You know, you're going to have to be a lot cleverer if you're going to take me on, *Rache*. You think you're so great. You haven't changed. Once a loser, always a loser. Even your so-called friends like me more than they like you.'

'Oh, get a life, Rebecca.'

'I have one. It's yours.' She smiles.

Everything stops. I wasn't imagining it. She's been love-bombing Sarah and Alex to turn them against me, zoning in on Sarah, the most vulnerable – doing anything she wanted and pretending to be into it, pretending to be so caring when all she was doing was using her to get at me. There was always something in it for Rebecca – to take from me the one thing I have now that I didn't have then. My friends. I stare at the smug face that has ruined my life once already. And I hit her. I actually hit her. Finally after all these years. The sound is surprisingly loud and my hand stings. Satisfyingly.

She holds her cheek. 'You will be sorry you did that,' she says slowly.

'Oh, I don't think so,' I say and turn.

'Just wait,' she says through gritted teeth.

I march down the corridor wanting to punch something, anything. Jack was wrong. She has changed. She's got worse. I can't keep still. I have to get out and walk. I march around the grounds. I march down Nutley lane, remembering all the times I talked myself out of suspecting her. She made me late on purpose that time, after I got the nomination. She did mean I wasn't good-looking in real life. Just like she meant I was fat when she said I shouldn't put on more weight.

Suddenly, I see everything the way it really was. She introduced me to everyone to remind me I was new. The one time she actually did help – the time I got the dates mixed up – she was trying to gain my trust. Or maybe she tampered with my schedule, changed the dates. All she'd have needed was a scissors, some glue and a photocopier. She's done worse.

There has to be a way of getting her back. I try to think, to plot, like she plots, the evil cow, but I don't have that type of brain. I just can't think like that.

In the afternoon I'm on set and, once again, have no problem working up some anger. When I get back to the dressing room at four, there's a note asking me to Emily's office. Rebecca smiles as she sees me reading it. My stomach knots. What has she done?

My heart is pounding as I knock on Emily's door. Her 'come in' sounds cold.

Slowly, I push in the door.

She's not alone. The taste of fear is metal.

'Rachel, this is Maeve Dwyer from Human Resources.'

)I(

I swallow. I don't even know what Human Resources is, but it sounds serious. Maeve Dwyer nods curtly. No hand is offered. This is not a friendly meeting.

'Sit,' Emily says.

I do. In silence.

'We've had a complaint from Rebecca French. Have you any idea what it might be about?'

'No.' *What, did, she, say*?

'Rebecca was up here with me, earlier, crying. She said you assaulted her and that you've been bullying her. Is this true?'

It takes a second to recover, a few more to know what to say. I go with the truth. Don't know what else to do. 'I'm not bullying Rebecca. It's the other way around.'

'Rachel,' Emily says. '*If* you were being bullied, why didn't you come to me? I've always told you I'm here if you've a problem. It's something I've emphasised, isn't it?'

I nod. Feeling sick. 'I didn't want to bother you with it, make it your problem. You're running a whole show.'

'If there's bullying on my set, it's my problem.' She folds her arms. 'In what way were you being bullied?' she asks, like she doesn't believe me. Then it hits me – I've already told her I'd no experience of bullying. She must be thinking of that now.

I take a deep breath. Where do I start? What is classed as actual bullying? And turning my friends against me has nothing to do with *D4*.

'She's been posting up stuff about me on moan.ie under a false name.'

'What name?'

'BatmanReturns.'

Emily stares. 'Let me get this straight. You're accusing

Rebecca of being behind BatmanReturns,' she says, as if to stress how serious this is.

'Yes.' I look her in the eye so she knows I'm telling the truth.

'I'm sorry,' Maeve says. '*Who* is BatmanReturns?'

What is she doing here? She's freaking useless.

Emily explains about moan.ie. And tells her that BatmanReturns is one of the most influential people on it.

'What proof do you have of this?' Maeve asks.

I take a deep breath. Let it out slowly. 'None. She's just deleted the account.'

'How inconvenient,' she says sarcastically.

I look at Emily because that's who I'm talking to from now on. 'I caught her posting something this morning as BatmanReturns. I told her I was going to you. I came up to but you'd left for lunch. I waited but then Rebecca came up to tell me she'd deleted the account. And now, only hours later, she goes to you saying *I'm* bullying *her*.'

'Did you assault her?' Maeve asks coldly.

Assault. It sounds so serious. Like a crime. 'I slapped her face. Not just because of what she did to me but also what she did to Maisie and Holly.'

Emily runs her hand through her hair.

'So you admit to assaulting her?' Maeve says.

'I slapped her, once, on the cheek.'

She takes notes. Then finally looks up. 'So, when you say you caught her posting something, what exactly do you mean?'

I glance at her then explain to Emily. 'I went on her computer to look something up. She'd closed it in the middle of a post.'

'You went on her *computer*?' Maeve asks, like she's horrified.

Emily is holding her hair in her hands in two clumps now. Finally, she lets them go.

'Anything else we should know?' she asks.

Desperately, I try to think of something to convince her. 'It started when I was nominated for the IFTA. She wants me off the show.'

'Is that everything?' Maeve asks coldly.

I look at Emily. 'There's other stuff but I'm not sure it's important.'

'What stuff?'

'She got in with my friends and turned them against me. We were in junior school together and she bullied me then.'

'Funny,' Maeve says. 'She said the same thing about you.'

'What? Oh, my God. She really *is* evil,' I say before I can help it.

'All right,' Emily says. 'Enough. Some very serious allegations have been made here today, none of which can be ignored. There will have to be an investigation.'

'I'm sorry.'

'For what?' Maeve asks, like I've admitted to something.

I look at Emily. 'The hassle. This is why I didn't say anything.'

'You let me deal with the hassle,' Emily says. 'In the meantime, you'll have to change dressing rooms. And I'll have to change your schedule. You'll be working flat out for the rest of this week. Because, next week, I don't want you in.'

My heart stops. 'Am I being suspended?' I ask slowly.

'No, but we're asking both of you to take a week out while the investigation goes ahead. OK, that's it.'

)|(

I stand up, every bit of me shaking. They believe Rebecca. And they're not going to change their minds. She's been here longest. She's one of the most popular members of the cast. She even produced tears. The bully played the victim perfectly. She deserves an IFTA.

Rebecca's on the phone when I get back to the room. I ignore her and just get my bag.

'Yeah, she's here,' she says looking at me. 'Yeah, I know. I'll see you in a minute.' She hangs up. Grabs her bag. Then she smiles at me. 'My best performance yet, I think.'

'Fuck off, Rebecca.'

'Happily.' She goes.

I'm surprised she didn't rub it in a bit more.

I wasn't going to change out of my costume, but now that she's gone, I do. Ten minutes later, I walk outside.

Rebecca is standing in the porch with Béibhinn Keane. It's like they've been waiting for me. So that's who she was talking to on the phone.

'Well if it isn't "The Nerd",' Béibhinn says. They look at each other and smile, and I'm right back there. I am ten years old. And I've lost my shell.

A car skids to a halt at the kerb metres away. We turn. It's Millie! Suddenly I remember who I am – and it's not who I was. Mark gets out of the car and towers over it.

'Yo, Dunne. Taxi's here.'

I smile. 'Well, guys, I'd love to stay and chat, but my very hot boyfriend is here. I guess you guys have each other.'

They just smile like they know something I don't.

'Can't wait till tomorrow,' Béibhinn says to Rebecca.

And I can't help worrying. *What's tomorrow?*

'Who was that, talking to Rebecca?' Mark asks, as we pull away.

'Some friend of hers.'

'Were they giving you a hard time?'

I can't believe he got that.

'Don't worry, I can handle Rebecca,' I say, because I've learned one thing: you tell people, they worry and that just adds to your worry, when they can't help anyway – and talking about it only makes you a bigger victim. The only person who can fight this is me. And I will. Somehow.

'Are you still hanging out with her?'

'No.'

'Good. I didn't like the way they were looking at you, Rache.' He looks concerned.

'They don't bother me.'

'I'd stay away from Rebecca.'

'I plan to.'

'Maybe change dressing rooms.'

I feel like laughing. 'Yeah. Anyway, forget about that. Let's get *sweeties*.'

'Here, give us a kiss,' he says while still driving.

I reach over. He turns his head. And I get a lovely kiss that has no pity in it. And I'm glad I haven't moaned to him.

We go for pizza and I try to put the worry on hold.

When Mark drops me home, I go to my room and try to do some homework. But I can't. This is too huge. What if they kick me off the show? And what if that goes public? I'll never get another acting job. I'll always be the bully. While the real bully gets off. I walk in circles around my room. When really I want to be out, running, moving, not staying still. There's nothing I can do. Except wait. Try to stay calm. Go back into *D4* and do my scenes. Go in there, not knowing who knows, who doesn't. Go in there and try not to kill Rebecca. I've no other choice. If I don't go back, she'll win. What *did* they mean about tomorrow?

EIGHTEEN
Make-Up

I'm standing in the doorway of Maisie's dressing room, clutching my bag to my chest. The place is a chaos of colour – shawls, throws, furniture, cushions, clothes and candles. There's just so much stuff. She's trying to tidy it away, when she realises I'm there. She throws the cushion she's been picking up from the floor behind her shoulder. It lands, perfectly on the bright pink chaise longue.

'Here you are!' she says, like she's delighted. 'Company at last. And someone *young* for a change. You wouldn't believe the amount of moaning you get from your average wrinkly.'

I wonder how much Emily has told her.

'Come in, come in. I won't bite.'

I close the door. And stand just inside.

'Sorry,' I say. I feel like crying.

'No. I'm sorry. The state of the place. Here, let me get that boa.' She sweeps it off what must be my dressing table. It could be a boa constrictor for all I care.

I sit at the dressing table she's been clearing and put my bag out of the way.

'Maisie, you don't have to move your things. I like it the way it is.'

'You do?' She looks so relieved and immediately stops

tidying. Instead, she lights an incense stick. 'Technically this is against the rules,' she says, shaking the match to put it out.

I take out my books. I open one, doesn't matter which. I put both hands on either side of my face and lean on my elbows, like I'm concentrating. I'm thinking of Emily, how I let her down. She believed in me. Put me up for the IFTA. Now, to her, I'm a bully and a liar.

'Put that away,' Maisie says.

I look up. 'Sorry?'

'Study! What a waste of time.' She waves a dismissive hand. 'We're playing Scrabble,' she says, like it's non-negotiable. 'Come on. Let your hair down. Have a bit of fun.' She roots around, checking under various coloured heaps. 'Here we are,' she says, finally, pulling a tattered box of Scrabble from under a cushion.

'I forget how to play Scrabble,' I lie.

'Then it's time you remembered.' She shifts stuff from a low coffee table, then throws two giant cushions onto the floor. 'Come on. Sit down.'

The only reason I do, is that she's making such an effort – for me, the supposed bully. I sit on a bright orange cushion. She tosses a tiny, grey bag at me.

'Pick seven letters.'

I start to take them from the bag.

'No! Don't look!' she says.

'Sorry. I forgot.'

'OK, pop them in their little holder. *But don't let me see. I will take advantage of you.*'

I believe her. I place my seven letters in their holder.

'I'll go first,' Maisie says.

I don't stop her.

)(

She places down five letters – that spell 'whore'.

I stare at her. And laugh.

'I knew she was trouble,' she says.

So she knows.

'Your turn,' she says.

The best I can come up with is 'poo'. Which you might say is expressing myself.

'Good one,' she says.

I look to see if she's joking. She's smiling.

She moves again.

I go next.

We're playing for a while when I get suddenly brave and challenge her. 'Is "looper" actually a word?'

'In this room it is,' she says, raising her eyebrows.

I love the way she plays. Like a total messer. And just as I'm beginning to enjoy myself, the cast manager calls her on set. She continues to play, though.

'Eh, Maisie. Don't you need to go?'

'He knows to give me fifteen minutes.'

I watch the clock for her.

'No need. He'll call again.'

He does. At last, she gets up. She stretches like Maggie. Like she's really into it.

'Thanks for the game,' I say, reaching for the box.

'Hey! We're not finished.'

I look at her.

'Just leave it there. We'll get back to it.'

I think of old men dressed in black, playing chess in France.

'No cheating,' she warns and is gone.

I sit looking at the words. They're like messages. Poo, at what happened. Whore, Rebecca. Looper, anyone who believes the whore. I smile and go back to the dressing table, lay my head on my hands and close my eyes.

In Make-Up, Damien's acting weird. He's totally quiet and won't look me in the eye. It's like I've done something wrong. Who told him? Rebecca? Maybe she's going around telling everyone to influence the investigation. Knowing Rebecca, I'd be surprised if she wasn't.

'There you go,' he says at the end. I look at his face in the mirror but his eyes are still avoiding mine.

Back in Maisie's dressing room, I try to blot everything out and just do my homework. For French, I have to write a letter to an imaginary pen pal inviting her to come and stay. On my laptop, I flick between the letter and Google Translate. Before I can finish, I'm called on set.

On the minibus, I sit beside Josh. He gives me this look.

'What?' I ask because at least he'll tell me. Or maybe he won't.

'What do you think?'

'I don't know. That's why I asked.' Jesus.

'So you haven't seen the paper?'

'What paper?'

'Today's. There's an interview with the girl you bullied.'

'*What*?'

He shrugs.

'What girl? What's her name?'

'Béibhinn something. She said you bullied her in junior school.'

They've gone professional.

'Then there's Rebecca.'

I shake my head like I can't believe it. But, of course, I can.

'Are you saying it's not true?' he asks.

'Look, believe Rebecca if you want. I don't care.'
Because I can't stop her. She can say whatever she wants
to whoever she wants (except Maisie) and she'll be
believed. She is adored in this place. She has worked hard
enough to make it that way. And now her friends in the
media have made everything official.

'Have you got a copy of the article?' I ask.

'No, but Rebecca has.'

'I bet she does.'

After my scene, I go back to Maisie's dressing room.
Someone has left the newspaper on my dressing table. So
I torture myself.

'I was bullied by Rachel Dunne,' is the opening line,
a quotation from Béibhinn Keane. The article outlines,
in detail, everything she, Rebecca and their evil bitch
friends did to me. But, of course, it says I did it all to her.
My heart is thumping. My breaths are coming short and
fast. Why didn't they check their facts? Didn't they *want*
to get it right?

The phone rings. It's Emily's assistant, calling me up.
Slowly, I hang up.

Upstairs, the newspaper is open on the desk in front
of her.

'Is it true?' she asks.

'No. She's Rebecca's friend, the ringleader of the group
that bullied me. I can't believe the paper never called the
school. The principal would have told them the truth.'

'Rachel, I want to advise you. We're getting a lot of
press queries, looking for your contact details. Don't
worry, we'd never give out that kind of information.

)|(

They know that. They're just chancing their arm. I just want you to be prepared. In case they turn up. Outside the studio. Or at your school.'

'Oh, God.'

'Don't worry. It's not ground-breaking news. I just want you to know what to do if someone does confront you.' I'm very still. 'Say nothing. Don't even say, "No comment." Just go about your business.'

'Emily. I know I told you I was never bullied. I just couldn't talk about it. Not publicly. If you contact the school …'

'We're onto it, Rachel.'

'I'm so sorry to bring all this on you and *D4*.' I try not to cry.

'Rachel, as far as *D4* goes, no publicity is bad publicity.'

'I might go now if that's OK,' I say, starting to well up. I hurry away without waiting for an answer.

I can't face school. I go outside, ready to duck back in if there's press, but there's no one. Just my mum, waiting in the car. Seeing her, I start to cry. Because it's back. And there's nothing I can do to stop it.

In the car, she smiles that smile that says she hates where I am but doesn't know how to stop it.

'Come here,' she says gently and pulls me into a hug. I try to stop crying but can't.

Finally, I pull back. 'I'm fine.'

She rummages in her bag for a tissue and hands it to me.

I blow my nose.

'I want you to stop *D4*,' she says. 'It's too much.'

'*No!* Then she'll have won.'

)(

'Is that what she's doing?' she asks. She's talking about Béibhinn. I can't tell her about Rebecca.

'I think so.'

'Then, let me talk to Emily.'

'No.' If she talks to Emily, she finds out about Rebecca. In her face, I see it all – the doubt, the worry, the fear that I won't be able to cope, just like I wasn't able to last time. And I do feel like giving in, just going home, climbing into bed and staying there. But I have to fight. Not just for me, but for my parents. They can't know how bad it is.

'OK, then let me talk to the newspaper.'

'No! Emily said not to talk to the press. It'll just keep the story going.'

'They need to know the facts.'

'They don't *want* them. Don't you see?'

'They can't print untruths and get away with it.'

'I don't want people to know the truth. I don't want people knowing I was bullied.'

'It's better than them thinking you *are* a bully.'

'No, Mum. It's not.' Because being the victim means you're weak. And being weak is the worst thing you can be.

Later, Mark calls over. His hug is strong and his eyes soft. Without a word, we go upstairs. We sit on the bed. My whole body is tense, like it was back then. My teeth are clenched so tightly, it feels like my jaw could break.

'I know you didn't do it,' he says. 'I know you couldn't.'

It is such a relief when someone has faith in you. 'Thanks.'

'Who is she anyway?'

'That girl you saw talking to Rebecca. Her friend.'

)Ӄ(

'They're bullying you, aren't they?'

'D'you know the really funny thing? In *D4*, Rebecca's accused *me* of bullying *her*.'

'Jesus.' He looks at me like he can't believe it. 'That's *evil*.' He hugs me tightly. Finally, he says, 'Let's kill her.'

I pull back immediately. 'Why do you have to make a joke of everything?'

'Sorry,' he says. His face.

'No. I am.' I hug him.

'What are we going to do?' he says, moving my hair out of my face.

'Nothing. There's an investigation.'

'Who can back you up?'

'Let's not talk about this now, OK?' It's just stressing me out and there's nothing he can do.

'The paper ...'

'Mark. Seriously.'

'I want to help.'

'So distract me.'

'I tried that, remember?'

I smile. 'OK, so let's just hug. Till I hatch an evil plan.'

About an hour after Mark leaves, I go downstairs to get a glass of water. I stop just outside the kitchen.

'We have to get her off that show,' Dad's saying urgently.

'No. It's her dream,' Mum says. 'She can handle it.'

'Like she handled it the last time?' he snaps.

'She doesn't want us to get involved.'

I want to run and hug her and thank her for backing me up even though she doesn't want to.

)(

'We didn't do enough last time. And look what happened.' And that is directed right at her.

She lowers her head.

Don't cry, I think. *Don't cry.*

But he doesn't stop.

'We need to do something,' he says. 'It's not just about Rachel. It's about Jack. How many fights is he going to get into, standing up for her?'

What?

'I've told him to stop,' Mum says, desperately.

'Has he?'

Silence.

I walk in. Dad sees me first. He looks shocked, embarrassed. Mum turns. She has been crying.

'It's OK,' I say. 'You don't have to do anything. I'm quitting the show.'

Mum stands. 'You don't have to.'

'It's not as if it's Hollywood.'

'We're just worried about you,' Dad says.

'So you can stop now, OK? I'll hand in my notice tomorrow.'

They look so relieved. Especially Mum.

I turn to go.

'Rachel?' she calls, like she wants to ask if I'm sure.

'I'm going to talk to Jack,' I say without turning back.

I go straight to his room. Earphones in, he's attacking his punch bag. I have to walk right up to him for him to notice I'm there. He stops punching, gloves in the air. Then he gestures to his ears with them. I reach over and take out his earphones.

'I don't need you to stand up for me, Jack.'

'Who said I was?'

'Mum and Dad.'

'Well they're wrong. It had nothing to do with you.'
He goes back to pummelling the punch bag.

'Good because I don't need your help. OK?'

'I can see that, yeah,' he says sarcastically.

'What's that supposed to mean?'

'Nothing.'

'If you keep fighting my battles, they'll have split us
up for nothing.'

He stops punching. His whole face changes. Softens.

'I'm quitting the show.'

'*Why*?'

I shrug like it's no big deal. 'Too much hassle.'

'But it's your dream.'

'*Was* my dream.'

'So you're going to let her win?'

'Didn't you know? Bullies always win.' I smile.

'They don't have to, Rache.'

'Mum and Dad are fighting again.'

'I'll talk to them.'

'And say what?'

'I don't know. Tell them to have faith in you.'

'Like you have?'

'I don't let people diss my sister and get away with it.'

I smile. 'Yeah, well, that'll all stop when I quit.' I punch
him lightly on the arm and wink. 'See you later, Rambo.'

'Rache—'

'I've made up my mind, Jack.' That's all I have to say.
He knows.

And so, Rebecca wins.

NINETEEN
Trespassing

The next day, people in school blank me. Like I'm the only bully in the world – which reminds me, I'm not one.

'Did you really bully someone in junior school?' Sarah asks in the canteen at first break.

I give her a look. 'Thanks, Sarah. For the faith.'

'Rebecca said she knew you in junior school and that you bullied her too.'

'Right, well, you believe Rebecca.' I get up, take my tray and go sit on my own.

Alex comes over. 'Are you OK?'

'No.'

'Do you want to talk?'

'No.'

'I believe you, by the way.'

'Thanks,' I say. 'I'm only your friend for five years.'

'Ouch.'

'Sorry.' I take a deep breath. 'OK. Look, I *was* in school with Rebecca. But *she* bullied me. And she's been doing the same in D4. She love bombed Sarah to get in with you guys so she could turn you against me. And it's worked.' *Crap, I'm going to cry. Right here in the middle of the canteen.*

'No, it hasn't.' She looks into my eyes to send the message home.

'I have to go,' I say.

'Right. Let's go. I'll talk to Sarah later.'

)(

'Don't bother.'

'Are you kidding? She'll kill herself.'

We grab our coats and go outside.

'Why didn't you tell us?' Alex asks. 'Do you really think we'd have hung out with her if we'd known what she'd done?'

'In the beginning, I thought she'd changed – the way she was with Sarah. When I discovered she hadn't, it was too late. She had you.'

'She never had me.'

I smile.

'I never liked her.'

'Really?'

'Too good to be true.'

'Wish you'd said.'

She shrugs. 'I thought she was helping Sarah. And you were working with her.'

I get to *D4* half an hour early. I go up to Emily's office.

'Hi, can I talk to Emily for a second?' I ask her PA.

'Let me check.' He buzzes her. Tells her I'm here, then hangs up and says I can go in.

'Rachel,' she says, standing up.

'I just want to hand in my notice or resign or whatever.'

Her face softens. 'Come in, Rachel. Have a seat.'

I don't really want to. But I do it. I sit looking at her, remembering all the times I've been up here, good and bad. I can't believe I'm walking away. I start to well up.

'What's up?' she asks gently.

'Sorry,' I say as the tears spill over.

She reaches for a box of tissues and holds it out to me. I take one and blow my nose.

'Take your time,' she says.

'I need to resign.'

'Why?'

'I love the show but it's hurting my family.'

She looks concerned. 'How?'

'I don't really want to talk about it.'

'Rachel, that's OK. But you've signed a contract. You can't just resign. We must see Naomi's story through.'

'But I *have* to.'

'Why?'

'Last time I was bullied, my parents almost split up. They've started arguing again. This is their marriage we're talking about.' And I'm crying again.

She hands me another tissue. And waits for me to stop.

'OK,' she says. 'Here's what we do. You take your week off. I'll call your mum and have a chat.'

'You can't tell her about Rebecca!'

'I thought you said they were worried about you being bullied.' She looks suspicious.

'They know about Béibhinn – only because it was in the paper. I didn't tell them about Rebecca because of what happened last time.'

'Would you prefer it if I didn't call them?'

'Yes.'

'How can we stop them worrying about you?' she asks.

'I can't think of any other way outside of quitting.'

'Who's you agent? Charley Bloomfield?'

I nod.

'Let me have a word with Charley.'

Today is the sex scene. I don't care. In Wardrobe, Rita is freaking out.

'That dress is meant to *cling*. You've lost weight.' She whips out a measuring tape. Quickly measures me up. 'Jesus. You've gone down a whole size. I *thought* the uniform was beginning to hang. I'm going to have to alter this. Now. Before your scene ... You should have told me you were dieting ... Don't move.'

OK, so she's seen the paper. She quickly runs pins up the side of the dress then tells me to take it off. She hands me a robe. I start to put it on.

'Wait. I need to see the underwear.'

I have to not only stand, but turn around while she looks me over.

'*Luckily*, I bought two sizes,' she snaps. She gives me back the robe.

I totter back to the dressing room in the robe, underwear and five-inch boots to try on the smaller size. I hurry into it. Go back to Wardrobe where I'm told 'it will do'. The dress will also 'do'.

I hurry to Make-Up, where Damien makes me up in total silence. Apart from one comment.

'You *do* know, I was bullied ferociously all through secondary school by a bunch of homophobes.'

'So you know how I feel,' I say.

He looks confused.

'Doesn't matter. You wouldn't believe me if I told you.'

I'm standing around in my, now, clingy dress and boots. Josh is beside me. I wish they'd just get it over with.

'You OK?' he asks quietly.

'Yeah, you?'

'No.'

We laugh. A break in the ice.

He winks. 'We'll be grand.'

I wonder if he's just being nice because we've got to do this scene together. Not that I care.

Oh, God. Here comes Emily. If this is about the investigation, now is *not* a good time.

'Just here to offer some moral support,' she says to me.

She's holding a robe. To help cover me up afterwards. And I can't believe I forgot to bring mine.

'Guys, can we get a move on?' Emily calls.

I take a deep breath.

The scene starts with us bursting into a (fake) bedroom, kissing. He kicks the door shut. We kiss and undress our way to the bed. It's a relief to get under the quilt. From now on it's upper body shots and the bra stays on. There's only one problem. The weight of Josh's whole body is on mine, pressing air from my lungs. His hands are moving over me. In between kisses, his breathing is heavy. It's so real. Too real. Oh, God. I feel him, hard, through his boxers. And start to freak. I tell myself to calm down. I can do this. Eyes closed, I pretend I'm with Mark. He pulls himself up onto his arms. Air shoots into my lungs. Relief. But then he starts to move over me. I remind myself of all the sex scenes I've ever seen. I pretend I'm in pain. I moan. I tilt my head back, let my mouth fall open. He speeds up. Then he groans. *Let this be over. Please God, let this be over.*

'And cut!'

He jerks off me like I'm on fire. Someone hands him a robe and he's gone.

Then Emily's beside me, handing me mine. I hurry into it, wrap it round me. I pull the chord tight. Make sure I'm completely covered before I emerge from the bed.

'Well done,' she says.

We look at the floor manager, who's talking to the director on his walkie-talkie.

'OK,' he says, at last. Then looks at me. 'We've got it. Thanks, Rachel.'

'I gotta go,' I say to Emily as I take off.

Maisie's dressing room is empty. I close the door and lean against it. I run my eyes over everything in the room, concentrate on every little thing. So I don't remember. I pull up the hood on the robe and sink to the floor, my back against the door, my arms around my knees. I knew it would be bad. Just not that bad. I'm shaking.

After about ten minutes, there's a knock on the door. *Go away. Whoever you are. Just get lost.*

For a moment, there's silence. Then another knock.

I'm afraid they'll open the door so I get up quietly. I'm sneaking towards the bathroom when the door opens. It's the last person I want to see.

'Just wanted to check you were OK,' Josh says. He's standing at the door, grimacing. At least he's dressed.

'I'm fine.'

'Can I come in?'

I make a face. 'I'm kinda tired.'

'Look, I just wanted to say sorry,' he says, still at the door.

'You didn't write the scene.'

'Can I come in? I don't really want to explain from here.'

'Explain what?'

'Can I come in? Please?' He puts on the nicest face.

I fold my arms defensively. 'OK.'

'Thanks.' He looks relieved. He comes in, closes the door but stays by it. Luckily. 'I just wanted to say sorry.

It wasn't, you know, *personal*?' He gives me this look, like he's trying to tell me something. I realise, in horror, he's talking about the hard-on. I want to die. He looks like he does too. 'I was just getting into it,' he says. 'You know, *in my head*. I was thinking of someone else.'

'Yeah, I know,' I rush. Dying of embarrassment.

'I just thought if I got into it, we might get it done in one take, you know?'

'You don't need to explain. You *really* don't need to explain.'

He smiles. 'So, we're OK?'

I nod. 'We're OK.'

He lets out a long breath. 'Sometimes I wonder why we're even doing this. It's not exactly saving lives, is it?'

Finally, I smile. 'I know.'

I get a taxi straight to Mark's.

'What's up?' he asks, knowing straight away that something's wrong.

'I just wanted to see you.' Any minute I'm going to burst into tears.

'Come on up to my little love nest.' He puts an arm around me and walks me to his room.

I burrow my face into his chest and breathe him in. He smells safe, warm, cosy, familiar. He lays his chin on my head and pulls me close. I feel his chest rising and falling, rising and falling. His hand rubs my back over and over.

'Hey,' he says gently when I start to sob. He pulls back and looks at me. 'What is it?'

'Today was that scene.'

His face clouds over. 'What happened? Did he go too far? Tell me, Rache.'

)¦(

'No. He was fine. It was just … the whole thing. I've never had sex, Mark. And it was kind of like I was. '

'I wish I'd never let you do it.'

'I'd have done it anyway.'

'At least pretend I've *some* influence over you,' he jokes.

I turn my face up to his. 'Kiss me.' Because I need to be kissing the person I love. Not some guy with a hard on the size of a— *Oh, God, I have to stop thinking.* 'Kiss me, Mark.'

He does. With those lips that I know. And love. I kiss him back, so passionately. I push him backwards towards the bed until he stumbles onto it. He laughs. I stop him with another kiss. I hold his face between my hands and gaze into his eyes like I want to imprint them on the back of my brain, tattoo them there forever. He smiles. And I think how lucky I am to have him. How he's always around to cheer me up. Make me laugh. Be Mark.

'I want to do it, Mark,' I say, looking into those eyes. 'I have to.'

He carries on kissing me and stroking me, like he couldn't stop if he wanted to. But then he does stop.

'Are you sure?' he whispers.

I nod slowly, holding his eyes with mine.

'Let's just see what happens,' he says.

'No. Let's do it.'

I pull him to me. And finally, finally, finally, we let ourselves go. We stop stopping. And just let it happen. Like nature. But in the end, it's still a shock. I feel at the same time powerful and vulnerable, happy and sad. I laugh and cry. And I shake. He pulls me close and holds me tight. Finally, he pulls back and looks into my eyes with so much emotion that I forget myself.

'I love you,' I say.

He smiles widely and kisses my forehead. He pulls me close again, so close. But he never says he loves me. I lie very still. And wait. I've wanted this for a very long time. Right now though, right this minute, I need it. But it never comes. Panic builds in my chest. Was I wrong, all this time? Doesn't he feel it too, this overwhelming love that I would kill for? If he does, then why doesn't he say it? All these questions flood my mind. Until I go cold and rigid and afraid in his arms. It feels like I've lost him. No. Worse. Like I never had him. I feel so *stupid*. So alone.

And he must sense something because he pulls back.

'Are you OK?' he asks, frowning.

'Yeah, fine. I gotta go.' I'm swallowing back all this emotion.

'*Now*?'

'Yeah. Now.' I grab my clothes and hurry into them.

He sits up. 'What's going on, Rache?'

'Nothing.'

He puts his hand to his head like he's realising something. 'You're sorry we did this. Aren't you?' He closes his eyes. 'I knew it was a mistake. I'm so sorry, Rache.'

A mistake? He's sorry? I shove my feet into my shoes. I step down on the backs, something I never do.

He's jumping into his boxers. 'Hang on. Wait. Don't go.'

I stop. Turn. I look at him, my heart pounding. Was I wrong? *Does* he love me? Maybe I just didn't give him a chance to say it.

'Come here,' he says, smiling. He's sitting on the side of the bed, patting his lap. How could I forget that this is

Mark? He loves me. Of course he does. I smile and go to him. He puts his arms around me. Kisses my cheek.

'This is my fault,' he says. 'I should have known you were just upset.'

I stand straight up. 'I'll see you tomorrow,' I say, feeling like I never want to see him again. I hurry from the room and downstairs before he can dress, feeling like Cinderella, trying to get away before everything turns to shit. *Too late*, I think. *It already has*.

I lie in bed and can't stop crying. Through everything, I always thought I had Mark's love. It was the one thing that kept me going, even when I thought I'd lost Alex and Sarah. Inside my chest, my heart aches, like it really is broken, bruised, trampled on. Smashed. I see everything differently now. All those times I thought meant something, meant nothing to him. I feel so stupid. I've always been alone. I just never knew it.

I cry all night, silently, so no one hears. I'm pretty expert at that. You just stick your face into your pillow. If I could just stop loving him. Switch it off. Pretend we were never together. That I dreamed it all.

TWENTY
Sausage

I so don't want to go to school, to face Mark. But I have to keep the show going for my parents. I'm walking (slowly) to the DART when Charley calls.

'Hello, sweetie,' she says, like she feels sorry for me.

'Hey, Charley,' I say, not wanting her pity, just wanting to know that I can quit *D4*.

'Emily called,' she says. 'Are you OK?'

'I'm fine Charley. Can I quit?'

There's a pause. 'Can you keep going till your contract is up?'

'I don't know.' I don't know if I can keep going at all.

'Shall I talk to your parents? I could tell them how great you're getting on in *D4*. How much they love you. And that they want to give you a week off to recover from the newspaper article.'

'You mean lie?'

'Effectively, yes.'

'OK.' I breathe out in relief. 'You won't tell them about Rebecca?'

'God, no.'

'OK.'

'Good, because you're the most talented actress I've ever met,' she sounds emotional. 'And I'm not going to let anything get in the way of your dream.'

)(

I'm getting a little emotional myself.

'I've never said this, Rachel. But you're like one of my own.' Her voice wobbles.

A tear spills over quietly.

'We'll get through this, sausage,' she says.

I smile. She's been calling me 'sausage' as long as I can remember. 'Thanks, Charley.'

'I tried to call you,' Sarah says on the DART to school the next morning.

'Yeah, I'd my phone off.'

'Did you get my messages?'

'I haven't been looking at my phone.'

'They're all sorries.'

'Thanks.'

'She seemed so nice.'

'I know.'

'I kinda want to kill her. Slowly. Painfully.'

I half smile.

'Are we OK?' she asks cautiously.

'Yeah,' I say.

'You don't sound OK.'

'I'm OK, Sarah.'

'You don't forgive me, do you?'

'Sarah, I forgive you, OK?'

'OK,' she says uncertainly. Then a lot more certainly, she says, 'I'll get her back.'

When I get to school, I can't look at Mark. All through class, I feel him looking at me. When break comes, I get out fast. I grab my coat from my locker and go. Outside the air is cold, clear. I need to think. No, I don't. I need to act like Naomi acts.

'Rache?' I hear his voice behind me.

I turn.

He's running up to me. No coat. Looking so caliente I want to hit him. He slows to a stop. I look at him and think, *Why couldn't you just love me?*

'What's going on, Rache? Why aren't you answering your phone? Why aren't you talking to me? Why aren't you even *looking* at me?'

Just say it, Rachel. Just tell him it's over.

'Why did you go, last night? Talk to me, Rache.'

I open my mouth to tell him it's over. But that's not what comes out. 'Let's see other people.'

'What? What are you talking about?' He looks at me in total shock.

The words keep coming. 'You're always saying we should live a bit. Well, let's see other people.'

'I didn't mean it like *that*.'

We stand facing each other.

Then his eyes narrow, 'Why? Why now? Why all of a sudden?'

'You don't want a serious relationship, Mark,' I say instead of 'you don't love me'.

'Don't tell me what I want.' His face hardens. 'It's OK, I get it,' he says. 'You know what? Let's just forget it, OK?' He turns and walks back to school.

That's it? It's over? Just like that? After last night, I shouldn't be shocked. But I am.

'Right,' I say, but he can't hear me. 'Fine.' It's what I wanted anyway. Just didn't have the guts to do. I wish

I had. Why could he say it and not me? And why did I even say that about seeing other people? I don't want to see other people. Him doing it would kill me. What's wrong with me?

I can't go back to school. So I turn and walk out.

I go to *D4*. I'd have had to anyway in an hour.

When I walk in, Josh is coming along the corridor, shoving an arm into the sleeve of his jacket.

'Hey,' he says awkwardly. Yesterday hasn't gone away.

I don't care.

'Want to go for coffee?' he asks.

Nothing else to do but cry. 'Sure.'

'I wanted to talk to you anyway. There's some kind of investigation going on.'

'I know.'

'You *know*? Why didn't you warn me? Emily had me up in her office quizzing the living daylights out of me.'

'Sorry.'

'She wanted to know if I witnessed either of you bullying each other.'

I don't ask what he said.

'And, you know, when she put it like that, and I thought about it, I remembered all the times Rebecca dissed you behind your back.' He shrugs. 'And that's what I told her.'

I nod. 'Thanks.'

'By the way. I've been offered a part in a movie.'

'Really?' I try to get excited for him. And because we all dream of it – I kind of do. 'That's brilliant.'

'It's the real deal. Hollywood.'

'Wow.'

)K

'So I'll be leaving the show.'

It feels like I'm losing my one ally. Apart from Maisie.

'Don't say anything. I haven't made the big announcement.' He grimaces. 'I keep putting it off. They've been so good to me, here. If it wasn't for *D4*, I wouldn't even have a profile. I wouldn't have got this part.'

Then I think of something. 'Aren't you on contract?'

'They've only ever given me three-month contracts, which they've kept renewing. My last one was up two weeks ago.' He checks his watch. And reaches for his coat. 'Listen, good luck with the Rebecca thing. She hasn't as many friends in here as she thinks she has. No matter how many cheesy presents she buys.'

He winks at me.

And I think, *Mark*.

I've finished all my scenes and am sitting, resting my forehead against the dressing table. Maisie comes in. I sit up and produce a smile. She smells of cigarette smoke. And frustration. She lifts up her script and grimaces.

'Don't suppose you'd help an old woman with her lines?'

I put my hand out for her script.

We go over her lines a few times.

'Tell me if you need to go,' she says.

'I'm fine.'

After a few more minutes, she asks. 'You sure you don't need to go?'

'Yup.'

)(

Then she says, 'These times pass, you know. It's easy to think they won't, but they do.'

Sometimes they pass, I think, *and then come back again.*

Finally, I leave. I don't take a taxi. I'm not ready to go home. I walk to the DART. My phone rings.

It's Sarah. 'Hey. What's up with Mark? I asked him if you were in school tomorrow and he nearly bit my head off. "How should I know?" he said. Are you guys OK?'

I stop walking, close my eyes. I take a deep breath. 'We broke up. But it's fine.'

'How could it be fine? You're mad about each other.'

'Not true.' One of us isn't. 'Look, I gotta go,' I say because I feel tears coming and there's no way I'm going to cry out here on Nutley Lane in rush-hour traffic.

'How're you doing, sweetie?' Mum asks when I get in. 'I made your favourite. Curry.'

I produce another smile. Like a vending machine. 'Thanks.'

'I got a call from Charley, raving about you. She said they love you in there. And were really upset about the Béibhinn Keane incident. They've given you a week off.' She beams like that's it, problem solved.

I smile. 'Yup.'

I long for my bed, for my squidgy pillow and my cool quilt. I long to hold Uggs and fall sleep. Black out.

'She spoke about the contract. How you can't really leave yet. Is that OK?'

'Yeah, fine.'

'You've only a few weeks left anyway.'

'Yup.'

'She said they're like family in there.'

I actually smile. Because Charley may have over-acted there. Something she's always warned us against.

TWENTY-ONE
Hansel and Gretel

'I was thinking,' Maisie says. 'Would you like a holiday?'

'I'd love a holiday.' From my life.

'Will you come and stay with me for the week? Starting tonight?'

'Are you serious?'

She shrugs. 'I think you could do with a break.'

'I'm not exactly great company right now, Maisie. But thanks.'

'I don't like great company.'

I smile.

'Where I live,' she says, 'you can walk for miles and not see a single person.'

It sounds like where I need to be. 'But we don't really know each other.'

'Yes we do.'

I smile again. Because she's right, we do.

'So, what do you say?'

'Maybe for a day or two. I'd have to check with my parents.'

'Of course,' she says, like it's a done deal, like I'm really staying with her.

I look at her. 'Why are you doing this?'

'We all hit a wall at some stage. When that happens it's good to have a bolt hole. Just don't expect advice, I'm not much good at advice.'

'Good,' I say.

She laughs. 'We'll get along just fine.'

'I'll ring my mum.'

'Great.'

'Hey, Mum,' I say cheerfully. Maisie Morrin has asked me to stay with her for the week.'

'The actress?'

'Yeah.'

'She asked you to *stay*?'

'Yup.'

'Where does she live?'

I hesitate. 'In the country somewhere.'

'Could you narrow it down a little?' she jokes cheerfully, no clue what's really going on.

I look at Maisie. 'Where do you live?'

She holds her hand out for the phone. I pass it to her.

'Hello, Mrs Dunne. It's Maisie Morrin.' Her voice is so commanding and calming at the same time. I feel myself relax. 'If it's all right with you and your husband, I've asked Rachel to stay for a while.' She explains that she lives in a cottage in the Dublin mountains. I imagine a thatched roof and smoke curling up from a chimney. I imagine peace.

Maisie's car is a tiny, ancient, yellow Fiat. It rattles along happily. I just want to drive up into the mountains and breathe. But we have to call home first to pick up my stuff. Mum looks so happy, it almost makes me happy.

'I'll just go get my stuff,' I say, and run upstairs.

I throw a load of clothes into a case, not really thinking about what I'll need, just wanting to go.

Mum and Maisie are talking in the hall. That's when I remember – Maisie doesn't know that Mum doesn't know. I hurry the bag downstairs.

'Great,' Maisie says. 'You're ready.'

I scan Mum's face. Still cheerful. *Phew.*

'Maisie was just telling me you're going to practice some scenes,' she says enthusiastically. 'It's a great idea. You'll have a great time.'

I look at Maisie. She winks.

'Yeah,' I say.

Mum hugs me. 'Well, have fun,' she says, like I'm going to Eurodisney.

'How did you know I never told Mum about Rebecca?' I ask Maisie, in the car.

'Just worked it out from how she was.'

'Thanks for not telling her.'

She gives me an 'as if' look.

After that, we drive in silence. I look out the window, watching the houses go by, the parks, a shopping centre. It feels like I'm leaving my life behind. I text Alex and Sarah to tell them where I'm going. I gaze at Mark's number for ages. Deleting it is like losing him all over again. I put my phone in my bag and stare at the world outside. Not wanting to think about my own. Maisie's car rattles along. When we start to climb, though, it sounds like it's under pressure. I look at Maisie. She doesn't seem to notice. So the engine must be OK. It makes this trip every day. I look back out the window. Fewer and fewer houses, more and more sky. Bogs, hills, wind in the trees. It's like a painting that moves.

Up in the mountains, the road levels off. Everything is brown and heathery and wild. Maisie rolls down the window. The air smells fresh and alive.

'You don't mind?' she calls above the wind. 'I always let the air in when I get to this spot.'

'No. It's lovely.' I roll mine down too. It feels like we're part of nature and not just driving through.

Slowly, the light leaves the sky. Maisie turns on the headlights.

The road narrows. We take a turn off, onto a country lane. Grass grows up the centre. Overhead, branches reach over us, blocking out what light was left in the sky. I glance across at Maisie.

'Nearly there,' she says.

We drive into a clearing. And when I see the cottage, I think *Hansel and Gretel*.

She pulls up outside, kills the engine and looks at me. 'So, what do you think of my little bolt hole?'

'I love it.'

'Me too.'

On the windowsills, there are herb gardens. A hanging basket hangs beside the front door – which is purple. A wind chime tinkles in the wind. Logs are stacked up on her little porch. I follow her up to the door, which opens with a creak. I can't believe she forgot to lock it.

Inside, she switches on a table lamp and the room fills with cosy light. It's even messier than the dressing room. Patchwork quilts are thrown over two armchairs by the fire, reminding me of log cabins in the Rockies. Bookshelves look like they're groaning under the weight of all the books. The paintings on her walls are abstract with layers and layers of paint. I love them.

'I'll get a fire going,' she says. 'Why don't you light some candles?'

I drop my bag by the door. There are candles everywhere. I go around creating tiny pools of light. The flames near doors and windows flicker in the draught. It's beautiful.

I leave my coat on till the fire takes hold. As it does, the smell of turf fills the room, reminding me of my grandparents, who are now dead. I loved my granddad especially. He used to chase me with his false teeth. We called him Pop.

I follow Maisie into a tiny kitchen. The cupboards are turquoise and genuinely old.

'I'm not a big eater,' she says. 'But I've home-made soup.'

I smile. It's the most perfect thing to eat in a place like this.

I start to set the table.

'Oh don't bother with that,' she says. 'We'll use mugs and sit by the fire.'

Yaay.

I cut some bread, put it on a plate with butter and set it on this wooden chest that's between the armchairs by the fire. Maisie takes a chair. I'm heading for the other with my mug when she says: 'Careful, that one's a rocker.'

Pop had a rocker.

We sit, watching the flames, hands cupped around our huge mugs. Silence except for an occasional crack from the fire. As I rock, I remember Pop's jokes about chickens crossing roads. And cars called Ladas. Jack loved the Lada jokes. I think they've stopped making them now –

the cars, not the jokes. Though the jokes have probably died with the cars.

After a while, the flames dim.

'Will I go get a log?' I say.

'Do.'

And that's all we say to each other for the rest of the night. Which is lovely.

I have my own tiny room. My own tiny bed. I'm in it by ten, feeling like a kid staying with her grandparents. I lie under patchwork, listening to rain on the roof, getting heavier and heavier. I love the sound. And I love that it's the only sound. No music blaring from Jack's room. (Move bitch, get out the way.) No cars on the road outside. No one on the stairs. Just peace.

I wake to the sound of birds. It feels like spring. *It* is *spring*, I think in surprise. It's February. I hear Maisie humming in the kitchen.

The bathroom has an old door with a latch on it. So cute. There's a wooden seat on the loo that looks antique and the sink has the kind of taps that you have to twist for ages to get water. I love this place.

When I come out, Maisie is putting on her coat.

'Hello!' she says. 'Sleep OK?'

'Like a log.' It's what Pop used to say.

'Good. I'm off to get some shopping.'

'I'll come.'

'No. Stay where you are. Help yourself to breakfast. Go for a walk. There's wellies in the hall.'

'I'd like to help.'

'No you wouldn't,' she says. 'Not really.'

I smile.

'Anyway, I shop alone.'

I take out my wallet and try to hand her a fifty, hoping it's enough to cover my share.

'Don't insult me. You're a guest. If you want to do something useful, clean out the fire.'

'OK,' I say, feeling better.

I sit eating muesli, looking out at Maisie's bird table, trying to identify the birds. Pop used to tell me their names when I was little. Once, I knew them all. Now, I pick out robins, blue tits and a black cap. There's one I don't know. It's bugging me. Because I should know it. I switch on my iPhone to check Safari. No service. I get up and go into every room except Maisie's. Nothing. I go get my laptop. I can't believe it. No wifi. Which will mean no Facebook, no Twitter, no moan.ie. I look outside again. *Is it a goldfinch?*

I check the bookshelves. Maybe Maisie has a book on birds. I run my finger over the spines. They're in no particular order but a lot of them look interesting. Books on photography. Travel. Buildings. Animals. Nature. Oh, my God, she has the very same book Pop used to teach me from. I pull it out. And smile at the cover. The big brown owl is like a familiar face. I hurry back to the kitchen with it. I sit at the table. Going through it is like travelling back in time. The pages are worn. The birds are in the same order. I remember whole pages. I forget my quest, getting lost in birds, ones that don't come to Ireland, all the types of eagles and hawks and birds of prey that I once loved. Finding this book is like finding my childhood.

There's noise outside. I look up from the book. A magpie

is swooping down at the smaller birds. They scatter but return to the table. He is turning around, about to come back. I jump up and race out into the garden clapping and waving.

'Bully!' I shout at him as he flies away. 'Yeah and don't come back.' I stand, looking after him, just to make sure. Finally, I go back inside. I watch the smaller birds come back, one by one. And then without even looking at the book, I have it. A chaffinch. I double-check the book.

'Yes!' I say, making a victory fist.

I clear away the breakfast stuff. There's no dishwasher. So I fill the sink with hot water and bubbles. Lots of bubbles. So many bubbles that I scoop them up in my hand and blow them into the air. Light catches them, turning each one into a tiny sphere of rainbow. I chase them with a finger, trying to burst them before they hit the sink.

I wash the dishes and leave them to dry. I go to put the book back. Sun bursts in through the windows, showing up layers of dust. I clean out the fire, bring in more logs and pile them next to the turf. I tidy up but not so much that it would bother her. No one wants dust. So I get rid of that.

She's still not back.

I could go for that walk – but a walk is a walk. I go to the window. It is seriously nice out there. Actual blue sky – which is always a surprise in Ireland. I go to the hall to check the wellie situation. They're my size, which gets rid of that excuse. I pull them on. They make me want to find puddles to smash through.

I go outside, sit on the porch. I turn my face to the sun and close my eyes. I guess I could walk a *bit*. I go back in for my coat. And a key. I find the coat. No key. Anywhere.

Her landline starts to ring. It's got this bossy ringtone that reminds me of old detective movies. I find it under a cushion. It's one of those genuinely old ones they've started to sell again as novelty phones, the ones with the dials. I instantly want to stick my finger into one of the holes and turn it. It rings again. I look at it thinking, it's not my house. But what if it's Maisie? She's no other way of getting me. I pick it up and wait for the other person to speak.

'Haven't you gone for your walk yet?'

I smile. 'Why are you ringing if you thought I'd be gone?'

'To make sure you did. Head back up the road, through the trees and take the first left. It leads to a lake. Should be nice today.'

'Eh, Maisie? You didn't leave a key.'

'Oh, I never lock the door.'

'Oh, OK. Sure.' No mobile coverage. No wifi. No lock on the door. We're doomed.

When she said lake, I thought, small circular thing. This looks like the sea. It's got tiny waves and sparkles in the sun. The trees leading down to it look like they came from Kenya. Way off in the distance, at the other side of the lake, there are pine trees that rise into a hill. It's so beautiful. And there's no one here but me. Two swans swim together, their heads curved like they're sharing secrets. I think of Mark and how stupid I was to let myself love someone who never takes anything seriously. Why would he be any different with me? I stomp down to the lake and start to lob stones in. A heron flies up, spreading his wide wings.

'Oh, sorry.'

I plonk down on the ground. It's kind of beachy where I am, with actual sand. The sun's in my eyes, so I look down. There are so many stones. They're small and smooth, different sizes and colours. When I was really young – like maybe two – I'd spend hours looking at stones. I don't actually remember this but Mum's told me. She said I'd sit on Killiney Beach, surrounded by stones. I'd pick one up and stare at it for ages, turning it over in my fingers and putting it right up to my eyes, then licking it wet to see it change colour. I asked her how she didn't worry about the dirt. She said, simply, that the sea had washed the stones clean. She seems like a different mum, a relaxed one, who didn't worry. She told me how she loved watching me. It was as if I saw more than just the stone, like maybe something spiritual; she didn't know. Now I pick up a stone. And do everything I used to do – apart from the licking. But instead of something spiritual, all I can think of is geography – weathering and freaking erosion – and how a person can be eroded by life too. If she's not careful.

Maisie's car is outside when I kick my way up the lane. It's sitting, bright yellow in the sun. It looks like a Betsy. Or a Charmaine. Or maybe a Petulia. I touch it as I walk by, the way you'd rest your hand on a dog's head.

On the porch, I take off the boots and leave them there to dry.

'Hello!' I call so I don't surprise her.

'In here!'

Already, she has lit the fire. The smell of fresh coffee fills the room.

'Can I help put away the shopping?' A job I usually hate. But this feels like a partnership. Like I should do my bit.

'Done,' she says. 'Would you like coffee?'

'No, thanks. Is it OK if I get a glass of water?'

'Don't ask. Just help yourself.'

She takes her coffee over to the fire. 'How was the lake?'

'Like the sea. Peaceful though.' From the pockets of my coat, I take out pine cones and stones I collected for her. 'There weren't any flowers,' I say. I feel kind of embarrassed giving her something so babyish. There really was nothing else.

She smiles immediately, puts the cones on her lap and the stones on her open palm. She examines each one with a finger. I swear to God, she licks one.

I laugh.

'What?'

'I used to do that when I was a kid.'

'Why did you stop?'

'You can get Weil's Disease from rat pee.'

She laughs. 'Live dangerously, Rachel.' She arranges the pine cones and stones on the mantelpiece. She makes them look like art. 'Thank you,' she says, sounding like I've given her something special.

I smile, take off my coat and sit down on my rocker. I don't think I'll mind being old. Everything's so simple. I sip water and rock a bit. I wonder if I'll be alone.

I look out the window. 'Does your car have a name?'

'Graham.'

'A boy car?'

'Of course.'

'But he's yellow.'

)(

'This is true. He's still a boy.'

We laugh. Then fade to easy silence. The fire sparks and a lone bird sings outside like he's just discovered his voice.

'By the way, you've the same book as my granddad.'

'Really? Which one?' She turns around to look at the book case.

I get the book and hand it to her.

She smiles and runs her fingers slowly over the cover. She looks up. 'My daughter loved this book.' She opens it and goes through the pages like memories.

'I didn't know you had a daughter.' I'm happy for her. That she's not alone.

She looks up. And I know straight away something's wrong. Her eyes are full of pain. Still, she smiles. 'Jules didn't stay in this world.'

'I'm so sorry,' I say immediately.

She shakes her head.

I want to know if she was ill. But don't want to ask.

'She wasn't strong enough,' she says.

It's like she wants me to know. 'Was she ill?'

She looks at me. 'She took her own life.'

Oh, my God. 'I'm so so sorry.' I don't know what else to say.

She looks into the fire like she's looking into the past. 'She was thirty-four. For twelve years, she had fought depression.' She looks at me. 'It won.'

The fire sparks. She looks at it, then back at me. She smiles. 'That's when I found this place.'

I think of Mum and how devastated she'd have been if I'd gone through with it, back then. But how devastated she must have been anyway that I'd tried it.

'Hey,' Maisie says gently. 'Are you OK?'

)(

I look up from my lap. I've never told anyone. 'I took pills when I was twelve.' I shrug. 'I wasn't strong enough either.'

She reaches forward, grips my hand and squeezes it. She doesn't ask.

So I tell her everything. About the bullying. How it started. How it went on for two years. How I began to believe everything they said. How it nearly broke my parents' marriage. How I blamed myself. I tell her about the pills. How Jack found me. How I was taken out of school for the last term. And how I spent that term and a whole summer seeing a shrink. And how, under the surface, it has never really gone away.

'I thought you'd a lot on those spindly shoulders,' she says, finally.

'Spindly?'

'Yes, spindly,' she says firmly. 'You need more of my soup, young lady.'

'Why? Is it *magic* soup?'

'Now that you mention it. It *is* magic soup.'

'In that case ...'

We sit smiling at each other.

Then hers fades. 'Are you glad you didn't do it?'

No one's ever asked me that – not Mum, not Dad, not Jack, not even the shrink. I think about all the things that have happened since, the good stuff, the bad stuff. Then I think of all the things that I'd have missed. Alex. Sarah. Maggie. Even Mark. And though things have been pretty damn shitty lately, I've never once felt like doing it again. I look at her, realising that somehow, somewhere, I must have got stronger.

'Yeah, I am.'

She smiles. 'Me too. Come on, let's have some of that magic soup.'

We stand up.

'Thanks, Maisie.'

'Well, it mightn't be *that* magic,' she admits.

'Why don't you have a lie down?' she says, after lunch.

'It's three in the afternoon.'

'Perfect time for a siesta. I'm having one. You should too, seeing as I'm going to kick your ass in Scrabble later.'

'In your dreams.'

In my little room, I lie on my back, not actually planning to sleep. I listen to the birds. Then close my eyes to hear better. I can tell a blackbird now. Listening to the sounds, I feel my breathing ease, feel myself drift. And when I wake again, it feels like a new day.

Later, we make stew. Then, we sit by the fire. I flick through a book called *The Great LIFE Photographers*. It contains photos from *LIFE* magazine going right back to the 1930s. Shots of the Vietnam War, shots of stars, of ordinary people with extraordinary faces, of weird hats and the Second World War, of children crippled by thalidomide, of rockets and a frog plopping into water. *This* is the kind of book we should have at school. Because *this* is life. And life is what we should be learning about. And learning about it ourselves, exploring, instead of being force-fed all this information *they* want us to know. It starts with colouring inside the lines. Do it this way,

)(

our way. Not your way. Until you forget what your way ever was.

Maisie is writing into a leather-bound notebook. She's spending more time sucking the end of her pen than actually writing though.

'What are you writing? I ask, after a while.

'Oh, poetry,' she says simply.

'Seriously?' Poetry's so *hard*.

She just nods like it's no big deal and looks back at her notebook.

'Can I read it?'

'Not till I'm finished.'

'Sorry.'

'On the shelf over there, there's a book of poems.'

'*Your* poems.'

She nods.

I'm so excited. She's an actual published poet.

On her shelves, there are loads of poetry books, but none by her. I look again more carefully.

'Oh.' She looks up like she's just remembered. 'Maisie Moore,' she says. 'Look under Maisie Moore. I use a pseudonym.'

'Oh, you mystery woman.'

She smiles. 'I do it for peace.'

'Why don't you want people to know it's you? It's such a huge achievement.'

'Judge that for yourself when you read the poems.'

'Still, wouldn't you sell loads more if people knew it was you?'

'Which is why I don't tell them. I want people to buy my poetry for what it is, not who I am. Anyway, my private life is private. And my poetry is the private me.'

I can't wait to read it now.

Yaay! I've got it. I hurry back to the fire with it. 'I can't believe you're published.'

'Shut up,' she says.

'No.' But I do shut up because I want to read.

The poems are short. And the words simple. There's one about a birthday party for a little girl. I know it's about Jules and that it's been written since she died, because it's so full of longing. I look up at her, sitting there all alone, writing away. And I am so glad that I am still here for my mum, that I can go home and hug her and slag her and tell her to go out for the night. With Dad. I'll do that when I go back. But I don't want to go back.

I read a poem about missing a man – missing his body, his touch, missing him in bed. I get up suddenly because I'm thinking of Mark. I go outside to get more logs for the fire. I throw two in and watch the sparks. I stack the others. Then I pick up Maisie's book and read about herons and shape shifting and a life lived.

I say nothing to her until she finally closes her notebook. Then I tell her the truth. 'I love it.'

'You do?' She sounds surprised.

I nod. 'I really do. You're amazing,' I tell her. And I don't just mean the poetry.

TWENTY-TWO
Some Kind of Angel

Sunday, we're planting bulbs in Maisie's garden. Judging by the packets, there's going to be a lot of colour. We kneel side by side – me digging, Maisie mixing the fertiliser and top soil, then sprinkling it into the holes I've made and planting the bulbs. A robin keeps us company.

'We're a bit early with these,' she says, 'but I'm an optimist. The sun's shining and the soil is soft.'

I love learning how to do this. I love being outside, feeling the breeze and sun on my face, smelling the soil. Digging my holes with my little trowel reminds me of when I was small and at the beach. I did a lot of humming back then. I remember. Jack and I used to bury Harry. I used to love slapping the sand hard with the back of the spade when he was covered.

'Emily's not as stupid as she looks,' Maisie says.

I look up, surprised.

'What I mean is, more people than you think can see through Ms French.' She carries on planting like she's just commented on the weather. I remember what Josh said. But they're wrong.

'She's actually really popular, Maisie.'

'Rachel, actors act. On and off stage. Most of us have been in this bitchy business long enough to recognise a trouble-maker.' I must look doubtful because she points her gardening fork at me. 'The truth will out.'

)(

Even if it does, I realise in shock, 'I don't want to go back to my life.'

She looks at me for a long time. 'That'll change,' she says so confidently.

She doesn't understand. 'They worry so much about me – that I'll do it again – that they end up fighting. I'm so afraid they'll break up because of me. I tried to quit the show to stop them worrying even though I wanted to stay and fight. I love them so much but they *crush* with their worry.'

Our eyes lock and I think, *Jesus, what have I said? She must have been so worried about her daughter.* 'It's not like it's their fault. They can't help it. I mean I'd worry if it was my daughter.'

She thinks for a moment. 'You just need to show them you're strong. And you are. Standing up to Rebecca took a lot of courage.'

'Only now it looks like I'm the bully.'

'The truth will out,' she says again.

'I wish I'd listened to Jack. I wish I'd never trusted her. I wanted to believe she'd changed. That we'd moved on. I was so *stupid.*'

'The only one who was stupid was Rebecca.'

'No. She was so clever. She tied me up in knots.'

'And look at the hassle she's brought on everyone. Including herself. And, by the way, she'd still have bullied you even if you hadn't trusted her. Because your acting threatened hers. This wasn't personal, Rachel. This was business.'

I look at her, surprised.

'Some day, Rachel, you'll see all of this from the outside. That's when you'll recognise your own strength.' She waves the fork. 'Now, dig.'

)(

I do dig. It is so good to be with a person who knows my life and isn't the tiniest bit worried about me. She actually thinks I'm strong. I look at her and think, *You are some kind of angel.*

The hail starts at eight, hammering against the roof. It's so heavy that it comes down the chimney. It gets colder. I put another log on the fire and go to get a hoodie. I flick through books, just looking at pictures. Pictures of the world, of places to be seen, pictures of war and pain, of love, of fun and of life gone by. It feels like I'm travelling the world and travelling through time.

'I'm going to have an early night,' Maisie says. 'I'm up early for *D4.*'

I'm so relieved, now, to have the week off.

'Do what you like tomorrow,' she says. 'Stay in bed all day, if that's what you want.'

I smile. 'Thanks.'

I'm in bed by nine. All snuggled up, listening to the rain. Nothing to do – but not bored. Happy in my own company.

When I wake, the room is pink. I kneel up in bed and pull back the curtains. The sun is coming up. And it's amazing. Slowly, the colours change. Pink to yellow to blue. And lots of in-betweens. Every day, I miss this. Too busy trying to stay ahead, to not fail. A waste of time. Because here I am and here is the sun. Like a miracle, doing what it does every day. What it's been doing since way before I was born. What it will keep on doing after I die. Making me feel tiny, and my worries even smaller.

I hear Maisie moving around, getting ready to go in to *D4.* I collapse back onto the bed like I used to do when I

)(

was a kid. A falling tree. I cover myself up and enjoy the feeling of drifting back to sleep.

I wake at eleven. Now that I've nothing to do, I want to actually do stuff. Like make breakfast, proper breakfast, not just boring old cereal, something different, something interesting. I want to teach myself to light a fire. I want to explore, go for an adventure not a 'walk'. Into the woods, off the track.

I make French toast. And smear it with Nutella. (Go, Maisie, for having it.) I slice it into soldiers. And, just like it did when I was a kid, it tastes better that way.

It's sunny out – but, being Ireland, that could change in five minutes. I grab my coat and borrowed wellies, and go. I don't turn left by the lake. Just walk straight on up the tiny road. Gurgling streams of rain water gush down either side. I splash through them, kicking up water then stomping down my feet. Kids have got it sussed. I pass a rusty old gate that's being held together with rope. In the field, there's a farmer with his sheep. Oh, my God, there are tiny lambs. I stand watching them frolicking around and feeding. The farmer sees me and waves. I wave back then move on. I turn down a tiny road. I pass a cottage. At the door, basking in the sun, is a small black dog. When he sees me, he gets up, comes over, tail wagging. Friendly.

'Hello,' I say, and keep on walking.

He follows me. Then trots beside me. Then passes me out and takes the lead. He has a tail like a fox and I imagine he's a cross between the tamed and the wild. That'd be so cool. He runs ahead a bit, then waits. He's like a little spirit, coming along with me. A free spirit, owned by no one. He turns into a wood. Wow, he's led me here. The trees are like huge, silent men, standing

)(

around waiting for something to happen. We walk along the nature trail. Up ahead something moves. It's a squirrel making tiny, silent leaps. His bushy tail is leaping after him like a second wave. I freeze. But the dog shoots after him. The squirrel darts up the nearest tree. The dog, at the bottom, barks.

'Nice try,' I say. 'But you haven't a hope. Come on.'

He takes the lead again. And when he goes off the track, I follow him. It is wild. Amazing. Autumn leaves have become part of the undergrowth, spring shoots coming up through them. A blackbird scoots along the ground in a hurry to get away. Shafts of light are coming through the trees, landing on bright-green moss on the side of a rock. Clusters of snowdrops spread out around the base of a wizened old tree whose branches almost reach the ground. Ferns are starting to unfurl. He runs under a fallen tree. I climb over. It's so pretty. The ground is covered in light-green shamrocks. And tiny purple flowers, like the flowers you'd draw as a kid, with oval petals and a simple circular centre. Like embroidery flowers. They tremble in the breeze. Some aren't even open yet after the night. I'd forgotten flowers did that, close at night. I take out my phone to photograph them and realise I've left it behind.

It starts to rain. Tiny splatters all around me. I stand with my back to a trunk, feeling like a kid again, listening to the rain and watching pine needles shake when the drops land. The dog sits beside me. I crouch down and put my hand on his head, happy with this little companion. I don't miss anything. Anyone. I know I should. But it's like a rest, to be just me.

When the rain finally stops, the dog leads me back. Outside his cottage, he trots up to the door and settles

)(

down again. He closes his eyes without a goodbye. I like that.

The farmer has gone from the field.

By the time I get back, I'm starving. It feels good to have an appetite again – to want to eat. I've time to make something nice. So I do. Bruschetta al pomodoro. I cut up the tomatoes. I take the leaves from the basil plant standing on the window sill. Then I have an idea. I'm going to have a picnic.

I sit out on the porch and take my first bite. Food really does taste better outside. I think of how I've been starving myself and how mad it seems now that I let some anonymous person (who turned out not to be anonymous after all) change how I felt about myself. I gave her that power, handed it over. I, will, never, do, that, again.

The magpie is back, strutting around the garden like he's important, head poking forward with every step. Does he *realise* how stupid he looks?

After lunch I teach myself how to make a fire with just newspaper, logs and turf. I am a ninja.

I find an old deck of cards and play Solitaire. I build a house of cards. And blow it down. I draw a house on condensation. It's got four windows and a door, smoke comes from the chimney. A sun and two clouds. A flower and a bee. A little family. The girl is the smallest. She's holding her brother's hand. Not the biggest brother. The one that's the same size. This is how my pictures were when I was a kid. I rub the picture away.

I run my finger along the spines of Maisie's books. I smile when I find *The Lord of the Flies*. I take it out, sit in the rocker and start to read. It isn't just about boys on an island. It's about boys on an island being cruel to each other. It's about a struggle to survive. It's about survival of the fittest. I'm reading about my life. I get so lost in the book, I almost forget dinner. Only the fire, starting to burn out, reminds me to get up off my ass. I put on two logs, stretch, then go to check the fridge. Everything I need to make my mum's chicken casserole is there. So, I get to work on my surprise for Maisie.

I've always helped Mum cook, for as long as I remember. When I was small, she'd sit me up on the worktop, beside the cooker while Jack played on the floor with his trains (he was obsessed). She never tried to explain what she was doing. We'd just chat. About anything really. Every so often, she'd lift me up and I'd add stuff, throwing it into the boiling water, pretending I was a witch and this was my potion. It surprises me how much she trusted me then not to do anything stupid, like touch the cooker or fall off the worktop. She'd so much faith in me then. Then worry took over our world.

Maisie gets back at five.

'My goodness. Fire on. Dinner cooking. I think I'll keep you.'

Do, I feel like saying.

The next day, I'm back in the woods, looking up at a tree, checking it out for possible arm and foot holds. I plan a route, then take off my coat and boots. I put my knapsack back on. Slowly, I start to climb, enjoying the stretch of my arms and legs, enjoying the challenge. It's years since I've climbed. Jack and I used to do it all the time. We'd have races. Pop built us a tree house. We'd spend hours up there, planning pranks on Harry, childminders, babysitters – anyone really, we weren't

)(

fussy. We were a two-man operation, a team. Mum didn't want people calling us 'the twins'. We were 'individuals', she'd say crossly. But we *were* the twins. We *liked* being the twins. We *liked* that it was us against the world. It felt like she was insulting Jack when she said that. He'd distract me though. With water fights, pillow fights, snowball fights. And then it stopped. And I had to fight alone.

I crawl out onto a branch and when I get to a spot where another smaller one sprouts from it, I lower myself into sitting position. I smile down at the dog who's looking up at me, barking. I love that I don't know his name, that we don't need that.

'Victory,' I say to him.

He stops barking. Now, just looks confused.

I laugh.

I love the feeling of my feet not touching the ground. I swing my legs, like a kid and there's nothing to worry about. I'd forgotten that feeling. The birds are making so much noise. After a while, it stops being noise and becomes conversation. Question. Pause. Answer. Another question. A joke. Laughter. It's so amazing what you hear when you stop and be still. For five minutes.

I've packed a picnic. Cheese sandwiches with mustard and pickles. Pop's speciality. I take it out. And drop the crusts down to my pal. I can't believe that he's still here. I thought he'd have toddled off ages ago. Tail wagging, he noms it in seconds.

I take Maisie's book of poetry from my bag. It opens at my favourite, the one about missing her husband. It's so full of love and longing. Reading it, I think of Mark. His face, his hands, his body. His smile. And how easily he walked away. The dog barks again. I look down and

)(

smile. He starts to trot off. I think how alike they are. Two
free spirits. Mark was never mine. And there's no rule
that a person has to love you back.

When I get back, there are two cars in the drive. Graham
and a big, flashy Merc. I don't want to walk in on
whoever's there. It's starting to rain, so I sit in the porch.
The door opens.

'I thought it was you,' Maisie says. 'What are you
doing out here?'

'You've company.'

'Actually, *you* have.'

'I do?' I didn't think I wanted it. Now I'm kind of
excited. 'Who?'

'Emily.'

'Oh.'

She laughs. 'Come on in. She wants a word.' Then she
whispers, 'The investigation's over.'

I look at her.

'It's OK.'

The real surprise is that I'm not more excited. I follow
Maisie in.

'Here she is,' Maisie says cheerfully.

Emily stands up. 'Rachel, hi. Come and sit down.'

'You didn't have to come all the way out here,' I say.

'Actually, I did. I wanted to let you know in person
that you've been totally exonerated.'

I'm not sure what to say. Finally, I opt for, 'Thanks.'

'Your old school backed you up. And apparently
you're not the first member of the cast to have been
bullied by Rebecca. Also, our technical department hired
some amazing people who specialise in retrieval of

information. It's amazing what they can do nowadays. Anyway, suffice it to say, Rebecca French will not be on the show much longer. I know I can trust you to keep that to yourself.'

I nod. Shouldn't this be sweeter?

'Do you've any questions? Anything you want to say?'

I'm a complete idiot because my questions are for Rebecca. What'll she do now? Who'll employ her? Ireland's a small place. She doesn't have a Leaving Cert.

'Not really. No.'

She nods. Then looks at Maisie. 'I need a drink. Why do you live way up here in the boons?'

'To get away from you,' Maisie deadpans.

TWENTY-THREE
Cinderella

'Thursday night is the IFTAs,' Maisie says later, over Scrabble. I can't believe I'd forgotten. 'Do you still want to go?' she asks.

The thought of leaving here, even just for a night … 'I don't know. It doesn't seem important any more.'

She nods. Then looks back down at her letters. After a few moments, she smiles and places down a word. It's only 'jugs' but *j*'s are worth eight points and she's put hers on a Double Letter Score. The *s* is on a Triple Word Score and it's stuck onto the end of another word.

'I haven't a hope,' I say.

She looks at me, crossly. 'Of course you've a hope. You're the bookies' favourite. And I for one, would really like to see you hold that award high for everyone who has given you grief to see.'

I smile. 'I was talking about the Scrabble.'

'Oh. The *Scrabble*. No. You haven't a hope.'

After a while, I ask, 'Am I really the favourite?'

'I've even put money on you, though the odds are appalling.'

I smile. 'Thanks.'

'Don't thank me, just win. So are you coming?'

'I don't have a dress.' I can't believe we never spoke to Marsha. Life just seemed to spiral out of control.

'No problem. We'll get you one tomorrow.'

)(

The thought of going back to the city makes me nervous.

'Come in with me in the morning. Entertain yourself. And we'll shop when I've done my scenes.'

'Thanks, Maisie.'

Coming down from the mountains, my phone comes back into coverage. There are messages from everyone. Except Mark. I text back to say I'm fine. I tell Charley the investigation is over. And Jack that Rebecca is being fired. I know he'll enjoy that. Then I switch off the phone.

I've brought my laptop but when we get in to *D4*, I use it to watch music videos on YouTube and play computer games, not to check what people have been saying about me. Progress.

Maisie has just been called on set. Which means she's fifteen minutes before she has to go. I rush out to grab her a coffee in the canteen. And just my luck, Rebecca's coming the other way with one of the cameramen. She doesn't see me and I'm so tempted to turn around. But I force myself to keep going, meet her eyes. Hers are filled with hate. Which is how I know she's already been given her notice.

I don't feel sorry for her now, though, like I did in the mountains, because seeing her brings it all back, everything she's done and how she's the opposite of sorry. She blames me, I know, for getting fired. She'll never see things the way they really are. I smile as I walk past. Because, for once, the bully has got what she deserved and she brought it all on herself. I know that as long as I'm acting there'll always be people like her who'll put me down to push their own agenda. But thanks to Rebecca, I know it won't be personal. It'll be about them not me. And it's something I'll have to live with. Like lots of people do. She's done me a favour. I should tell her. Because she'd so hate to know it.

As soon as Maisie is finished, we go shopping.

I pick out a dark green dress and hold it up. She takes it off me and puts it back on the hanger.

'Think big,' she says. The one she picks is white. It's fitted. And off one shoulder. 'Try it.'

'I don't think it's me.'

'Trust me. It's you.'

I make a face. 'It's too—'

'What?'

'I don't know. Obvious?'

'That is your *exact* problem, right there. For someone so beautiful you put an incredible amount of energy into not being noticed.'

I laugh. 'No I don't.'

She shoves the dress at me. 'Prove it.'

I exaggerate a sigh, take the dress and go to the dressing room. 'We're just wasting time, Maisie.'

I strip to my knickers because that's what you have to do with a dress like this. I put it on, muttering in my head. Then I look in the mirror. It's just a piece of material but it's turned me into something I'm not. I stand staring at myself for a little too long.

Finally, I come out, knowing she's going to say, 'I told you so.'

She smiles. 'Ha!'

I laugh.

'Say it.'

'What?'

'You were right, Maisie.'

I smile. 'You were right, Maisie.'

)(

'Not just about the dress, but about the other thing.'

I can't stop smiling. 'Not just about the dress, but about the other thing.'

'Maisie, you're a genius,' she says.

'Maisie, you're a genius. And I love you.' I give her a hug.

'Don't look now,' she whispers, 'but I think you've a fan club.'

I turn around. People in the shop are staring. A woman asks if they have the same dress in her size. I'm smiling and I don't really want to take it off.

'Right,' Maisie says. 'Hurry up and get out of it. We need to get you shoes.'

'Magic shoes?'

'*Magic* shoes.' She winks.

I hurry back to change. When I come out again, Maisie is taking out her credit card.

'No *way*!' I say.

'Let me do this,' she bosses, pushing her way ahead of me to the counter.

I catch up and take out my wallet.

She looks at me and her whole face softens. 'Let me have this,' she says, quieter than I've ever heard her speak. 'I lost my little girl.'

I throw my arms around her and squeeze her so tightly. It's only then I realise that, without Rebecca, I'd never have what I have with Maisie. And I wouldn't change that.

Thursday night. We're in the auditorium after a gala meal, everyone is dressed up and facing the stage. I feel like Cinderella – I even have glass slippers. We've had our hair and make-up done professionally. Damien insisted on coming to the cottage. He spent his time apologising. And calling himself naïve. Eventually, Maisie told him to just shut up and make me wonderful. Now, she's on my right and Charley's on my left. That helps. Because even though I thought the IFTAs didn't matter any more, now that I'm here, they do.

The very first award is the one I'm up for, Actress in a Supporting Role in Television.

Good, Jesus. Colin Farrell is presenting it. Sarah will die when she hears this.

'And the nominees are ...'

The lights go down.

They start to show clips of us. It's a reminder of how tough the competition is. I'm shown last. It's my very first scene. Where I say nothing. There are so many better ones they could have used. And that's how I know I haven't won. They haven't bothered. *It's fine,* I think.

There's polite applause. This is not a major award. And most people here are just waiting for their turn. As the lights go up again, the cameras zoom in on all four of us. I swallow and keep very still. On stage, Colin Farrell is opening the envelope.

'And the winner is ...' he pauses – for ages. 'Rachel ...'

There's another Rachel and I'm thinking, *OK, it's her.*

'Dunne,' he says.

I turn to Maisie in shock. It's like my brain's frozen. 'Is it me?'

She's beaming and nodding like a psycho. 'It's you. Now get your spindly shoulders up there.'

I can't help it, I start to laugh. I hug her. Then get up. I can't pass Charley without hugging her too. Then I'm in the aisle. My knees are shaking. Actually shaking like little islands on jelly. I'm breathing funny. I feel the cameras on me and every head turned in my direction. I can't believe they picked me.

I reach the stage. I lift my dress to climb the steps. I think of Meryl Streep, losing a shoe at the Baftas. I curl my toes to hold mine on. I reach the podium. And Colin Farrell. He is even better looking in real life.

'Hi,' I say, by accident.

Everyone laughs.

'Hi,' he says and winks, like he's trying to say everything's OK.

He hands me the award. He actually kisses my cheek. *Never* washing it again.

'Congratulations,' he says, then turns to the cameras. 'Watch this space, people. This lady's going to be *big*.'

I'm torn between not believing it and thinking, *Eat that, Rebecca*.

I turn to face everyone. Because now I have to say something. Christ.

'Eh, hi.' I smile.

They laugh again.

'Eh, I just want to say thank you so much to everyone who voted for me.' I clear my throat. 'And to everyone in *D4* for believing in me, especially Emily Liston.' I look down at her, sitting on the other side of Maisie. 'I want to thank my family and friends. My agent, Charley Waters. Who is the best. But I especially want to thank Maisie Morrin, who has been the best friend to me.' My voice wobbles and my eyes well up. I better get out of here before I do a Gwyneth. But Maisie is raising a power fist. So I raise the award.

I grin all the way back down. I could skip.

The ceremony goes on all night. Every so often, I look at my award, to prove I didn't imagine it. Charley whirls

)(

me around, introducing me to directors, producers, talent scouts, casting agents. People look at the dress and see someone I'm not. A star. Or maybe I am a star. For one night. I wonder if Cinderella, travelling back in the carriage, knowing it was going to end, thought it was worth it. Bet she did.

It is the best feeling climbing into Graham after our victories and heading back into the mountains.

The show didn't go out live, but the results must have gone out on Twitter or something because when I turn on my phone, there are missed calls and texts from everyone. And I realise something great. I'm happy on my own. But I'm not on my own. My phone bleeps again.

Oh, God, it's a text from Mark.

It's just him saying congratulations. I imagine what the words would be if we were still together. 'Caecilius superbus est.' I smile. Then burst into tears.

Maisie looks over. 'Are you OK?'

'Yeah, sorry. Sometimes I just miss my boyfriend.'

'Do you want to go home?'

'It's not that kind of miss. We split up.'

She reaches over and squeezes my hand. 'There's always Colin Farrell.'

Next day at around five, Maisie comes home.

'They want us to go on the *Late Late Show*.'

'The two of us?'

She nods.

'*Why?*'

'Two people from *D4* who won IFTAs. One at the winter of her career; the other, the springtime.'

I make a face. 'Winter? They didn't say that, did they?'

She laughs. 'They actually did. That's what happens when you get the geriatric award. So, what do you think, do you want to do it?'

'Not if they're talking about winters.'

She laughs. 'It would be good for your career. And I've a very thick skin. There is one thing though,' she says, her face growing serious. 'They might ask about the newspaper article? I don't think they actually would – it's not that kind of show – but you should be prepared for anything.'

I consider that. And realise something huge. I'm not afraid any more. 'Then I can set the record straight.' I look at her. 'I'm tired of hiding, Maisie. Whatever they ask, I'll answer.'

'Good,' she says, like my problems are over.

TWENTY-FOUR
Quiet

It's well into the *Late Late Show*. I'm in a hospitality room with Maisie, waiting to go on. A rock star is draped on the couch opposite, halfway through a pint of Guinness. There's a bunch of people with him, also dressed like rock stars. They listen to everything he says. He doesn't listen back. They don't seem to mind, they look like they're used to it. He gets called to go on. He brings his pint with him. They wish him luck and, when he's gone, order more drinks.

Ever since we got here, people have been telling me I'll be 'grand'. Which makes me nervous.

'Tell me I'm going to be crap,' I say to Maisie.

'You're going to be crap.'

'Thanks.' I feel better already. Because now I've something to prove wrong.

There's a huge flat-screen TV high on the wall. We watch the rock star turn on a charm that wasn't there before. For the first time, he looks like he's enjoying himself.

The door to the hospitality room opens. A guy in his twenties in denims and a checked shirt comes to get us. I look at Maisie.

'Don't worry. You'll be crap,' she says.

⚸

The guy laughs. He brings us out along corridors. My heart is pounding and I'm wondering why I'm putting myself through this.

The red 'On Air' sign is on above the backstage door. Once through, we whisper and walk quietly.

A sound guy mikes us up.

Out on set, the rock star's interview is finishing up. I get a jolt of nerves. But then I realise, with relief, he's going to perform his latest hit. I try to focus on the music, just the music.

It's coming to an end.

Oh, God. We're being called out. I take a deep breath. Then we're walking out into the lights. The host, Ryan Tubridy, is standing, waiting, smiling. He shakes our hands, Maisie first. We take our seats, me farthest from him. I catch my breath. I'm facing an audience of real, live people. I can see individual faces. *D4* goes out to hundreds of thousands of people but it never feels that way when you're on set. It's just you and the cast and crew. It's not live. It's not even you. I look at Tubridy and try to pretend it's just him.

He welcomes us, congratulating us on the IFTAs. Then he zones in on Maisie. He asks about the award – her life, her achievements, her big breaks. He doesn't know about the poetry. And I love that she has her secret.

Then, just like that, he turns to me.

'And, Rachel, you're at the other end of your career, just starting out. How are you finding it all?'

'Good.' I can't think of anything else to say. Any time I think of *D4*, I think of Rebecca.

'Must be a challenging role to play. Your character, Naomi, is terminally ill.'

'It's fine.'

'She's also a bully,' he says.

Suddenly, I've something to say. 'Yeah and people think *I* am one because a newspaper reported it. But I'm not a bully. I never was. The person who said I bullied her, bullied me.'

'Wow,' he says in surprise, like he'd given up on me talking and now this.

'I wish people treated bullies in real life the way they've treated me since Naomi started bullying. They should be isolated, blanked. They should be expelled – instead of the people they bully being forced to move school. And they should keep getting expelled until they can't get into a school unless they treat people properly. That's the way it should be.'

'When were you bullied?' he asks.

'In fifth and sixth class.'

'For *two years*?'

'It's not unusual.'

'How did it start?'

'I was moved back a year.'

He doesn't ask why, which means he thinks I'm dumb. Which is better than blaming my parents on national TV.

He asks me to tell him what else the bullies did. And I do. In detail. There's complete silence in the studio.

'Didn't the school help?'

'Not really, no.'

'Your parents?'

'They tried. But if the school isn't behind you, you can pretty much forget it. In the end, I just pretended to my parents it had stopped. It was easier.'

)I(

'How did you feel?'

'How the bullies wanted me to feel – stupid, sad, a loner, a loser.'

'But it stopped eventually?'

'Yeah.'

'How?'

'I tried to commit suicide.' I hear people breathe in. While I'm breathing out.

'What age were you?' Tubridy asks quietly.

'Twelve.'

'*Twelve*?' He looks like he can't believe it. Then he asks me about it.

And while I'm telling him, I realise something. I have to talk to Jack.

For a moment, there's total silence.

Tubridy clears his throat. 'There might be people watching who are going through what you've been through. Have you anything to say to them?'

I look directly at the camera. Because this is important. My one chance to make a difference.

'I'd say, hold on. You think that things will never get better, but they do. And when they do, you can't believe what you almost did. When people are trying to ruin your life, you have to fight. You can't take it personally. Because it's not personal. It's about power. They don't care who they pick on as long as it's someone. You have to believe that you are better than them and you deserve better. And I know that's so easy to say. It's so hard when you're in the middle of it, when you feel so alone. And that's why I think people shouldn't have to face it alone. The only way to stop bullying is together. By not tolerating it in our society. We need to treat it like a crime – an actual crime. And it is. It's stealing. Stealing a person's happiness, stealing their confidence, stealing their lives. The most important things we have. From the time they're tiny, kids need to be told that they're as good as everyone else. They need to know that bullying is wrong – and it will be dealt with, that all they have to do is speak up. Right now, so many people are out there, too afraid to say anything in case they get it worse for speaking up. What I'd say is, speak up. At the very beginning. And if your school doesn't back you up, then move. Start over with new people. It's just bad luck they picked you.' I stop. And take a breath.

'Did you move school, Rachel?'

I nod. Then I look at the camera. 'And I don't know if my friends Alex and Sarah are watching, but they were real friends to me when I needed friends.' I look back at Tubridy.

'Rachel,' he says. 'I know you've so much more to say. And I know that people are listening. Unfortunately we've run out of time. Maybe you'll come back and talk to us again?'

I nod, then shrug. 'Sure.'

There's a huge round of applause. I look at the audience for the first time. And I can't believe it. One by one, they're starting to stand up. Till they're all standing. While still clapping. And I know that this is because everyone knows someone who has been bullied. And they want something done.

Tubridy wraps up the show. He hugs Maisie and me when we stand up and go.

'Thanks for being so brave,' he says to me.

I don't feel brave. I feel free. I've nothing to hide

anymore. But I need to talk to my parents. I need to talk to Jack. I really need to go home.

I walk out with Maisie. She puts an arm around me and gives me a little squeeze.

'You were a sensation.'

I look at her. 'Maisie, I have to go home.'

She smiles. 'Good.'

I think of her going back in Graham on her own. 'Will you be OK?'

She winks. 'I think I'll manage.'

'Thank you so much for everything. Without you … I don't know.'

'I just provided a bolt hole. No more.'

'Yes more.' I hug her.

'See you Monday,' she says when we finally pull back.

I *love* that we'll still be sharing a dressing room. 'See you Monday.'

'Till then, how're you fixed for Internet Scrabble?'

I smile. 'That would be amazing.'

We take our time leaving. Finally, we walk out of the TV Centre. It's cold and our breaths fog up.

'I'll drop you home,' Maisie says.

'It's fine, I'll get a taxi.'

'Rachel!' comes a voice from behind me.

I turn. It's Mark, walking towards us.

'On second thoughts,' she says. 'I'm going to say goodbye.' She winks and whispers, 'Good luck.' Then she's gone. Leaving me standing, facing the guy who walked away. So easily.

'Hey,' he says when he gets to me.

'What are you doing here?'

He shrugs. 'Don't know.' He shoves his hands into his pockets. 'Saw you on TV, got in Millie. Here I am.'

We stand looking at each other. I hope he can't see that I still love him.

'You were good,' he says.

'Thanks.'

We're quiet again.

'If I'd known all those things she did to you, I *might* have actually killed her. And I'm not joking, this time.' He sounds angry, hurt. For me. Which would probably be nice if he hadn't let me go. 'Do you want a lift?'

It seems weird. 'I don't know.'

'Since I'm here. And I'm going your way.'

I shrug. 'OK, if you like.'

We walk side by side to the car. His car, now. He's looking at his feet. I don't talk. Just watch my breath frosting up. Bizarrely, I think of our bulbs and hope they'll be OK.

He looks up. 'I think you helped people.'

'It takes more than someone on TV.'

'I don't know. I wish someone like you was on TV when I was going through it.'

I stare at him. 'You were bullied? *When*?'

He makes a face like it doesn't matter. 'Before we moved back to Ireland.'

'Why didn't you tell me?' I start, but I know the answer. He wanted to leave it behind.

But it's not his answer. 'I'm a guy. We're supposed to be the tough ones.' He smiles. 'I didn't want you to think I was a wimp.'

'Mark, some of the *best people* are bullied,' I joke.

He smiles.

'What happened?' I ask him.

He looks away for a moment, then back. 'They were my friends. They just turned on me. Don't know why, but it was suddenly like they didn't want me around any more. And they kept reminding me about it. The thing about friends is they really know how to hurt you.'

'I'm sorry.'

'It was only for eight months. You had two whole years of it.'

'How did it stop?'

'I started to pretend I didn't care. I hung out with other people. Became the class clown, the joker.' He looks at me apologetically. 'It's become a bit of a habit.'

Wow, I think. It's like everything's changed.

'They backed off eventually. Anyway, it's over now.'

'You sure?' I ask.

'What d'you mean?'

'It wasn't over for me till tonight. Well, it still isn't. I need to talk to my parents. And Jack. But it will be. Then. I hope.'

We get to the car. I run my hand along Millie's bonnet. Remembering. Then we get in.

He looks at me. 'Do you ever think that good can come from bad?'

I shrug. 'Sometimes.'

'For me, it was good that we split up.'

Ow.

'I never thought I was good enough for you, Rache. All the time we were together. Before that, really. I don't know how I ever got the courage to ask you out.'

'What?' I whisper, not believing.

)(

'Until you said you wanted to see other people, I was the most easy-going person in the world. I was cool about everything – even things I wasn't cool about. I was the class clown, hiding behind jokes, never being serious about anything. Those scenes with Josh – I encouraged you all the way – I couldn't watch them. And then, finally, because of you, I had to make a stand. I couldn't watch you with other people. It would have killed me. And if I wasn't good enough for you, then I had to let you go. But the thing is, everything's changed. By standing up to someone I loved, it meant that I can stand up to anyone now. You kind of set me free.'

'*Loved*?'

He looks at me as if to say, 'of course'.

'Hang on. You *loved* me?'

'You know I did.'

'*No*. I told you I loved you and you said *nothing*.'

'Yeah, because it would have been a response.'

'*What*?'

'I didn't want the first time I said "I love you" to be because you'd said it first. Or because we'd just had sex. Or because you were upset. I wanted it to just be, "I love you." Me to you, no reason.'

I'm so completely stunned. By how sweet that is. By how wrong I got it. But mostly by the fact that, after all this time, Mark Delaney is as sensitive as I am.

'I was going to tell you, the next day. But that was the day you announced you wanted to see other people.' A look of hurt passes across his face. 'For the record, it was my first time too.'

'What?'

'You weren't the only virgin. People get better, you know?'

'You think I wanted to see other people because you weren't *good* enough? Mark! I said it because I thought you didn't love me.'

He looks confused.

'That day. I wanted to end it because I thought you didn't love me. But when I opened my mouth all the stuff about seeing other people just poured out.'

He stares at me. 'So it *wasn't* that I was no good?'

'No!'

'Then why were you so upset, after?'

'Because you never said you loved me.'

He puts the car into gear and takes off. Fast. We're both totally quiet. No music. Just the sound of the engine, and my heart thumping. As we drive, I go through everything in my mind. He loved me. And I stopped trusting that. So I hurt him. Insulted him. Made him think he wasn't good enough, which he believed anyway. Jesus.

He pulls up outside my house.

I look at him. 'I'm so sorry.'

For a second he says nothing, then he turns to me. 'Do you know how hard it is not to crack a joke right now?'

I smile.

'Maybe we could start over?' he says.

I'm so relieved. I open my mouth to say yes, but he gets there first.

'Be friends again.'

Friends? I want to say we were never friends, but I'm so shocked that I don't say anything.

Ж

'We could hang out a bit,' he continues. 'Get to know each other properly, no secrets, without all that boyfriend–girlfriend stuff getting in the way.' He smiles innocently as he crushes my heart.

I tell myself it's logical. But for once, I don't want logic. I want Mark. More than ever. He, loved, me.

'Cool,' I say. I start to open the door.

'Millie missed you,' he says.

I feel like asking, 'How about Caecilius?' But I just smile and get out of the car.

TWENTY-FIVE

}|{

I let myself in and go straight up to Jack's room. There's a crack of light under his door. I knock and go in. He's in bed with his laptop. He looks up.

'Hey!'

'Hey yourself,' I say, smiling.

'You were great.'

'You saw?' I ask, walking in and sitting on the bed.

'Everyone saw. The phone never stopped ringing.'

'I never thanked you, Jack.'

He looks at me for a long time. 'You think I wanted thanks?'

'I wouldn't be here if it wasn't for you.'

Another long pause. 'Sometimes I wonder if I did the right thing.'

'What d'you mean?'

'I took the choice from you. Stopped you doing what you wanted to do. Like, what right did I have?'

'Jack, you saved my life. I am *so* glad you did. And *so* sorry I never told you that.' I think of him fighting for me, standing up for me, and I start to get upset.

'It's OK,' he says.

'No. It's not. I hated you for stopping me. I hated that you knew. I hated everything back then. And that was OK. I was messed up. But it's never been the same between us since you found me like that. And that's because of me. I should have thanked you. I should have made it OK.'

He shakes his head. 'I should never have let you copy my stuff. If I hadn't, you'd never have been moved back. None of this would ever have happened.'

I smile, remembering. 'It was our rebellion. Us against the world, remember?'

'It was dumb. If I'd known what was going to happen—'

'How could you?'

'I'm the oldest.'

'By six minutes.'

'Six and a half.' He looks at me. 'I left you behind.'

'It wasn't your idea to hold me back.'

'I bought into the individuality thing. I thought I was squishing you. Blocking you out. Otherwise I'd have put up a fight. I thought they were right.'

'So did I.'

'Were they?'

'I don't know.'

'It was hard,' he says.

'Like losing a part of yourself.' We'd shared everything. Birthday parties. Friends. Illnesses. I hadn't wanted a party when I was eleven, so he didn't have one either. When he asked if I was OK, I told him I was. What was the point in going through the pain of becoming an individual if he bailed me out? I look at him, as realisation hits.

'They were wrong. We always were individuals.' All the memories that came to me in the mountains come flooding back. Me looking at stones on the beach while he tore around. Me cooking while he played with trains. Me trying to get him to act in my home-produced plays

)(

and failing. 'You were stronger than me, bolder, more outgoing, a better plotter of pranks.' I smile. 'But I was me, I was always me.'

'I should have protected you though. Then – and now. I did try this time. For what it's worth.'

'I know you did. And I'm just saying, not accusing, that trying to protect someone is like saying they can't do it themselves. And I can. I can handle myself now. I'll never let myself be bullied by anyone ever again. I swear to God.'

'I believe you,' he says, like he's afraid of me. And we laugh.

'When are you coming home?'

'I am.'

'Good. So I'm having a problem with this guy in school, maybe you could sort him out for me.'

I roll up my sleeves. 'Just give me the name.'

We smile at each other.

'Where's Mum?'

'Downstairs, ironing.'

I check my phone. 'At *half-twelve*?'

'After you were on TV, she just got up and started cleaning. When there was nothing left to clean, she took out the iron.' He looks at me. 'She'll be glad you're home.'

I go down to the kitchen. Mum looks up from the ironing board.

'Rachel!' she says. She puts the iron down, hurries over and hugs me.

'I missed you so much.' She holds me out to look at me. She's been crying. 'You were amazing tonight. So *strong*.'

)K(

I look her in the eye. 'I *am* strong, Mum.'

'I know, pet.'

'No you don't. And neither does Dad. You worry about me. And then you fight. And I worry about that. And it's just this big cycle of worry. And that's why I had to go away.'

She looks shocked.

'You have to stop,' I say. 'You have to trust that I can handle things.'

She nods, her face serious.

But I have to make sure. 'I'll never do anything stupid like that ever again. OK? Ever. And I'll never put up with any shit from anyone either. It's over. It really is over.'

She takes a deep breath and her whole body deflates.

'So you trust me, right?'

She looks into my eyes. 'I trust you.'

'Good.' She hugs me again and I let myself relax in her arms. Finally, I pull back. 'Is Dad awake?'

'I think so. Go on up.'

I knock and go in. He sits bolt upright. He turns on his bedside lamp. His hair is sticking straight up. I feel like laughing. 'Rachel? Are you OK?'

'Fine. I'll talk to you in the morning.'

'No, no. Stay.' He looks like a little boy in his plain white T-shirt and sticky-up hair.

I say to him exactly what I said to Mum. But I'm stronger with him, firmer.

He looks all emotional. Then he says, 'When I was watching you on TV, I realised something ... You don't need us any more, do you?'

I smile. 'Well, I need your money. And, like, a roof over my head, and that.'

He laughs.

But the great thing is, I know that if I had money I could leave tomorrow and survive. And there's something amazing about that.

In bed, I turn on my phone. It bleeps with messages and missed calls.

From Sarah: 'I can't believe how awful they were. I can't believe you almost . . . I cried, Rache.)l('

From Alex: 'Always knew you were the strong one.)l('

From Peter Sweetnam: 'And I thought *Naomi* was a survivor.'

From half my class: 'I didn't know.' 'Thank you for telling my story.' 'Go you.' 'What's Tubs like?' 'Where did you get your top?'

There's even one from Amy Gilmore: 'You rock.'

Another from Sarah: 'I'm soooo sorry.)l('

And then, from a blocked number comes: 'U r such a loser.' I smile. Someone's obviously jealous.

It's too late to call anyone. So I text Sarah and Alex, telling them I'm home and asking if they want to come over tomorrow.

'Hey, Uggs, did you miss me?' I snuggle him under the quilt with me. I remember a time Mark put him under the quilt, with his tiny arms out over it, making him look like he'd just had sex. He kept putting his arm towards his mouth as if he was having a smoke. Why didn't I keep on believing that he loved me? Why didn't I hold on? Why didn't I have the confidence? Then I realise, I let

)(

Rebecca French break it. I make a promise to myself that that will never happen again.

Next day, Alex, Sarah and Maggie call over. Do babies really grow that *fast*?

'Oh, my God, she's got a tooth!' A tiny, bright white square. *So* cute.

Alex takes off her coat. Maggie's striped babygro says: 'I've done nine months inside.'

I burst out laughing.

Maggie looks hurt. And she's only four months. I put my face up to hers. 'I'm sorry, Maggie May. I'm not laughing at you. I'm laughing with you.' And I swear to God, she gives me a look that says, 'I'm not laughing.' So I tickle her. Her laugh is like energy. I look at Alex. 'How could she have got even more gorgeous?'

'That would be *my* genes.'

'Let's go upstairs.'

'I can't believe you mentioned us on TV,' Sarah says. 'I cried.' She touches her heart.

'You guys saved my life. Of course I mentioned you.'

'We didn't save your life,' Alex says. 'We liked you.'

'When I needed to be liked.'

'We weren't doing you a favour, Rache,' Alex says. 'If we didn't like you, we wouldn't have hung out with you.'

'Still —'

'Still, nothing.'

'I can't believe Rebecca was such a total *bitch*.' Sarah glances at Maggie. 'Witch. Total witch.' But it's too late. Maggie's laughing like she's just decided it's going to be her first word.

'She's being written out of the show.'

⅜

'Cow,' Sarah says, then looks at Maggie. 'What does the cow say? What does the cow say? Moo. Moo. The cow says moo, doesn't he?'

'She,' Alex says.

'She, jeez.'

I laugh.

'How much longer do you think you'll have on *D4*?' Alex asks.

'I don't know. Josh is leaving at the end of the month. So probably not much longer.'

'You'll get other stuff,' Sarah says optimistically.

'I'm not worried.'

'We missed you,' Alex says. 'You're the glue that holds us together.' She says it in a corny voice and we all laugh.

'I don't think we were the only ones who missed you.' Sarah raises her eyebrows.

'If you're talking about Mark, he just wants to be friends.'

'I don't believe *that*,' Alex says.

'What if you die next year?' Sarah asks.

I shrug. 'Then we'll die friends.'

'But you're mad about each other.'

'You know what? It's better this way. I need a break from all that relationship stuff. I just want to chill for a while.'

Sarah raises an eyebrow.

'So! What's been happening while I was away?' I ask quickly.

'Ab-sol-utely nothing,' Alex says.

And I know she means Louis.

TWENTY-SIX
Sleeping Beauty

On Monday morning, our first class is Double Biology. At the top of the lab, the teacher is going through the experiment, reading aloud from our textbook. I'm looking at a tuft of hair sticking up at the top of Mark's head, wanting to flatten it down and watch it spring back up again.

'Could Rachel Dunne please come to the principal's office,' announces a voice over the intercom.

People turn in my direction. I get the usual, 'Oooohs' and 'Raaachels'.

I get up, not caring.

In his office, I sit looking at the principal, remembering that scene in *Ferris Bueller's Day Off*, where Ferris breaks his girlfriend out of school by pretending to be her dad. It's the kind of thing Mark would do – or would have done, if I'd let him. He would have been right.

'I saw you on the *Late Late Show* on Friday night,' he says. 'You were inspirational.'

He called me out of class for this?

'As you know, we run an anti-bullying programme in the school. I'd love you to become involved. Your story, your *attitude*, are so powerful.' He looks at me hopefully. 'Would you speak to a class? Maybe every class, in time?'

'What would I say?' There's no point unless I make a difference.

'Just tell your story in the same honest way you did on TV. Take questions. That's it.'

'And you think that will change things?'

'I think we need to come at it from a few angles. We're about to review our anti-bullying policy at the school. Would you consider sitting in on our meetings?'

I smile. 'I would.'

When I get back to class, everyone's in pairs, dead frogs in front of them, scalpels in hand. Some are tucking in enthusiastically; others, looking pretty white, are standing back. I look to see if anyone's missing a partner. There is one person standing alone, back from the bench holding a scalpel, the frog in front of him, untouched. He's looking at me and mouthing the word, 'Help.'

Smiling, I go over to Mark.

'I thought you'd never get here,' he says.

I take the scalpel from him and step forward. 'Poor little guy,' I whisper. Then I cut him open.

'Aw, crap,' Mark says. He's gone kind of green.

'Don't faint,' I warn.

He faints.

At exactly the same time, two other people drop.

Everyone delightedly abandons their frogs.

I kneel beside Mark and open his tie. He looks so adorable, all pale and vulnerable, his eyelashes making long shadows on his face. It's so hard not to bend down and kiss him. Sleeping Beauty.

I control myself – but I do flatten the tuft of hair. It springs back up just like I imagined. I even know his hair.

I open his top button.

)I(

'Steady,' one of his rugby friends says.

'Just throw cold water on him,' Peter Sweetnam says.

'No!' He's not soaking my just-friend.

Finally, Mark opens his eyes.

I smile. 'Hello!'

'Hello!' everyone else mocks.

I try not to laugh.

'I didn't faint, did I?'

'Yup.' ''Fraid so.' 'Sure did,' come a load of male voices.

I just raise my eyebrows and nod.

He jumps up. 'Oh crap,' he says as he wobbles. He grabs the bench and manages to stay up. He is the colour of chalk.

The teacher is beside us now, having dealt with the girls first. 'Take him outside. Get him some air. But keep him sitting, OK?'

I nod. 'Come on, let's go.'

Out in the corridor we sit, side by side, on red plastic chairs.

'Frogs will never be the same,' he says wistfully, like they were his favourite animal.

'Poor frogs. Minding their own business.'

'Don't make me go back in there,' he jokes.

I smile. 'Suits me.'

It feels like nothing's changed, like it's just the two of us and we still love each other. I look at him.

'How's this going to work, this friends thing?' I ask.

'Oh, right.' He scratches his head.

I laugh. 'It's OK, I was joking.'

'No. We should meet up. Definitely. Go for coffee or something.'

'Honestly, I was only messing.'

'Jitter Mug. After school.'

I shrug. 'OK.'

At lunch, I sit with Alex and Sarah.

'Want to come to mine later?' Alex asks.

'I meeting Mark for coffee.'

They look instantly hopeful.

'As *friends*,' I say.

'Yeah, right,' Sarah says.

I glance over at him. He's laughing at something someone's said. I want to know what it is, which is not good. Maybe we shouldn't meet for coffee. Maybe I should move schools and never see him again.

'Hey, do you guys want to come?' I ask.

'Eh, *no*,' Alex says.

Sarah just smiles.

At the Jitter Mug, Mark orders me a fruit smoothie without asking what I want and pays without thinking. Our usual seat is free and he heads for it.

'This is weird,' I say, sitting down.

'Yeah,' he says, like he's just remembered. He looks out the window at the sea, which is wild.

I search my brain for something to say.

'I was thinking about *Ferris Bueller's Day Off* today.'

'I always wanted to be Ferris.'

I was right! 'He *is* kind of like you.' Oh, God, did that sound flirty? It wasn't meant to.

He looks at me. 'Yeah, well, you're a hell of a lot better looking than his girlfriend.'

Do just-friends say things like that to each other? Would Alex or Sarah say it? OK, they probably would. It wouldn't mean as much, though. God, this was a mistake.

After a silence, Mark clears his throat. 'I was wondering. Was Rebecca French as bad, second-time round?'

I tell him about BatmanReturns. And about trying to turn Sarah and Alex against me.

'Why do people like that exist?' he asks, squinting. 'Do they ever provide anything? Or do they just take?'

Exactly, I think. 'She's been fired.'

'You could probably sue her for libel or slander or whatever. Do you remember that talk we had in TY?'

I smile. I always thought he was the opposite of me. Now he's thinking like me. 'Yeah, I don't want the hassle, the publicity. I just want to get on with it now.'

He nods. Then, he's squinting again. 'How do people change? Grow from cute, innocent babies into monsters?'

I feel like saying, *I know.* 'Maybe we infect each other, or something?' I say instead. 'You know what I'd love to do? I'd love to teach the entire world of small children that if someone's mean to you, it makes *them* a lesser person, not you.'

'At least we'll know that for our children. Not *our* children. Together,' he rushes, actually blushing. 'Just, you know, our separate children.'

I laugh. 'Yes, Mark.'

'Shut up. You know what I mean.'

Unfortunately. I do.

'The principal wants me to talk about bullying.'

'To who?' he asks, surprised.

'All the classes, eventually.'

)(

'Are you going to do it?'

'Yeah. I can't give out about no one helping if I don't do something myself.'

He smiles. 'Careful,' he says, 'or I'll start thinking you're better than me again.'

I want to kiss him.

We talk till the Jitter Mug's closing. And laugh when we realise it is.

In the *D4* canteen next day, I'm finishing lunch and going over the conversation with Mark in my head for the hundredth time. I'm smiling at the whole 'our children' thing. I'm thinking maybe we could get back together. If we stay friends, keep seeing each other maybe . . .

Josh is pulling out the chair opposite me.

'Hello, Mr Hollywood. Still talking to us amateurs?'

'It's killing me but, yeah.'

'Two more weeks.'

'And counting. Hey, what did you think of Rebecca's quote in the *Evening Herald*?'

'What quote?'

'Oh, I thought you knew.' He looks awkward.

'What did she say?'

'It was pathetic. So obvious really.'

'Josh!'

'Something like …' He makes his voice all girly. '"Rachel's so *sweet*. When she was nominated for the IFTA, she said *I* should have been picked because *I'm* a better actress."'

I smile. 'You're such a good mimic.'

'You're not pissed off?'

And I don't want to sound smug or anything but, 'Who's got a job and who hasn't?'

'True. Have you started looking around for other work yet?'

'Nah. I'm going to take a break for a while.' Be a normal person.

Later, I'm called to Emily's office.

'Rachel, I just wanted to let you know that you'll be finishing with us at the end of the month.'

Even though I knew it was coming, it's still a shock.

'That you've stayed with us so long is a testament to your acting. You were so good, we kept writing you in. We'd have made your role more long-term – somehow – if Josh wasn't leaving. But he is. So that storyline is over. Our plan is for Naomi to die and for Josh to commit suicide. A modern day Romeo and Juliet.'

I nod. The storyline will generate loads of publicity. There's only one problem: 'Naomi's condition is going to have to get worse very fast.'

She nods. 'She's going to get MRSA.'

It's like a punch to the chest – that's what killed Shane. I can't let it happen.

'How about you really go down the Romeo and Juliet route? Naomi commits suicide first.'

She considers it.

I help her along. 'She's not the kind of person to go out without a fight. She'd want to do it on her own terms. I know Naomi.' So well now.

She nods slowly. 'I'll talk with the team. It would be very dramatic. But we shouldn't shy away from that.

〉〈

Leave it with me.' She looks at me. 'I'm going to miss you around here.'

Funny thing is, it feels like my time's up. Like I've learned all I can, got all I can. And it's time to move on – which is great, because I've always dreaded leaving.

TWENTY-SEVEN
Crunchie

I'm in *D4* all the following week. Dying. It's actually a relief to go back to school. I open my locker, after our last class, thinking, *Thank Crunchie it's Friday*.

Mark passes by. 'Have a good weekend.'

I smile. 'Thanks. You too.' So formal. For us.

He starts to walk off, then stops and turns back. 'Don't suppose you want to do something tomorrow?'

I try not to look enthusiastic. 'Like what?'

'I don't know.' He thinks for a moment. 'Bowling's quick, in case you've to go somewhere after.'

I'd spend the whole day with him if I could. 'OK, yeah, sure.'

We arrange to meet at two in Stillorgan.

I take ages to get ready. I wear skinny jeans and a hoodie he once said he liked. I put on just enough make-up to look like I don't have any on. I half-straighten my hair, then tie it up. So much effort to look like I didn't try. But then he knows me so well, he'll probably see right through me anyway.

We meet at Stillorgan Bowl. He's sitting on the steps outside, waiting. He's got a new hoodie. Purple with bright green writing. It suits him. A lot. He stands up. It feels wrong, not hugging or kissing, just standing there,

)(

saying, 'Hey.' All this awkwardness, like a first date. I tell myself to chill. We can be friends.

We go inside. Without touching. Without talking. I can't think of anything to say. It's weird being nervous with Mark.

At the till, he tries to pay. This time I'm ready.

'It's OK,' I say, handing over a twenty.

He looks at me.

I shrug. 'Friends pay for themselves.'

'OK,' he says, like he's agreeing to new rules.

'Can we put up the sides?' I ask.

'No.'

'What? Why not? I'm totally crap without sides.'

'I know. It's hilarious.'

'You know what? I'm fine with no sides,' I say indignantly. 'In fact, I'm a bowling ninja.'

He laughs.

'Let's put money on it,' I say. 'Twenty quid says I win.'

'It's OK.'

'No. Come on. I'm loaded. I'm a working woman. At least I am till the end of next week.'

He looks shocked. 'You're finished?'

'Yup.'

'Damn.'

'No. It's fine.'

'Let's get the sides,' he says.

'I don't want your pity,' I say dramatically.

I'm not totally hopeless. I've had two accidental strikes. No idea how, or I'd do it again. There's a bunch of cool Asians beside us. They are amazing. They've all this technique. I try to ignore them, but can't help watching in admiration. It's my turn now. I get up and wait for my favourite ball to pop back. Then try to use some of that technique. It starts off like it's got potential, then drops into the side and rolls away.

'Bums,' I say and turn around. Oh, my, God! I stare at Mark as I walk back. 'You were looking at my ass.'

'No I wasn't,' he says, like he's horrified.

'You *so* were. I caught you.'

He gets up and reaches for a ball. 'I'm a guy. Occupational hazard.'

No way. 'If I was a granny would you have been looking at my ass?'

He makes a disgusted face, then takes off with the ball. I sit watching him. Just before he throws the ball, I shout, 'Nice ass.'

He bursts out laughing and messes up his shot. He's still grinning when he comes back to take his second shot.

'What are you waiting for?' I ask.

'My lucky ball to come back.'

I roll my eyes.

This time he knocks three skittles.

'Hard luck,' I say, grinning.

I collect my lucky ball, go up, swing it, then turn suddenly to catch him out.

'What?' he asks.

'Just checking.'

He holds his hands up like he's innocent.

I shake my head then take my shot, hoping so hard that he still fancies me.

We play two games. He wins both.

'You were lucky,' I tease, not wanting to go.

'Maybe. Or maybe you were crap.'

)(

I hit him. Officially, a touch. I snatch back my hand. I'm starting to blush so I walk ahead. Outside, I wait for him. It feels like there's all this tension, like people who fancy each other but haven't got together yet. It feels like something's going to happen. I don't want to speak in case it breaks the magic.

'So,' he says.

'So.'

'That was fun.'

I hand him a twenty.

'I'm not taking your money.'

'A bet's a bet,' I say, shoving it at him.

'Yeah, well, I'm not taking it.'

I could try stuffing it in his pocket but I'm not going to risk touching him again.

He looks at the cinema billboard across the way. 'We could blow it on a movie?'

I try not to let him see how happy I am about that. 'Sure. What's on?'

He squints at the billboard. 'Don't know. Want to go over and see?'

'Sure.'

As we walk through the car park, I get a text. I take out my phone. It's Alex. Wondering if I want to call over. Halfway through texting back, I look up to see Mark looking at me.

'What?' I ask.

'If you want to go, it's OK.'

'I don't want to go.'

We get to the cinema and start to check out the movies.

'If you need to be somewhere,' he says. 'I don't mind. We can leave it.'

'I don't need to be anywhere.'

It's like the mood has changed. We pick a movie, buy popcorn and drinks. But he's so quiet, so gloomy, I start to think that this was a mistake, that I imagined the whole thing in the bowling alley. And now I'm gloomy too. We go inside. I wish now we'd just left. Everything's changed.

We get seats up at the back. Like we used to do. Of course, he keeps his legs to himself instead of throwing one over one of mine. The trailers start and I'm insanely aware of him beside me. Every time he moves, I notice. Hand to face. Fingers through hair. Shifting in seat. I'm so freaking stressed.

The movie's just OK.

'So, what did you think?' he asks, afterwards as we're walking out. He seems cheerful again.

I stare at him. It's like we're in two different places. 'It was OK.'

'Just OK?'

'I don't know, Mark.'

'What's wrong?'

I shrug. 'I don't think this friends thing is working out. Maybe we could be friends in a group or at school or something. But not like this . . . I should go.'

He blushes. 'OK.'

I so want to kiss him.

'Do you want a lift?'

'No thanks, it's fine. I'll get a taxi.'

He nods. And looks so alone.

All the way to Alex's I'm trying not to cry. I don't know what happened. What went wrong. All I know is that we'll never get back together now and I was stupid to ever think that we might. 'Somebody That I Used To Know' comes on the radio. I've listened to that song millions of times. Now it is my life.

By the time I get to Alex's, it's six.

'Where were you?' she asks.

'I met Mark.'

'Ooooh,' she says, bouncing her eyebrows around.

'The whole friends thing is crap.'

'What happened?'

'Nothing . . .' I sigh. 'It's just so hard when a person doesn't love you back.'

'Yeah, I know.'

I look at her.

'OK, so I don't just fancy Louis. I love him.'

'Are you *sure*?' I ask, like it's this awful disease. Which, it, is.

'I want to be with him all the time. When I see him, my heart flips. When he's not there, I'm thinking about him.' The classic symptoms. My symptoms. 'I love everything about him, Rache. I love the way he drums the air when he's no sticks. I love the way he sings to Maggie when he thinks I'm not listening. I love the way he nibbles on those freaking carrots. I love the way he never makes a big deal about the stuff he does, like giving up smoking or getting me to go out and have fun. I love the way he's got back into his music, turned his life around. I so love him, Rache.'

I think about everything I love about Mark. The way his hair does it's own thing. The way he frowns when he drives. And zones out when he reads. The way he follows Mum into the kitchen in search of home cooking. The way, at eighteen, he still draws fake eyebrows and wants to test them on the world.

)(

'How do you make a person love you?' Alex asks. 'You don't have, like, a magic potion, do you?'

'If I had, I'd have used it – I'd have given you some, obviously.'

'Maybe if we just tell them we love them anyway,' she says finally.

'That's how I split up with Mark.'

'What? You told him you loved him and he dropped you?' She sounds shocked.

'It's complicated.'

'Well, uncomplicate it for me.'

I do.

'Rachel, he's never said he *stopped* loving you.'

'He wants to be *friends.* He knows I love him. If he still loved me, he'd have asked me out. Today, I thought he *might* have *fancied* me? Then I thought the total opposite. Being friends is just too hard. I told him it wasn't going to work.'

'What did he say?'

I shrug with one shoulder. 'He offered me a lift home.'

'At least he cared how you got home.'

'He didn't argue, though, did he?'

We sit there for ages, just gazing at Maggie sleeping in her cot.

'It'd be so much easier if they'd never fancied us,' Alex says finally.

'I know.'

'And if they weren't so freaking caliente.'

'True.'

'What'll we do?'

'Put them out of our heads,' I say.

'Louis has a gig next Friday. I'll probably die of

)(

frustration watching him up there, banging away on his kit.'

'Don't be such a perv.'

She laughs.

'Does he want us all to come?' I ask.

'He's holding us a place.'

And I get how frustrating that is for her.

TWENTY-EIGHT
Red Dress

My last scene in *D4* is the way I wanted it – and the way Naomi would have wanted it. There will be even more publicity than when we covered bullying. If it helps just one person, it's worth it. I'll miss Naomi. And, now that I'm finishing up, I'll miss *D4*. I'll miss Maisie. Emily. The life.

They throw a party for me and Josh. Which is more like a little fuss – with cake. They show some clips. I remember what was going on at the time. All that stuff with Rebecca. I look at Josh and think how great it must be knowing that, from here on, it's the big time. Or at least a giant step in that direction. After some short official speeches, Emily comes over to me.

'I'm sorry you couldn't stay longer,' she says.

I smile. 'It kind of feels like my time is up.'

'You were one of the most loved and hated characters we've ever had on the show.'

'I felt it,' I joke. Because I can now. She's not my boss any more.

'It was hard for you, sometimes.'

'I learned so much.' About life.

'Well, just so you know, I'll be recommending you to people in the industry. You won't be waiting long for a part.'

)H(

Wow. 'Thank you.'

She actually hugs me. 'I'll be in touch with Charley if I hear of anything.'

'Thanks.'

She goes over to Maisie.

I look at Josh. For a split second, there's no one with him. So I go up to him. It might be my last chance to say goodbye.

'Hey. Just wanted to say good luck.'

He beams like he is seriously happy. And I so get that. 'Here, give us a hug.'

As we hug, he pats my back, which makes me smile.

He pulls back, then whips something from the pocket of his jeans.

I laugh. 'Are you serious? A business card?'

'That's *Hollywood*,' he says in an American accent.

'You'd actually need them, there, wouldn't you?'

'Hey, email me some shots and links to your work. I'll be meeting people out there, talent scouts, casting agents. I'll do what I can.'

'Really? Oh, my God. Thank you so much.'

'Can't promise anything.'

'I know, I know.' It's the thought. And it's such a surprise. He didn't have to. But then I think, not everyone's like Rebecca French. Good people do exist.

'Take it easy,' he says and bangs me on the upper arm. Then he's gone.

People are starting to leave. Maisie comes over and we walk back to the dressing room together.

I start to pack up my stuff. There isn't much.

Maisie watches me. 'I'll miss you around here.'

I stop what I'm doing, look up. 'I'll miss you too. More than anyone. By far.'

)(

She smiles. 'You know, I've been thinking of calling it a day. Taking some time off. Do the Camino.'

'The what?'

'The Camino. It's a pilgrimage in Spain.'

'Are you *religious*?'

She laughs hard. 'No. But after watching Martin Sheen in *The Way*, I've decided that I need adventure. I'm no spring chicken. I've more money than I need. And here I am stuck in a day job.'

'You should do it.'

'I should, shouldn't I? Who knows, I might meet a decent man.' She pauses. 'Or an *indecent* one,' she says, like it's a better option.

I laugh. Then remember the passion in her poems. 'Do it.'

She nods slowly, like she's making her mind up. 'All right. I will.'

'Yay.' I smile and hug her. 'You better get an iPhone, because we are playing Internet Scrabble no matter where you are.'

'Deal.'

In school, Mark avoids me completely. Doesn't even look at me – or even sneak-look. It's like I don't exist. Sometimes I think I've made a mistake, that being friends would be better than this. Then I think, no, at least this is honest. I don't want to be his friend. I wonder how two people who were so together can grow so apart. And how, in that apartness, one of them can still love the other, so freaking much. And hate him at the same time.

On Friday night, Undertow are playing their first real gig. Alex's dad's driver, Mike, drives us into town. Alex is chatting all the way in. Sarah's quiet, the way she goes sometimes, and I know that, for a few minutes, she's forgotten about living till she dies, and is thinking of Shane.

'I hope they fill the venue,' Alex says. 'I think there are some music journalists coming. God, I wish they'd a manager.'

'They'll be great,' I say.

Mike pulls up outside. It's raining and we hurry inside.

The place is mobbed. Louis has kept us a place. This time, though, he doesn't come out to say hello. Alex goes a bit quiet. When they finally come on stage, though, her eyes go straight to him.

I recognise the first song from before – but it's better. It's like they're more comfortable with each other now, more confident. Alex sings along to all the songs but I forgive her. Love, right?

It's well into the concert when they stop playing. The stage goes dark. A spotlight is turned on Louis. Then he looks over to where we're sitting and says, 'This one's for Maggie.'

Alex touches her heart. We all look at each other and smile. It's like our baby is up on stage.

Louis starts up on the drums. Then he is singing – just Louis. And the song isn't just *for* Maggie, it's about her. How she's changed his life. I know that people listening think Maggie is probably some girlfriend somewhere. That she's his little girl makes it so much better.

'Oh, my God,' says Alex. 'Can we tape it? Can we tape it? Who's got their phone?'

I fumble mine on. I hit video and zoom in on Louis. And I don't know if it's because I'm focused so closely

on him and only him but it's like a light going on. I see
everything Alex does. His love for Maggie. The way he's
turned his life around. His passion for music. And his
general hotness. I want what she wants – for him to love
her, for them to get together.

The song ends. There's a second's silence then huge
applause. Someone shouts out his name. But Louis just
sees Alex. He smiles over like only they can really share
this moment. And I think, the way he's looking at her right
now *has to* mean something. Even I have goosebumps. I
switch off the video. And look at Alex. She's smiling up
at him, a tear sneaking down her face.

The stage lights up again and James is back up front. It
hits me, suddenly. They're going to be huge.

When the show's over, Louis comes out to us.

'That was amazing,' Alex says. She looks so excited, so
young. 'I didn't know you could sing.'

'I can't.'

'Or write.'

'Can't either.'

'Eh, hello? That was amazing.'

'That was Maggie. It was different.'

'You can say that again.'

People start crowding around, looking for photos
with Louis, looking for autographs. It's happening so fast
for them. Louis is really generous to everyone but as soon
as he can, he escapes.

We go outside and queue up for our coats. After a
while, my phone goes off. Only it's not my phone. It's
someone with the same ringtone. I can't find mine.
Damn.

'I left my phone inside,' I say. I rush back in.

Already they've started cleaning up. There's a couple

)(

kissing at the door to the stage. I recognise the red dress. But not just the dress – the girl. It's Rebecca. Oh, my God, the guy is Louis. I think of Alex, so excited out there. So freaking in love. Then, I think, if I don't hurry up, she'll come looking for me and see *this*. I dive onto the seat, jabbing my hands down the back. There it is! I grab it and turn to go. Rebecca is walking towards me. Louis is watching her go. He sees me. They both do, at the same time. He looks in total shock. She looks happy.

'Hello, loser,' she says just as she's about to pass.

I don't think, just stick out my foot. She stumbles forward trying to stay up but she's going too fast and after four steps falls onto her hands and knees. It is the most beautiful sight. I don't kick her ass as I pass but I'm so freaking tempted. When I look back, Louis is gone.

'Did you find it?' Alex asks me, all concerned. I want to punch Louis in the face. I know he's not going out with Alex, I know that technically he can kiss whoever he likes. Still, I hoped he'd changed. I hold up my phone.

'Cool,' she says. Then she turns to Sarah. 'You never told me about the song for Maggie.' She touches her heart again.

'I didn't know.'

'If Dad heard it, he'd change his mind about Louis. I know he would.'

I should tell her. I can't, though. Not now. Not when she's so happy. Maybe tomorrow.

Then again, maybe not.

My phone wakes me at ten the next morning. I don't recognise the number.

'We need to talk.'

)(

'Who's this?' I ask, though I'm pretty sure I know.

'It's Louis. Sorry. Got your number from Sarah's phone.'

'What do you want?' I ask coldly.

'Can you meet for coffee?'

'Why?'

'To explain.'

'So explain.'

'Not on the phone. Can you meet up? It's important.'

'For who, you?'

'For Alex – and Maggie.'

I sigh. 'All right. What time?'

'As soon as you're free,' he says, like he's relieved that we're going to talk.

We arrange to meet at twelve in a coffee shop we never go to.

'Rebecca French,' I say when we're sitting. 'I thought you'd have better taste.'

'I do.'

'So why were you snogging her?'

'She was snogging me.'

I laugh and shake my head. Guys.

'Look, I got a message to say my sister was looking for me urgently. I came out and that psycho jumped me. I pushed her off. You saw that, right?'

'No.'

'Well that's what happened.'

Sure, I think.

His eyes narrow. 'You've never liked me, have you?' So now I know why he never looks at me.

'Actually, I'd started to.'

It's like he hasn't heard me. 'Not that it matters what anyone thinks.' His voice softens. 'Except Alex.'

)H(

I look at him.

'Look, don't tell her what happened. Please. I know we're not together, but I don't want her to think there's anyone else – because there isn't and there never will be.'

I stare at him. 'Never?'

'She and Maggie are my life. I'd never do anything to risk that.'

'You love her, don't you?'

He says nothing but his eyes give him away.

'Tell her.'

He shakes his head.

'Why not?'

'She's seventeen. She doesn't want a big heavy relationship in her life. And that's the only kind I'd want with Alex. Anything else would end and I'd lose them both. This way, we stay together, the three of us. We see each other every day. Like a family.'

'She thinks you don't like her.'

He smiles sadly. 'I love her.'

'Explain. I don't know, you could make a pact – if it doesn't work out, you stay friends.'

'Tell me one person who's stayed friends after they've split up.'

I feel like laughing. And crying.

He looks at me for a very long time. 'Don't say anything to her. Please.'

'She loves you, Louis.' I know she'd want me to tell him. 'And you know what Sarah says – live till you die. You could die next year, Louis.'

'Or I could lose them both. Don't say anything, Rachel, please. Especially, don't tell her I love her.'

'You're making a mistake.'

'Maybe.'

)K(

'All right, I won't say anything.' Because there's always the future.

'Thank you.' He looks relieved.

'By the way, you're wrong, Louis. I do like you.' And it if it wasn't for Rebecca I wouldn't know just how much. So, thanks again, Rebecca for being so accidentally helpful. I wonder why she did it. Because she fancied Louis? Or to hurt me by hurting Alex? Whatever her reason, it hasn't worked.

TWENTY-NINE
Cold

Monday morning, Mark comes over to my locker. I'm thinking, *Please let him want to try again. Friends is fine. Friends is better than nothing. Stop, Rachel. You don't want friends.*

'Saw your friend, Josh, has got some big movie deal,' he says.

I look at him in surprise. 'Where did you hear that?'

'He was on the *Late Late Show* on Friday. Didn't you *know*?'

'I never watch the *Late Late*.' He knows that. The bell goes and I turn to get my English books.

'You'll miss him.'

'What?' I turn back with my books.

'I said, you'll miss him.'

'Not really. This is a great chance for him.'

'You don't sound too concerned.'

'About *what*?'

'He's moving to the States.'

'So?'

'You're *not really* going to miss him.'

'No.'

'That's a bit cold.'

)(

I stare at him. 'What's a bit cold?'

'You're not going to miss him.'

'Oh, my God. You're so weird.'

'And *you* are so cold.'

'*What?*'

But he's already walking away. Ahead of him, Sarah and Alex are waiting at the door. I shut my locker and go up to them.

'What was that about?' Alex asks as we walk along the corridor.

'I have *no* clue.'

'He looked upset,' Sarah says.

'I know, it was so weird. He kept giving me a hard time because I wasn't more sorry that Josh was going to the States. He called me *cold*.'

They look at the back of his head as he disappears into class.

Sarah's quiet for a moment, then she turns to me. 'Maybe he was trying to tell you that you were cold to *him*.'

'I was *never* cold to him. It was the total opposite.'

'OK. Then I don't know.'

'That makes two of us.'

'Three,' Alex says.

Monday night at eleven, I get a call.

'You're not going to believe it,' Alex says.

'What?'

'We kissed. We were just watching Maggie fall asleep. It was, like, the most peaceful moment, leaning over the cot, watching her eyelids get heavier and heavier. Next thing I knew we were looking at each other and everything just stopped. Then we were kissing.'

'What happened then?' I ask cautiously.

'He backed off. Totally. Said he wanted to stay friends, not ruin the way things were. So I kissed him again. *Then* – you're not going to believe this – he told me that *I* didn't want a serious relationship. I said, "*Excuse* me, but after Maggie, it's the *only* kind of relationship I want." I told him I loved him, Rache. He seemed so stressed. All he could talk about was what would happen if it didn't work out; would we stay friends? I told him I felt closer to him than anyone. No offence, Rache.'

I smile. 'None taken, bitch.'

'I told him we'd always be friends, no matter what. He actually made me promise. Weirdo,' she says, with so much love in her voice.

'And then?'

'And *then*, he said he loved me. Oh, my God, I still can't believe it. He loves me, Rache. He, loves, me. I'm going to *die* of happiness.'

I laugh in relief. 'I'm *so* glad for you, Alex. Both of you. The three of you. He's a great guy.'

'Really? You're not just being Rachel?'

'What d'you mean?'

'You're not just being nice?'

'Shut up. I'm not nice.'

'It's not an insult.'

'Yes it is.'

'OK you're a complete bitch.'

'That's better.'

'I thought you didn't like him, though,' she says.

'I do like him. I guess I just didn't trust him to hang around. But you're right, he's changed ...'

'This is *it*, Rache. The real thing. You know what else?' She sounds so happy. 'He loved me when we were together. I always worried that Maggie wasn't made with love and that she'd somehow instinctively know. But he loved me, Rache. And now I love him. You should talk to Mark,' she says. 'You should have this.'

I go to see Mark on Tuesday and ask him out. No I don't. I think about it. I imagine a few scenarios. In all of them, he turns me down. Or gets angry. Or both. He's turned into such a grump. Why would I even *want* to go out with him? OK, I can think of a few reasons. Enough. I'm going to stop obsessing now. And think of leaves and trees. And puddles. And birds. I need to get back to the mountains.

'D'you know what's really weird,' Alex says at lunch on Thursday. 'After everything that's happened between me and Louis, we've never been on an actual proper date.'

'Seriously?'

'He's asked me to dinner on Friday night. Dinner.'

Sarah and I look at each other. 'We'll mind Maggie,' we say together.

'It's OK. Dad's offered. Well, Dad and Marsha.'

'We're doing it,' Sarah says firmly.

Alex smiles. 'You sure?'

)|(

'D'you want to live?'

'It would be so unfair to kill me now.' This girl is floating.

'Have you told your dad you're dating Louis?' Sarah asks.

'I probably should, shouldn't I?' she grimaces.

'He might actually make more of an effort,' I say. 'When he calms down.'

We laugh.

On Friday, Sarah and I call over to Alex's for our first official babysitting job.

'Where's Louis?' Sarah asks.

'Downstairs having a "chat" with Dad.'

'God.'

'I know,' Alex says, putting on more mascara.

Sarah and I start to get Maggie ready for bed. We opt for the Superman babygro.

Finally, Louis appears. 'Ready?' he asks Alex. His hair is jelled. He's wearing an actual shirt. I have never seen that happen.

'What did he say?' Alex asks immediately.

'He told me if I ever hurt you or Maggie, he'd kill me.'

'God. Sorry.'

'I thought it was kind of cute,' he says.

'It kind of is,' I agree.

He looks at me and smiles. And I know it's changed between us.

He goes over to Maggie. 'Night, night, sweetie pie.'

He kisses her forehead. I think how she's changed his life. Changed him. The person he almost ran from.

Alex goes over to them. They look like that song by REM, 'Shiny Happy People'. He calls them 'his girls'. And I think, *They don't just look like a family any more, they are one.*

'About time they got together,' Sarah says when they're gone.

'I know. It's so great.'

She looks at me. 'Even though you don't like Louis.'

'Shut up. I do like Louis. And don't call me nice.'

'What?'

'Nothing.'

'He's a good guy – even if he is my brother.'

'I know.'

'He's always been good to me.'

'I know.'

'He is actually a really caring person.'

'It's OK. I'm convinced.' I hit her with a pillow and we laugh.

We put Maggie to bed and bring the monitor downstairs to the screening room, where we fight over which movie to watch. *Mean Girls* or *The Devil Wears Prada*. I let Sarah win. So it's *The Devil Wears Prada*, which I like anyway. I've just seen it too many times. It's not possible to see *Mean Girls* too many times.

We're at that scene where Meryl Streep calls Anne Hathaway the 'smart, fat girl', when there's a little cry on the baby monitor. One by one, the green buttons light up.

'Shh,' Sarah says.

I pause Anne Hathaway with her mouth open. She

)(

still looks pretty. Silence on the monitor now. 'She might just be moving around.'

'We should check,' Sarah says.

Upstairs, Maggie is sitting up. She smiles at us.

'Hello, you little monkey,' Sarah says.

Maggie laughs.

I twist the knob on the mobile that hangs over her bed. 'Hush Little Baby' fills the room and tiny dolphins slowly turn. Maggie ignores them and just looks at Sarah with these pleading eyes. She knows what she's doing.

'You are such a softie,' I say as Sarah lifts her up.

'Want to watch a movie?' Sarah asks Maggie.

We bring her down. Sarah gives Maggie her soother. Maggie snuggles into her and in five minutes is asleep. 'Night, night, little monkey,' Sarah whispers.

We bring her back up and settle her.

'God, she's so cute,' I say when we're back in the screening room. I reach for the zapper.

'Rache?'

'Yeah?'

There's a long pause.

I look at her.

'Do you believe in reincarnation?'

'*Reincarnation*?'

'Yeah.' She looks at me like she really needs a 'yes'.

'Do you?' I ask carefully.

'Sometimes I think. I don't know …' her voice trails off.

'You think what?'

'OK, this is going to sound weird.' She stops. 'You know the way Maggie was born at the same time Shane died? You don't think …?' Her voice tails off.

Oh, God.

)(

'But then I think that Maggie is Maggie. Her own little person. And I don't *want* her to be anyone else.'

'Yeah,' I say, with such relief. Because, for starters, what would Alex think?

She looks at me, eyes so wide. 'I miss him so much. Sometimes, I just need him to be here.' She looks so suddenly lost. 'I'm trying, *so hard*, to live till I die. But it takes *so much energy*. I have to push myself *all the time* to get up, get out, do stuff. When all I want is to lie in bed. I knew I was going to lose him. I knew it was going to be hard. I'd no idea it would be this hard, that instead of living till I die, I'd just want to die. I have all this love for him and nowhere to put it.'

'Oh, Sarah.' I hug her tight. And for ages she just cries. We both do.

I stop first. Eventually she does too. She pulls back. Looks worried.

'Don't tell Alex what I said – about Maggie. She'd hate me.'

'No, she wouldn't. But I won't say anything.' I brush her hair back from her face.

'Do you think I'm mad?'

'No. I just think you miss him. How couldn't you? I'm glad you told me, though. I thought you we were doing so well. And I wasn't there for you. Then Rebecca was.'

She looks at me. 'No, she wasn't. Not really. She helped me forget because she never knew Shane and, with her, it seemed easier to do the whole live-till-I-die thing. It's all I wanted. Because it's what he wanted. And if I could do it, then he wouldn't have died for nothing. I can't do it anymore though, Rache. It's just so fake. And so freaking exhausting. I miss him too much.'

'That's OK.'

She shakes her head desperately. 'No it's not. It's like I'm giving up.'

Then it hits me. 'Sarah, sometimes, you need to give up.'

She looks at me.

'As long as you've known me, how hard have I worked?'

'Too hard.'

'And d'you know *why* I worked so hard? Because I was afraid of falling behind and being bullied again. I've stopped that, given up. I don't care any more if I fail. Because I know I can handle it if I do.'

'That's different. If I give up, it's like giving up on Shane.'

'But he only wanted you to be happy, Sarah. That's why he said it. And you're not happy.'

'I'll never be happy again.'

'You know where we're going tomorrow?'

She looks at me blankly.

'We're going to the mountains, OK?'

She shrugs. 'OK. Why?'

'You'll see.'

She thinks for a minute. 'It'd be good to get away.'

'You have no idea.'

'How'll we get there?'

'We'll work something out.'

Sarah borrows her mum's car. This involves a little white lie. Sarah has a provisional licence which means she should only drive with someone who has a full licence. She lets on that I do, so we can go.

)(

'I'm a great driver,' she says as she starts the car. 'It's a stupid rule.'

She checks the rear-view mirror, indicates and pulls out carefully. All the way up into the mountains, she drives confidently and well. We don't talk. The farther we go, the more my mood lifts because it's so good to be back. I roll the window down when we get to Maisie's spot. I close my eyes and breathe in through my nose. I wonder if I could identify this place in a line-up of different smells. Bet I could. I open my eyes and watch nature go by, remembering how I felt the first time I came here – angry. Angry and lost.

We park near the lake and walk down to it in silence. It's like the world has stopped. And everything is still. Sarah starts to throw a few stones. I walk away and sit on a rock, to leave her to her thoughts. I wrap my arms around my knees and close my eyes, turn my face to the sun. After a while, I feel her sit beside me.

'It's amazing up here. Like a break. Or something,' she says.

'I was thinking. Maybe we could go somewhere for Easter. I don't know. Rent somewhere in the mountains. And just walk and stuff. And play jigsaws. And eat soup.'

She smiles. 'Sounds good.'

'No TV or computers, just nature.'

'I'd so like that.'

'I'll check it out. It shouldn't be that expensive this time of year. And I wanted to do something good with the money from D4.'

'We wouldn't use it all up though?' she sounds worried.

)(

'God, no. Want to go for a walk? I want to show you the woods.'

She smiles. 'Sure.'

We walk for ages, then sit against a tree trunk on the forest floor.

'He was my life,' she says. 'Nothing makes sense without him. Except maybe Maggie. I see Alex and Louis together and I know I'll never have that again.'

I turn to her. 'You will. With somebody else.'

'I don't want anyone else. Just Shane.'

I shut up. Because I'm not helping.

She looks at me. 'Do you think Alex is right about sending thoughts to a person?'

'Yeah, I do.'

'I still send him messages on Facebook. Do you think that's weird?'

'No. I'd do it.' I think of Mark and how I'd die if anything happened to him. Still.

'You don't think I'm a failure, do you?'

'A *failure*? How can you even *say* that? Sarah, you've been super-freaking-natural. No one can be as positive as you've been for as long as you've been. You can trust me on that. Telling yourself you don't miss Shane is just a lie. You've lived it long enough.'

'I know,' she says. She looks relieved.

Driving back, Sarah has all this colour in her face. In my head, I'm already planning Easter.

She turns to me. 'You should try again with Mark. You can't just walk away from what you had. I didn't have a choice.'

And I know how annoying and stupid we must seem to her. 'He doesn't love me, Sarah.'

She looks at me. 'I feel like locking you both in a room. Jesus!' she says, as a car comes flying round the corner we're approaching, driving right into our side of the road.

'Oh, my God!'

Sarah brakes and swerves to avoid him. I can see his face, the shock on it. He has a beard. Oh, my God, we're going off the road. The drop-off is steep. The car is in the air. We are flying, front tipped down. My stomach swoops like on a roller coaster. Everything's happening in slow motion. We are totally quiet. No screaming. No sound. Sarah's hands grip the wheel, her knuckles white. Ahead of those knuckles, through the windscreen, the brown and boggy ground is coming up fast. We look at each other. I think, *My life is over.*

I'm lying on my back. My head hurts. I put my hand up to it and feel something. It's a hat.

'Why am I wearing a hat?' My mouth is so dry, my lips are stuck together, the words barely make it out.

'You're awake! Nurse! She's awake.'

I squint my eyes open, look to the sound. Everything's blurry. My thoughts scramble together. *Nurse equals hospital. OK, I'm in hospital. But why? God, I'm thirsty. Maybe I've rabies. Why would I have rabies? I live in Ireland. Don't I?* I close my eyes to help me think. There's movement beside me. The smell of perfume. I squint my eyes open again. An unfamiliar face. Smiling.

'Rachel, I'm Nurse Kelly. You're in hospital. You were in an accident.'

Rachel. Nurse. Hospital. Accident. OK.

'You were in a car accident in the Dublin mountains.' She's wrapping something cold around my arm. *Blood pressure,* I think. I remember a beard. Then a face. Then knuckles.

'Sarah!' I sit up suddenly. My head and chest roar in pain. 'Where's Sarah? Is she OK?'

Her cool hand lowers me back down. Then she moves aside and I see my mum. She's smiling. 'Sarah's great. Walked out of that heap of metal without a scratch on her. Then saved your life.'

'Where is she?'

'At home in bed. It's two in the morning. She was here all day. And all day yesterday.'

'I'm here two days? Am I OK?' *I could be paralysed,* I think. Then I remember I just sat up. And everything's sore.

'You've a little skull fracture,' she says.

'A *skull* fracture?'

'They're watching you very carefully. We're all just so relieved you're awake. Oh and you broke a few ribs.'

'Makes sense,' I say, closing my eyes in pain.

'Nurse, could she have something for the pain?'

'Absolutely.' The air moves and the smell of perfume eases.

'You'll be in here for a little while,' Mum says.

I think of Sarah and the licence. 'The accident. It wasn't our fault. This guy —'

'I know, pet. Sarah's told the police everything. It

was a hit-and-run. How a person could do that? Up in the mountains. With no one around to help. I hope he rots in hell.'

'He has a beard.'

'I know, pet. They need more to go on.'

'I know his face.'

'Don't worry about it now.'

The nurse is back with some painkillers, which I take. I lie back down and close my eyes. I've never been so tired.

When I wake again, it's bright. Sarah's sitting beside the bed looking at my face. She smiles.

'Hey! How're you doing?'

'I've a skull fracture.'

'I *know*. Oh, my God, Rache. I thought I'd killed you.' She starts to get upset.

'It wasn't your fault. That guy —'

'Drove off. Left us up in the freaking mountain. Never came back to see if we were alive or dead.'

'How did you get us down?'

'Mobile phone.'

'But there's no service up there.'

'I found service. Eventually,' she says proudly. 'I didn't leave you, though,' she rushes. 'I covered you with my coat. Then walked around like a lunatic till I found coverage. I could always see you. I never left you alone. I was so worried, Rache. I thought I'd lose you too. You were so pale. There was blood everywhere.'

I feel my head. So it's not a hat.

'You've a few stitches.'

I think of my face, my acting.

'They're in your scalp,' she says, like she can read my mind. 'So you can't go shaving your head. Unless you want to look tough. That'd work, though.'

'Are *you* OK?' I ask her.

'I thought we were going to die,' she says.

'Me too.'

'I didn't want to.' She sounds surprised. And I realise then what she's really saying. She laughs like she can't believe it. 'I don't want to die, Rachey.'

'Thank Christ.'

'I want to live.'

I smile and squeeze her hand. 'You're not the only one.'

'I'm going to call Shane's mum.'

I look at her.

'I thought we'd make each other sad, so I didn't,' she says. 'We could help each other though. Remember him together.'

I smile. Then remember someone else. 'You know, there *was* something else Shane wanted you to do. That you *could* do now.'

She looks at me hopefully.

'Look out for Peter.' Shane's best friend.

Her face falls.

'What's wrong?'

She looks guilty. 'He called a few times to see if I was OK. I blew him off.'

I remember a phone call. 'He'll understand. He's probably been blowing people off all over the place himself.'

She thinks about that. 'Probably not.'

'Look, all I know is, he's a good guy and Shane wanted you to look out for each other.'

She looks down, fiddles with her bag. After a while, she looks up, guiltily. 'I thought he'd remind me of what I was missing.'

'That's OK. But everything's changed now. You've stopped pretending now, haven't you? And you do miss him.'

She takes a deep breath, closes her eyes and breathes out. 'You've no idea.'

'But Peter will. No one knows what you're going through as much as him.'

No reaction.

'Maybe he called you because he needed you.'

'You think?' For the first time, she looks hopeful. Now that it's not about her.

'Call him. If it doesn't work out, you tried.'

She thinks about that, then smiles. 'Shane did say he was a pussy.'

We laugh.

She nods. 'OK, I'll call him.'

'Yaay. Now get up here and give me a hug.'

We hug. Which hurts. But that doesn't matter 'cause I know she'll be OK. In time.

She sits back down.

'Mark's been in, you know,' she says.

'Oh crap.'

She smiles. 'You two.'

'Did he say anything?' I ask like I don't really care.

'Asked loads of questions. Like he was a freaking doctor. Sounded a bit like you.' She smiles. 'He was terrified you wouldn't wake up, though.'

'Yeah, and now that I have, I bet he won't come near me.'

'Why d'you say that?'

'Because he's hot and cold and hot and cold and I don't know why he ever bothered with that whole friends thing if it's not what he wanted.' I can't believe I'm crying.

And then he's there. And Sarah's gone.

He pulls up a chair.

'How're you feeling?'

Like I need Sarah back. 'I'm OK when I don't move.'

He says nothing for ages, then finally, 'I was going to offer to drive you to the mountains.'

'Are you saying that if you were driving this wouldn't have happened?'

'No.'

'Then what?'

'I'm saying that I was going to offer to drive you to the mountains.'

'Why?'

'To see Maisie.'

'What do you want, Mark?'

'What do you mean?'

'I just don't get you any more. You're hot and cold and—'

He leans forward and stops me speaking. With a kiss. I pull back immediately. Pain shoots all over my body. 'What are you *doing*?'

'Sorry.' He gets up and turns his back to me. 'Sometimes, I just want to be with you,' he mumbles. Then turns back. 'On any terms.'

'What are you talking about?'

He shrugs kind of hopelessly. 'Can't live with you. Can't live without you.' He laughs but sadly.

I feel like crying suddenly. 'Mark, I don't know what you want.'

'To be with you. But just the two of us. I mean, I know Josh is going away and you'll be on your own again but that's not by choice.'

'You think I'm with Josh? I'm not with Josh.'

'You broke up?'

'I was *never* with Josh.'

'Then why?'

'Why *what*?'

'Why did you want to see other people? Was it someone else?' He looks confused.

'Mark. There was no one else. Ever. Just you. I told you why I said it. Because I thought you didn't love me.'

'I know but I still thought you wanted to see other people.'

I bite my lip. 'No.'

He shakes his head like he doesn't get me.

'I don't know why I said it. It just came out. Maybe because I didn't want you to know how much I still cared.'

He stares at me for ages. 'You're a complete eejit, you know that?' But then he's smiling, and beside me, and kissing me. And I really don't mind that my head hurts.

'I love you,' he says. 'I love you so much it freaking hurts. And, by the way, I've loved you since way before you loved me.'

'How do you know? Maybe I loved you first.'

'Did you love me on my first day at Strandbrook? Did you even notice me?'

)(

'Of course I noticed you – you were new.' I think back. 'But I was caught up with Alex back then. She'd just lost her mum. And that was everything.'

'I know. You were like that song, 'You Don't Know You're Beautiful'.'

'That's so corny,' I say, but I'm thinking, *Aw*.

He kisses me again.

'We've been kind of stupid, haven't we?' I say.

'Speak for yourself.' He smiles

'So, that whole friends thing ... What was that about?'

He looks embarrassed. 'That was me not being able to go out with you because I thought you were with Josh, but still not able to let you go.'

Aw. We look at each other for a long time.

'Are we going to get better at this?' I ask.

'Jesus, I hope so.'

We laugh.

'So, you *love* me?' I tease.

'I love you,' he says, like it's the easiest thing in the world to say.

And my heart is singing.

'And there I was thinking you were a free spirit.'

'*What*?'

'Nothing, Caecilius.'

Being in hospital reminds me of the last time I was here, the awfulness of it, how I couldn't listen to my parents, how I wouldn't see Jack. He sent me letters, none of which I opened, all of which I kept. Now I can't stop thinking of them. I need to get home.

When I do, the first thing I do is go looking for them.

)(

I find them at the back of the top shelf in my bedroom cupboard where I'd flung them. I use the swivel chair to get them, risking death.

I sit on my bed, dust them off, sneeze, then open the first.

It's a list. Called 'Reasons to Live'.

We love you.

You can't let them win.

You're better than them.

You haven't fallen in love.

You haven't seen Africa, Asia, California, The Rockies.

You haven't ridden a camel. Make that 'ridden ON a camel'.

You haven't beaten me in *Halo 3*.

I smile. At least I've done the most important thing, fallen in love.

I'm so glad I didn't open the letter back then. It wouldn't have made a difference to how I felt (I was too low). And actually, I'd probably have torn it up, thrown it away. Now I have it. And it makes me see. I have won. I *am* better than them. And I still haven't seen Africa, Asia, California and The Rockies. But I will. I'll ride ON a camel. And I will beat him in *Halo 3*. If we still have it.

I look at Uggs, sitting up on my pillow like he's been waiting for my return. I reach over and pick him up. I smile at the face I love so much. I remember how I looked into it the night before it all started, before I got a place in *D4*. I was so sure about rhino hide, how it can't be created. Turns out I was wrong.

Also available in the Butterfly Novels series

And By The Way . . .
(The first book in the Butterfly Novels series)

At Strandbrook College, Dublin, we are Kids Of. Kids of media stars, musicians, artists, actors . . . I'm the kid of a rock star. Means nothing to me.

When my mum died six months ago, I didn't just lose her, I lost my dad, 'The Rockstar'. To work.

Now I don't trust anyone or rely on anyone. That way, I won't get hurt.

My best friend Rachel won't let me pull back, though. And that's a problem.

Another one is David McFadden, a guy in my class (who calls me Ice Queen). He says he wants to help. Six months ago he could have – but he didn't. Now, it's too late. The very last person in the world I'm going to listen to is David McFadden. I'll show him who's Ice Queen. }|{

And For Your Information . . .
(The second book in the Butterfly Novels series)

Everyone thinks they know who I am – ditzy Sarah, who cares more about appearances than anything real. And yeah, I do care about what people think.

Take my friends Alex and Rachel. We're supposed to be best friends. But they tell each other things they'd never tell me. I try not to mind.

Then there's Simon, my sort-of boyfriend. We hardly see each other and when we do, I feel like he doesn't really 'see' me, you know?

And I'm not even going to discuss my family.

So … shoplifting. It wasn't exactly on my list of things to do before I die. But it makes me feel good. In control.

I'm sixteen and still waiting for my life to begin. Then it does. The day I get caught . . .)|(